Riches
Beyond
Measure

Books by Mary Connealy

GOLDEN STATE TREASURE · 3

Riches Beyond Measure

MARY CONNEALY

BETHANYHOUSE

a division of Baker Publishing Group
Minneapolis, Minnesota

© 2025 by Mary Connealy

Published by Bethany House Publishers
Minneapolis, Minnesota
BethanyHouse.com

Bethany House Publishers is a division of
Baker Publishing Group, Grand Rapids, Michigan

Printed in the United States of America

Library of Congress Cataloging-in-Publication Data
Names: Connealy, Mary, author.
Title: Riches beyond measure / Mary Connealy.
Description: Minneapolis, Minnesota : Bethany House, a division of Baker
    Publishing Group, 2025. | Series: Golden State Treasure ; 3
Identifiers: LCCN 2025004885 | ISBN 9780764244414 (paperback) | ISBN
    9780764245589 (casebound) | ISBN 9781493451173 (ebook)
Subjects: LCGFT: Christian fiction. | Romance fiction. | Western fiction. | Novels.
Classification: LCC PS3603.O544 R53 2025 | DDC 813/.6—dc23/eng/20250228
LC record available at https://lccn.loc.gov/2025004885

Scripture quotations are from the King James Version of the Bible.

Cover design by Dan Thornberg, Design Source Creative Services

Baker Publishing Group publications use paper produced from sustainable forestry practices and postconsumer waste whenever possible.

25 26 27 28 29 30 31   7 6 5 4 3 2 1

I've got a new editor, Rochelle Gloege, and as always I'm giving her a huge job to get my books ready for print. I sincerely appreciate all her hard work. The books are so much better once they've had her editor eyes on them.

Thank you to all at Bethany House for being beside me on this writing adventure.

ONE

Cordell Westbrook dropped a lasso over the head of a skittish calf. It was springtime in California, and they were rushing to finish up with the branding at the ranch. And Cord was a cowboy. A genuine cowboy. At last.

Grinning, he leapt off his horse, landing next to the bawling calf. He flipped it onto its side, hog-tied it, and held the animal still while Josh Hart, his boss and friend, made quick work of branding the little heifer.

The poor little heifer.

But Josh was fast, and Cord had gotten mighty good at this. He untied the critter's feet while Josh freed the lasso from around its neck and let the calf run off to an outraged mama to be nuzzled and fed and comforted.

"That's the last one," Josh said. He stood and watched the milling red-and-white Hereford cattle settle down. "Great calf crop this spring."

Cord studied the herd while he coiled his rope, recognizing

9

and appreciating all he'd learned since arriving at the ranch. These days he knew what he was looking at: good, sturdy cows and calves that were shedding their shaggy winter coats, revealing the shiny coats beneath. The cows had survived the winter well and without any worrisome weight loss. The weather here in the central California valley wasn't harsh, but it got cold often enough.

Cord understood all of this meant, to his absolute delight, that he was indeed a cowboy now. "This is so much better than being a banker. I can hardly believe I lasted so long in that cramped office."

Josh clapped him on the back. "You're a solid hand, Cord. You've got a job here on the Two Harts for as long as you want."

Nodding, Cord walked over to his ground-hitched horse. The well-trained animal stood patiently despite the noise and commotion and smoke all around it.

"I've always wanted my own place, Josh. I'd like to stay on longer if I can, but the plan is still to get my own land. Even Grandpa Westbrook has accepted that now."

He hoped.

The sound of steady hoofbeats caused him and Josh to turn to the north, just in time to see a chuck wagon pulled by two brown Morgan horses approaching the branding site. It was being driven not by the bunkhouse cook as was usual, but by Josh's pretty sister, Annie Lane. Cord wondered how such a beautiful widow had managed to stay single for so long. As she drew closer, Cord saw Annie's five-year-old daughter, Caroline, tucked up beside her ma.

They were a pair, those two. Dark hair, brown eyes, with pretty roses in their cheeks. Annie leaned toward being a solemn woman, and Cord knew she'd loved her husband. She'd watched him die from a gunshot wound, which seemed reason enough for her not to want to risk her heart again.

Annie pulled the wagon to a halt, and Josh slapped Cord on the back again, a little harder than before, jolting Cord back to awareness of his surroundings. Then he glanced at Josh. It did near to a physical injury to have to take his eyes off Annie.

As if sensing Cord's thoughts, Josh rolled his eyes and headed for the wagon. But Annie was already off the bench seat and on the ground, helping Caroline alight before any man could reach her. The cowhands stripped the saddles off their mounts to give the horses a break.

"Did Casey go to the south pasture?" Josh asked as he moved to the back of the wagon and folded down the gate to pull the food out.

Plenty of hungry cowhands stepped in to help him. They had a full crew today. The ranch boasted several pastures of livestock, and all the spring calves needed branding.

Josh and his brother, Zane, had hired a new bunkhouse cook just a few weeks ago to help their longtime cook, whose knee was giving him trouble.

Annie tucked a stray hair behind her ear and shook her head. "Neb went south, so Casey got pulled into helping make lunch for the orphanage and school. And Tilda had an extra-long morning class because whatever she hit on teaching today kept the whole class enthralled. Your wife has a rare gift for teaching."

"She does indeed." Josh smiled as he mentioned Tilda, his wife of less than a year. "I like sitting in on her classes, too. But I don't get much chance." He leaned down and kissed his sister on the cheek. "Thanks for bringing our food. We just got done with this pasture, so you timed it perfectly. We're all starving."

Suddenly a strange rumble had all the men stepping away from the wagon, most with their food already in hand. It was an earthquake. Normal enough in California, and nothing to worry about if it was a small one. And with no roof overhead to collapse on them, they just had to wait it out.

Then the shaking turned rougher than any Cord had felt before. Yet the men kept eating, legs spread wide for better balance. It seemed nothing was to disturb lunchtime.

"I hope they got the children outside back at the ranch." Annie drew Caroline close.

"I'm sure they did," Josh reassured her. "Zane stayed around today since Tilda's pa is coming out. I don't like it when there's no one to watch him, though he's turned into a man Tilda and I trust . . . mostly." Josh hadn't settled in to having a father-in-law close at hand. Especially a meddling father-in-law who Tilda, raised as an orphan, hadn't known existed until last fall.

The shaking worsened, and Annie pulled Caroline tight against her body. The earth rolled in a way unlike anything Cord had seen before, and he'd grown up in California. "Look at that—the ground's moving like waves."

Everyone turned to stare at an incoming ripple. Then came a deeper rumble, and a crack appeared in the ground.

"Step back!" Cord rushed to Annie's side to pull her away from the oncoming rupture, but he was too late. A crevasse appeared right between Annie's feet.

Annie screamed and jumped toward Cord, losing her tight grip on Caroline. Fortunately, Josh was there and grabbed his niece, who shrieked in terror.

The ground collapsed under Cord as he caught hold of Annie, a narrow slit that kept widening. Cord clawed at the edge of the crack with one hand and held on to Annie with the other as she plunged downward.

Mustering all his effort, Cord managed to push Annie up and out of the crack even as he slid deeper. Someone grabbed hold of his hand, and then a whole crew had him. They dragged him out of the collapsing ground and well away from where he'd been falling. Yet still the shaking and rumbling went on, causing the men who had him to fall as they scrambled backward.

With an awful creak, the chuck wagon sank into the widening crack. Cord took one look at the vanishing wagon and hollered. Josh sprang into action, passing Caroline to their foreman, Shad, then pulling a knife. He dashed over to the horses and slashed the reins, setting loose the Morgans before the ground could swallow them up.

Cord rolled onto one elbow, got to his feet, and caught the terrified horses' reins. Quickly, Cord began to lead them away when the earthquake tossed him to the ground again. Somehow he held on to the horses as they dragged him along, Cord clinging to the reins more out of instinct than anything else. Finally the pair halted. Everywhere, men were sprawled on the ground.

The sound of thundering hoofbeats alerted Cord and the others to the cows and horses charging away from the crack that was swallowing the still-smoldering fire, along with a couple of the Two Harts branding irons.

At last, the shaking stopped.

Shad brought Caroline to Annie, who remained sitting on the ground. She hugged her terrified, sobbing daughter, soothing her with quiet shushing sounds.

"We've got to get back to the ranch. There'll be damage." Josh looked around, then began snapping orders, rattling off four names. "You four are lightest. Ride the Morgans double back to the ranch house, rounding up enough horses for the rest of us wherever you can find them. One of you can bring them to us. The others should stay and help at the ranch. There may be injuries. In the meantime, we'll start walking home as fast as we can."

Cord thought of Brody MacKenzie, who'd gone back east to partner with a doctor he was indebted to. It'd sure be nice to have a doctor around the place right now. The doctor in the nearest town, Dorada Rio, would be needed there. That left them with Zane's wife, Michelle. While she was a knowing woman, she had a baby to tend, and of course she was no doctor.

Cord could only hope and pray there were no serious injuries.

The four cowhands rode off for home. Before they'd gone far, the ground trembled again, this time less violently. Even so, they all froze and swayed, looking in all directions for a dangerous new split in the earth.

The powerful aftershock stopped soon enough, and they hoisted their saddles and slung them over their shoulders. They'd stripped the leather off most of the horses and left them grazing, and now they had saddles to carry. They grabbed up the remaining branding irons and bridles, all that was left after the earth had swallowed their things.

They set off on foot toward home. They were miles from the ranch house, and Cord sure hoped they didn't have to walk the whole way. But considering what they'd just endured, and the possible chaos they might find when they arrived at home, he felt grateful to be in one piece.

——— ◆ ———

Annie made Caroline walk, though her instincts told her to carry her daughter. But they had a long way to go, and Caroline was getting heavy. At least she was finally calming down.

Of the eight of them left to walk, Caroline was probably the most tireless, judging by her little girl's constant motion all day every day.

Occasional aftershocks, small tremors in the ground, kept them all on edge.

They hadn't gone far when Bo, one of their cowhands, came trotting back while leading three horses. "I'll bring more if I can find them. We saw a couple ahead of us, still running and heading for the barn. Shad and I left our riders behind so that I could get back to you fast and he had a chance of catching more horses."

"Annie," Josh said, saddling the closest horse as Bo rode off, "those of us who can ride should go on ahead. There'll be work to do back there."

Annie nodded. There would be work for her too, but if buildings had collapsed, a lot of it would be heavy work, and the men needed to get on with it.

Josh jabbed a finger at five of the men. "You're with me. We'll all ride double. Cord, that leaves you out here with Annie and Caroline. More horses will be coming soon."

Josh galloped away with all the men except Cord.

They walked briskly along, Cord toting his saddle and

bridle. "Do you think he picked me to stay behind because he knows I'm still the most useless of his cowhands?"

Annie surprised herself by laughing. Not much made her laugh since Todd had died.

"And he left me behind for the same reason."

Cord turned to her and smiled.

"I'd say you are doing a decent job," she said. "Between Josh and Zane, neither of your bosses is real worried about anyone's tender feelings. If you were bad at your job, you'd know it by the way they tore the hide off you."

"You know, you're right. Because they've done it a few times, including with kids from the orphanage who want to do ranch work. Your brothers are good teachers, but they aren't exactly tactful. As for myself, I like straight talk. I'm going to have my own place one of these days. Nothing, I suspect, as beautiful as the Two Harts, but I spent four of my growing-up years on my grandpa's farm, and this life suits me."

"Mayhew Westbrook owns a farm?" Annie knew Cord's grandfather had gone back to his mansion in Sacramento for the winter. He'd cleared out when Michelle's family, five of them, had turned up to see her new baby and filled the ranch house. Not long after, Brody and Ellie MacKenzie had taken Brody's younger brothers with them to Boston, where he had a doctoring job. Thayne and Lochlan—who'd run away from New York in search of treasure, then lied their way onto the Two Harts, leaving mayhem wherever they went—had only gone on the condition that when Brody felt like he'd fulfilled his promise to Dr. Tibbles, they'd come right back. They had already found some of the treasure they'd hoped to find, and it seemed to Annie there was more out there still waiting to be discovered.

It chafed more than a little that practically everyone had gotten to go treasure-hunting except her. Being a teacher and a mother and the one who generally took care of everything and everyone slowed her down some. But a treasure hunt sounded like fun, and Annie wouldn't mind being a part of it.

"Grandpa Westbrook, farming?" Cord laughed and shook his head. "Hard to picture that. Nope. My pa's father has been a city dweller since birth. He owns a big bank in Sacramento, although he's mostly turned over the reins these days. My ma grew up on a farm, though, and when my pa died, and Mayhew was so grouchy with her that she couldn't take it anymore, Ma went to live with her folks and took me along.

"Grandpa Rivers's place was a small homestead, so when I grew up, there wasn't room for me. It was only then that I went back to Sacramento and worked with Grandpa Westbrook to earn enough to buy my own place. I've saved every penny I could scrape together, hoping to buy land someday. And I'm still waiting for my chance."

The ground rumbled, and they stopped walking to keep their balance until the tremors ceased.

"The other thing I would have loved to do is study music, but Grandpa Westbrook considered that useless."

Annie shook her head. "It sounds like your grandpa has a thing or two he still needs to learn. You play such beautiful music at church on Sunday. You could have made a career of it. I've been talking with Zane and Josh about buying a piano. It would be a good addition to our home."

"Maybe I could teach the orphans to play the piano. Music is a rich addition to a child's life." Cord looked down at Caroline, and Annie noticed his kindly smile.

"But music as a career didn't suit my grandpa's wishes for me, so I worked at his bank. My hope has been to buy land close to Grandma and Grandpa Rivers's place. Then Grandpa Westbrook sent me on this treasure hunt—not for the first time, mind you, since Grandpa knew from Graham MacKenzie that if it was found, half of it would be his. But it mostly ended up being a chase after Frasier MacKenzie, Graham's son and Brody's father, and he never looked in the right place. Grandpa was hoping I'd come back to Sacramento and continue working at the bank, but I saw a chance to learn cowhand skills from a first-class operation. So I hired on, and here I am."

"Are we going to have to walk all the way back home, Mama?" They were setting a good pace, and Caroline sounded tired. It was the time of day when Annie could tell a nap would still be a good idea. Caroline didn't nap much anymore now that her days were spent at school. But after the scare of the earthquake and the long walk, she was probably worn clean out.

"Uncle Josh will send horses for us. If they have to ride all the way back to find a horse, they will."

Cord walked alongside them, with Caroline in the middle. He looked down at her and said, "Would you like a piggyback ride?"

Caroline turned to him and beamed. "Can I?" She looked up at Annie. "Is that all right, Mama?"

Annie ran one hand over her daughter's dark hair, which was so like hers. "That would be very nice of . . . Cord."

She stumbled over the name. She should probably have said *Mr. Westbrook*, but Caroline didn't talk a lot with adults who weren't her aunts and uncles. She wasn't around the cowhands much, and everyone else called each other by first names.

Cord set his saddle on the ground. "I'll come back for that." He picked Caroline up to face him, then with a big boost upward and a playful growl, he swung her over his shoulder. She squealed, then clung to Cord's back like a monkey, her arms around his neck, her legs around his waist.

Annie hoped her little girl didn't choke the man.

"Even if we can't get a piano at the house, maybe you could use the piano at church for lessons. It's awe-inspiring the music you can get out of that old piano."

The Harts had twenty-seven orphans at their school, kids taken off the streets or out of the orphanages in San Francisco. They were sheltering, feeding, and educating them, and they took them to church every Sunday when the weather was decent. Cord always went along, as did Josh and Tilda, Zane and Michelle, and also any cowhands who were interested.

It wasn't long after his arrival that Cord, who'd moved to the bunkhouse after hiring on at the Two Harts, had taken over playing the piano for church. He had a talent that left Annie feeling humbled and inspired.

"That old piano, as you call it, is a wonderful instrument. I love playing it. I even got offered a job to play at the hotel." Cord smiled. "It didn't pay worth a lick, though, and it would have cut into my ranching time. And that's what I'm here to learn."

Striding along at a brisk pace to cover ground, Annie said, "I wonder what the others found when they got home. If it's bad enough, if people are hurt, we might have to walk the whole way back."

"If we have to, then we'll do it."

Annie saw Caroline's arm slide off Cord's neck. "Someone's falling asleep." Annie reached for her daughter, but Cord drew her around and cradled her in his arms. She snuggled her face against his chest before sighing and falling asleep in earnest.

Annie's heart was gladdened to see her little girl held by such a kind man. Her brothers were good men too, yet it was nice to have a spare.

Moving along, Annie tried to think of more to talk about. She'd found Cord attractive from the first moment she'd seen him, a disturbing sensation she'd felt for no one since her husband had died. But they didn't talk much, and now she found herself tongue-tied, with images of her husband invading every thought she had about this man. Being interested in Cord felt like a betrayal of Todd, even though he was such a good man he'd likely want her to let go of her grief.

The ground trembled again, then shook with greater force. Cord stopped, holding Caroline against him. Protecting her as the shaking grew worse.

Another big quake. A sudden heave of the earth threw Annie off her feet. Cord dropped down beside her as if to steady himself and keep from falling when he carried precious cargo.

"Be ready to move if the ground starts to give way." Cord didn't need to say that, because this time Annie was ready. But she liked knowing he was always thinking of what to do next.

At last the earth stilled. The two of them sat side by side on the ground, and Annie turned to check on her little girl.

"I can't believe she slept through that. When awake, she's always moving and talking, running and climbing whatever she can find to climb. But when she sleeps, she's out, and nothing much can bother that girl."

Cord ran a hand over the straggles of hair that had escaped Caroline's braid. "She's sure a pretty little thing. She looks like you." He raised his eyes and locked them on her.

For a long moment, Annie enjoyed what he hadn't exactly said. A pretty little thing that looked like her meant that he thought she was pretty. Her brown eyes met his blue ones, and the gaze held, then held some more.

"It's been a long time since . . ." She stopped. The words he'd implied had touched a place in her heart . . . a place she'd thought had died with her husband. She clenched her jaw to keep from saying something stupid. And right now, she could only think of stupid things.

Then, with Caroline still in his arms, Cord leaned forward, slowly but steadily.

Almost as if he were going to . . .

The drum of hoofbeats jerked them apart. And they'd been much too close. Annie scrambled to her feet. Cord stood only a bit more slowly than she, careful not to jostle Caroline, then wheeled to face the oncoming horse, which wasn't yet in sight, thank heavens. Quickly, he started walking again, faster than ever.

Josh rounded a jumble of rocks. He was leading two horses, one saddled.

"I left my saddle back a ways so I could carry Caroline."

"I'll get it." Josh rode on and was back fast.

Annie swung up onto her horse. Josh took Caroline so that Cord could mount up, and they all rode for home.

"Josh, w-what . . ." Annie started to speak and found her voice was a little hoarse, so she cleared her throat, almost— but not quite—clearing her head, too. "What did you find back home?"

TWO

Brody, Ellie, Thayne, and Lock MacKenzie dismounted after riding rented horses into the ranch yard. The ground started shaking before they could lead their horses into the barn. The plan was to get someone to return the horses to town without delay. If no one was available to do that, then they'd just unsaddle the critters and turn them out to pasture.

Brody was in no mood to ride to Dorada Rio to take the horses back, not if that meant returning on foot. It'd been a long, cold winter out east. He'd done the work he felt was fair to repay Dr. Tibbles, and a new partner had been found to take Brody's place. Brody's work in Boston was done, and he had finally come home. For good.

And now he was experiencing his first big earthquake.

Brody looked wide-eyed at his wife of less than a year, who seemed unfazed by the shaking.

Brody and his brothers had gone through a few mild earthquakes in their brief time in California, but they hadn't gotten used to the whole world shaking. Ellie, however, had grown up with them. She merely widened her stance a bit for balance to wait it out.

Then the shaking grew more violent, and Ellie looked around, alarmed.

Brody saw the doors of the orphanage fly open and all the children come streaming out, heading for an open spot away from the building next to Tilda and a man Brody didn't know. A man wearing an apron.

Brody caught one of Ellie's hands and held on as the earthquake kept getting worse.

Cowhands, including Zane, Ellie's older brother, hurried out of the barns and sheds, and Michelle exited the ranch house, carrying her baby. Seven-month-old Leah Suzanne was sitting upright in her arms, looking around, perfect whisps of dark curls on her head. Gretel followed right after Michelle, a toddler in her arms, with another hanging on to her skirts. Brody noticed her very round belly, indicating a new life would be joining them soon.

He thought of Ellie and corrected that: two new lives.

Unlike him, everyone seemed very matter-of-fact. Most of these folks were lifelong Californians. They knew they needed to get outside during a rough earthquake in case any buildings collapsed.

Zane led several cowhands into the barn, and together they led the horses out into the corral.

Then a scream switched Brody from watching into action, and a thunderous sound like that of a falling building set him to running. He took off in the direction of his doctor's office, barely aware he had his doctor's bag in hand. After a shout to Michelle, Ellie was coming fast at his side.

At the end of a row of buildings, a house had collapsed. Harriet Sears lived there with her husband, Bo, and a baby not yet a year old. A baby Brody had delivered.

"Did they get out?" Brody shouted at the small crowd already gathered near the collapsed house.

"No," said Nora, "and I can hear the baby crying." The ground still shook as Nora, Harriet's sister, shoved the toddler she held into someone's arms and rushed for the house, its front door blocked by debris.

"Wait!" Brody sprinted toward Nora and reached her just as she began tearing at the jumble of fallen wood planks behind the door. He caught Nora around the waist and tugged her away. "Stay back. I'll go through the window around the back. We can't get inside this way."

Nora, her eyes shining with tears, nodded and stepped back.

Brody heard wailing coming from the collapsed house. Harriet would never let her baby cry like that. "Thayne, Lock, come with me! Ellie, stay with Nora."

"Brody, be careful." Ellie went to Nora and drew her away.

He didn't trust the frantic woman to control herself, not when her sister was trapped in the damaged building. He sprinted around the house and found a window. Its shutters were tightly closed. Brody kicked at the window; the sturdy shutters rattled but held. It took two more kicks before the latch gave way and the shutters cracked open.

The earthquake took a sudden violent turn, knocking Brody and his brothers—now at his side—off their feet.

Brody lunged to his feet, then grabbed the window frame and hurled himself into the house. He charged toward the sound of crying and found Harriet pinned to the floor by a rafter, which had partly collapsed onto her chest and neck. She lay there unconscious and bleeding, though Brody couldn't yet tell from what wounds.

He scooped up the baby in the nearby cradle and handed the infant to his younger brother, Lock, who was there with Thayne. "Lock, get the baby outside. Now!"

As Lock hurried away with the child, Thayne began lifting the heavy rafter off of Harriet's chest. It was then Brody heard another timber snap.

Brody wasted no time in sweeping Harriet into his arms. While he did so, debris fell from the ceiling, striking him on the back. He staggered under the blow, but it didn't knock him down. The whole roof was caving in.

"Out! We've got to get out of here." Somehow he made it out of the room with Harriet even as the shattered roof rained wooden shingles down on them.

Thayne led the way to the back window they'd come in through. After Thayne clambered outside, he turned and plucked Harriet out of Brody's arms while more debris came down around them.

The earthquake continued wreaking destruction.

Once outside, Brody rushed around to the front of the house, close on Thayne's heels, just as the back wall of the house fell outward. He emerged from the choking dust and wreckage to find Nora, crying out with relief, Harriet's baby already in her arms.

Ellie rushed to Thayne's side, who knelt and laid Harriet gently on the ground.

Then the shaking finally stopped.

"Do you have many earthquakes this bad?" Lock had the baby again. Nora's two had fussed enough that she had to attend to them.

Nora tore her eyes from Harriet, who was still unconscious, and looked anxiously at Ellie. "I've been here just a bit longer than you, Lock. I've never felt one shake so hard."

"I was born here," Ellie said. "Except for six months in Boston, I've always been here, and I've never known such a strong quake."

Harriet started writhing and clawing at her throat.

"She can't breathe," said Brody, noticing her badly swollen throat. "Hold her still, Ellie. Thayne, toss me my doctor's bag."

Thayne had the bag beside Brody in an instant. He looked up from Harriet's bleeding shoulder and arm to the others gathered there. "Don't anyone go inside the buildings. We can't trust them not to collapse."

"Especially as there will be aftershocks," Ellie added.

As if to prove her point, the ground shook again. Everyone froze and rode out the much smaller earthquake.

Brody pulled a gleaming scalpel out of his doctor's bag. "I've got to open an airway." He reached for her throat with the wickedly sharp instrument.

"Dr. MacKenzie, no." Nora strode toward him.

"Stay back. Thayne, hold her back if you have to." Brody shot a look at his brother. "I know what I'm doing, Nora. Please don't interfere."

Working quickly, Brody wiped Harriet's throat clean, then dusted it with carbolic acid. "Ellie, I have some clean cloths in the bag. There'll be bleeding once I start cutting, and I can't see what I'm doing if the wound fills with blood. Keep it wiped away."

With the cloths in hand, Ellie bent closer.

He slashed a short but deep cut into the hollow of Harriet's throat, below the worst of the heavy swelling on her neck and very near to the airway to her lungs. Ellie dabbed at the flow of blood with the cloth. Brody was being extra cautious, knowing how close he was to the carotid artery.

"Now hand me an eyedropper." He knew Ellie had never seen him do this procedure before, and there was much debate about it. He'd seen only a handful of them performed and had done two himself.

Without hesitating, Ellie placed the eyedropper into his hand. He ripped off the rubber top and gently inserted the narrow glass pipette into the incision.

"Keep dabbing away the blood," he instructed, then bent over the tube and blew air into Harriet's lungs.

Her chest visibly lifted, and Harriet's struggles finally calmed. Brody eased back, letting the air flow out of the tube, then bent and blew into the tube again. Silence reigned around him as everyone watched while Harriet's lungs took in more air, the color slowly returning to her face.

The ground trembled again. Brody pulled away from the tube. He'd blown in about half the air this time because he didn't want to injure her neck further. He waited, letting the air escape while waiting for the shaking to stop. When it did, he blew into the tube again.

This time, as the air flowed out, Harriet's eyes fluttered open. She reached for her throat.

"Ellie!" Brody exclaimed.

Ellie caught Harriet's hands and pressed them against Harriet's waist, leaning forward until she was fully visible to her. "Harriet, I know you hurt, but you mustn't touch your neck. Brody and I are here, and he had to help you breathe by cutting a small slit into your throat. He used a tube to get air to your lungs."

Baby . . . she mouthed.

"Your baby is fine, Harriet," said Brody, reading her lips. "Not a scratch on him. He's a tough little frontiersman." Brody used the voice he reserved for his patients, hoping to soothe Harriet and offer comfort in the midst of her fear and pain. As he spoke, he petitioned God for healing and for His favor right now. "Lock, bring the baby so she can see him."

"Here he is, Harriet."

Brody was struck by how deep his brother's voice was, how reassuring. Thayne, the older of the two scamps, had shown real interest in doctoring. But Lock? His treasure-mad little brother? Was it possible the boy, now fifteen, might develop a serious side and go into medicine as well? He just might have a talent for it.

"He's fine." Lock lowered the baby—with a fuzzy head of blond hair that was only a bit of an improvement on bald—so that Harriet could get a good look at him.

Ellie moved back without releasing her hold on the cloth pads she'd used to stanch the blood, allowing Lock to lean in farther so that Harriet could see her son. The little tyke had calmed down once he'd been rescued from the shaking house. Now his arms waved, his feet kicked, he cooed and drooled and smiled at his ma.

Harriet calmed down, nodded, and moved her lips, unable to speak past the swelling that had blocked her airway. *Thank you,* she mouthed.

They'd barely gotten her and little Bo Jr. out of the house in time.

The earth shook again, more violently this time. Brody was glad he was kneeling on the ground or he might've fallen down.

"I'll go to the doctor's office when this shaking ends," Thayne offered, "and haul your examining table outside. Then we can get Harriet up off the ground."

"Good idea." Brody released his grip on the pipette, then watched her chest rise and fall without assistance from him. *Thank you, Lord.* "I don't see any damage to her neck beyond the swelling, thankfully. But she's cut badly on her shoulder and arm where the rafter landed." He looked up at Ellie. Now that the worst was over, he felt nothing but relief that his wife was there to help. "She's going to need stitches. Ellie, get the needle and thread ready."

Ellie went to work preparing for the next step as they waited for Thayne to return from the doctor's office.

Brody smiled up at her with appreciation. She was the perfect partner for him. "Thank you," he said.

She gave him a firm nod and returned the smile.

"Let's get this done fast." Brody lifted the cloth and saw that the bleeding from the surgery had slowed but was still stubbornly oozing. "Lock, could you hold the baby so she can see him? Harriet, please do your best to hold still while I stitch you up."

Harriet gave him a weak smile, then focused on her baby as Ellie presented the needle and thread to him.

As Brody reached for the cut, the ground trembled again and everyone paused. It was then that Thayne stepped out of the doctor's office, pulling the bedlike examining table toward them.

One of the cowhands, an orphan who wanted to learn how to do ranch work, rushed over once the trembling stopped. "What can I do to help? The children are scared, and we've all been watching over them, but Zane sent me over to help."

Thayne shouted, "Grab the other end of this bed!"

The young cowhand ran over to Thayne and helped move the bed over to Brody and Harriet.

"Is anyone else hurt here?" the cowhand asked.

"Dr. MacKenzie is stitching up my sister," Nora said. "She's seriously injured, but so far no one else is hurt. Are the children all right?"

"Yep, we got everyone outside, and fortunately no more buildings have collapsed. We're not letting anyone else go inside until these aftershocks slow down and we've had a chance to look everything over and make sure it's safe."

Brody motioned for the cowhand to come and assist him. "Help me lift Harriet onto the bed. Thayne, you and Ellie get on the other side. We'll lift her and move her forward. Mind that tube in her throat."

The cowhand glanced at Harriet's bleeding neck and flinched, then moved to stand by Harriet's legs.

Once everyone was in place, Brody said, "Very smooth now, on the count of three. I don't want to jostle the tube."

The four of them tucked their hands under Harriet.

"One, two, three, *lift*."

They lifted her in one easy move and settled her gently onto the bed.

Brody checked the tube. "She needs more stitches on her shoulder and arm. Lock, stay close with Bo Jr. Thayne, she may need to be held still."

Harriet, her eyes alert now, looked hard at Brody and gave him a small wave of her uninjured hand. He could tell she was determined to stay still regardless of what lay ahead.

Brody turned to the cowhand. "Go check again to see if anyone else needs a doctor."

He studied the nasty gashes on Harriet's arm and shoulder, cleaned the wounds thoroughly, then took the threaded needle from Ellie and went to work. He wished he'd've gotten to the stitches before she regained consciousness. This was going to hurt.

Brody loved this kind lady. She'd been a teacher and had accepted spinsterhood until she'd come west with a mission group that included her sister, Nora, and Zane's wife, Michelle. Now she was a married woman with her first child as she neared the age of forty. Even with an infant to care for, she helped at the school whenever she was needed, and she did it with a cheerful attitude.

"All right, Harriet, let's get you patched up. Keep your eyes on Bo now." Brody steadily and neatly put eight stitches in her upper arm, then fifteen more across the top of her shoulder. He tested the area for fear of a fractured collarbone, but it was intact.

"Ellie, you can bandage the wounds now." Brody took an assessing look at Harriet. Though she'd had her teeth clenched the whole time, she never flinched once from the needle's piercing.

"Yes, Doctor," Ellie said, reaching for the bandages.

His wife was the best nurse he could imagine.

Brody addressed the group around him, "If any women with children to tend find they've got a hand to spare, have them watch over Harriet and her baby. I need to check around, see if there are others with injuries."

Brody's eyes met Ellie's, and she gave him a look that warmed his heart.

He repacked his medical bag, then turned to leave just as

riders came galloping into the yard—Josh and Cord and the others returning from their work on the range.

After Brody finished up here at the ranch, he would ride to Dorada Rio to see if they needed his doctoring skills in town. They had their own doctor, of course, but he might need more help. This earthquake had been an especially bad one.

Brody rushed away, heading first for the orphanage.

THREE

Cord had his horse running flat-out for home, his head swimming with worry for Sacramento and Grandpa Westbrook. His ma and her parents, Grandma and Grandpa Rivers, lived south of California's capital city. What about San Francisco? An earthquake this powerful might have gone on for miles, maybe touching the whole state!

He leaned low over his horse's neck to urge more speed out of the critter, hoping for no more aftershocks. "I've never seen the ground crack open like that. I've heard of it but never seen it."

Glancing to the side, he saw Annie. She was astride her horse, galloping as fast as his mount was running. Besides Caroline, it was just the three of them. The other men had gone on ahead. While Annie mostly stayed in the house or schoolroom, she was a tough westerner just like her brothers. He'd heard Josh talk about what a crack shot she was and decent at following a trail.

Then he remembered that he'd almost kissed her. All right, so she was unlike her brothers in some very significant ways.

"Slow down!" Josh reined his horse to a walk just as Cord realized the ground was shaking.

Cord mentally scolded himself for not being more mindful. Josh was a skilled, knowing horseman. Cord still had a long way to go to come close to those skills, and if he wanted a place of his own, he would need to improve.

This time the quake was over quick, and they picked up the pace again. They'd be home in another ten minutes, if they didn't have to stop and walk again. "Not a bad one," Annie said, giving Caroline an assessing look. She was riding in front of her Uncle Josh, snuggled up against his chest.

One more stop and the ranch came into sight. From a distance, there was no visible damage, but there'd surely be some. Cord had lived in or near Sacramento his whole life. He knew earthquakes always left their mark. The buildings left standing could still be so damaged that they couldn't ever be used again and had to be torn down. His time at Grandpa Westbrook's bank working with the inspections people had taught him a lot about earthquake damage. He'd be sure to go over all the buildings thoroughly.

The horses were milling around in the corral. A Hereford cow calmly walked away from the buildings to the first patch of good grass and stopped to graze, her baby pressed up against her side. The little one looked skittish, and who could blame it? It settled in for a comforting nip of milk.

"Is that Brody?" Annie pointed at the dark-haired man carrying a doctor's bag, rushing toward the mob of children being corralled in their own way. As expected, everyone was outside.

"He said he wouldn't be back till spring, but it's great he's here in time to help us through this. Thank God." Josh closed the distance to the ranch house, but instead of taking his horse to the barn to groom it, he trotted over to the hitching post and dismounted.

— ◆ —

Annie swung down from her horse as well. Her head jumbled with all the possible trouble they'd find. "Stay by my side, Caroline, and be careful around the horse. Get too close and it might step on your little toes."

Five-year-old Caroline had lived on the ranch since birth. She knew about keeping her distance from the powerful hooves of horses and cattle. Her little girl was growing up fast.

Josh and Cord made short work of stripping the leather from all three horses and shooing them into the corral.

Annie didn't wait for them. "Good time for Brody to get here, though I hope no one needs doctoring. Caroline and I are going to see how the children are doing." She rushed toward the school building, holding Caroline's hand while following in Brody's footsteps.

The doctor quickly went from one child to the next to assess their condition. Meanwhile, Tilda told him which ones she suspected needed care, indicating a child here and there. Though Brody no doubt wanted to check for himself, his expression said he was taking Tilda's words seriously.

Annie reached them just as Ellie, her little sister, came running up.

"Ellie! You're home! A fine welcome we've arranged for you."

Ellie had blood streaked down the front of her dress and

on her hands. She'd noticed some blood on Brody, too. "What happened?"

"Harriet got hit by a falling rafter and had cuts to be sewn up. But she's awake and alert. She should be fine. Brody had to do some real doctoring. I'll tell you more later."

Annie nodded. "It looks like the children are going to be all right."

Ellie took Annie's arm and gave it an affectionate squeeze. "I'd better stick with Brody." She grinned. "He gets to ordering people around when he's involved in doctoring, but I like helping him."

Annie smiled back. "Should I go help with Harriet?"

"That's a good idea. She's outside resting on the examination table near what's left of her house. No one's going inside the buildings until we can be sure it's safe to do so. A lot of young children are there. Thayne and Lock are out tending the herd of women and children, so you'd be a big help. Caroline can go with you."

Annie and Ellie hadn't seen each other since Ellie had followed Brody to Boston last fall, but Annie knew from letters that there was a baby on the way.

"You look good, Ellie. I'm so glad you're here."

They hugged despite the blood, then Ellie ran after her husband while Annie and Caroline went to see Harriet. Seeing Ellie's devotion and respect for Brody had Annie remembering that for one moment, she'd thought Cord was going to kiss her. What's more, she was going to let him. She hadn't kissed any man since her husband had died nearly three years ago. Hadn't had such a thought even.

The grief and loss had left an ache in her heart that was so painful, she'd vowed she would never risk loving another man again. And it had never been difficult to stay true to that promise.

They'd just gone through an earthquake. She was upset by it all. Cord had been so careful and sweet to carry her little girl when Annie didn't have the strength to do it. Strange things could happen to a woman when she was upset and grateful.

Thank heavens Josh had shown up and put a stop to any nonsense that might've taken place had he not come along.

Annie rounded a building to see every cowhand's wife on the place, standing outside their row of homes and looking rather bewildered. The women were gathered in front of Harriet's collapsed house. Many of them had a baby or two. Since Michelle had married Zane, they'd done some things differently on the Two Harts, including offering any cowhand who wanted to marry and settle here his own cabin with some space for a garden. They'd found that married men made for a steadier working crew who tended not to wander off. As a rule, cowhands were known for having itchy feet.

The noon meal was long past, and fussy babies whined in their mamas' arms. Annie sighed, wondering what she could do to help, then realized it was naptime. And no one could go inside.

But it was a beautiful spring day, and there was a grassy stretch with young fruit trees just past the bunkhouse. A nice day to sit in the sun with a sleeping baby on your lap.

She hated to see Harriet's house in ruins. Thankfully, though, it was the only house so badly damaged, its roof caved in.

"Thayne and Lock." The two boys were hovering around Harriet, whose throat was all bandaged up. She was watching

38

her baby, Bo Jr. Lock held the child up so that Harriet could see the little one was all right.

The boys looked up at her. "What do you need, ma'am?" Thayne asked.

Because Annie worked with the older children most afternoons, she'd been their teacher since the day they'd arrived. She'd venture to guess that she knew these two as well as anyone. Tilda had ridden across the country with them on the orphan train they ran away from. So maybe Tilda had a good notion about them. But she probably knew them even better than their brother, though maybe they'd become better acquainted while the boys had lived with Brody and Ellie through the winter in Boston.

Annie had been a witness to all their antics. She'd found all the gaping holes in their education and devoted herself to filling those gaps. While they were smart boys, they were utterly undisciplined. They had no qualms about lying to get themselves out of trouble. And they were obsessed with their grandfather's treasure map and the journal it was hidden in, sent from California to their mother and father back in New York City.

But they seemed to be calm and helpful right now.

"Can we move Harriet?" she asked them.

"Brody said we can move her if we're very careful of her throat." Thayne explained about the surgery Brody had performed on Harriet so that she could breathe freely.

Annie shuddered to think of having to slit someone's throat to open their airway. "You both stay and watch Harriet while I get the other women settled over by the orchard. Then I'll come back and hold the baby while you carry her bed there to join the others."

They nodded, serious looks on their faces. These two scalawags were long overdue for some sign of maturity. Right now, at least for this moment, they were behaving like fine, dependable young men.

In really hard times, they could be counted on. She hoped.

Cord staggered as he turned to the last building. They'd checked the rest, so he had an idea of what to look for. He was glad for the years working in Grandpa Westbrook's bank. He'd been among those sent out by the bank when someone wanted a loan to repair a damaged house. In some cases, a building was too damaged to save or the repairs were too costly.

He'd heard once that California averaged five hundred earthquakes a year. He didn't experience that many himself, of course, but most of the ones he did were so small that they barely caught his attention before they were over.

Not this one.

In full darkness, he approached Michelle's laboratory, the final building. Since no one was going to sleep in it, he felt no urgency to inspect it tonight, especially with only the light of a lantern. He would have put off even stopping by the place, except the door was ajar. Michelle usually kept it locked. It must've been broken open by the quake.

He'd just see if the lock wasn't so badly damaged that he couldn't simply close and relock it. If he couldn't, well, so be it. Every person on the ranch was exhausted. Her laboratory would be safe over one night, as well as the one remaining piece of Spanish armor still stored there, the one they'd found before the winter weather had forced them to abandon the search for more treasure.

He reached the door and stared at the splintered wood around the lock. Strange-looking earthquake damage. He didn't think he'd ever seen anything quite like it. In fact, if it wasn't for the quake, he'd have guessed someone had kicked the door open or maybe battered it with something heavier than a boot.

Mindful of possible danger from falling debris, he inched the door open. It dragged across the floor, requiring him to shove and lift at the same time. That worried him even more. The whole building might be askew.

A chill of fear struck him for no reason he could understand. Not like any other he'd felt today. He silently prayed, wondering if that fear was a message from God. He listened to unexpected feelings like that, allowing God to guide him.

He got the door open enough that he could slip in, but approaching footsteps spun him around. He was definitely spooked.

Annie emerged out of the darkness, and the worst of his nerves eased. He liked having company, especially Annie's.

"The day's over, Cord."

Her crisp tone always made him think of her as a teacher and a mother. Annie knew how to make things run smoothly.

"Josh and Tilda and Ellie and Brody and the boys have finished supper at the bunkhouse and are off to bed, so come and eat with me . . . uh, I mean *us*." She fell silent for a moment, then rushed on. "Zane and Michelle should be on their way soon. You're the last. Leave this place for tomorrow."

"I almost skipped this one." Cord pointed at the smashed door. "But it was open, and it never is. I'm not going to assess quake damage. I'll just glance at that armor and make sure nothing harmed it, then see if the door will lock. You should stay outside, though, just in case the building is on the verge of collapse. Budging the door farther open was tough."

"Make it quick. I'll wait out here." She crossed her arms as if annoyed at anyone who thought they knew better than she did.

He bit back a grin, then stepped into the darkened building. Enough moonlight came through the windows that he could see a few things tipped over, and something was smashed on the floor, as if it'd fallen off the table.

And then he looked at the armor.

Or the spot where the suit of armor should have been.

"It's gone, Annie." Cord rushed to the far side of the room and looked around the table. But he could see well enough to know that no suit of armor had toppled onto the floor or was lying on the table.

Annie was beside him before he could protest. "Did Michelle take it somewhere?"

Cord thought he would have noticed Michelle toting a suit of armor around, but then they'd have noticed anyone doing that . . . and yet someone had sure taken it. "Let's go ask her."

FOUR

Cord sank down onto a chair at the kitchen table at the end of a long, hard day. The sun had set, and they hadn't felt a tremor in hours. "We got the last family moved back inside, all but Harriet and Bo and the baby. They had an extra bedroom in the bunkhouse, and they're settled in there. We'll start building a new cabin real soon, but first we have to finish branding. We gotta find those artifacts, too."

It wasn't just the suit of armor that was gone; also missing were a spear tip and a sword, both nowhere to be seen. He realized how jumbled his thoughts were and knew he had to eat and get some sleep before he could do anything else.

Annie set a plate in front of him filled with beef stew and biscuits. She hadn't bothered sitting down herself. Instead, she'd started serving food, Michelle's baby Leah on her hip. Gretel, who'd prepared their supper, was round with a third baby on the way. She'd gone home to get her two youngsters to bed.

"You shouldn't be serving me, Annie. You've had just as long and hard of a day as any of us."

She gave him a tired smile. "It's been a day to remember, I'll grant you that."

Cord caught her wrist gently. "Let me hold the baby at least."

Annie smiled and handed Leah over. "Like you, Michelle has been checking for damage on the buildings. We've debated it and decided it's safe to sleep inside."

He could see the worry in her expression. Aftershocks could sometimes go on for days.

Cord turned to his food.

Annie pushed his plate away from the edge of the table. "This one's got a reach that surprises us every time. Watch out for her grabbing your food or she'll dump hot stew on your lap."

Cord had little experience with babies, but he'd seen a few in action and so watched the child's grasping fingers. He managed to hold Leah back and still eat.

Zane came in with Michelle right behind him.

Annie looked at Cord. They both knew they had to tell Michelle about the missing armor, and both were dreading it.

Cord squared his shoulders as the two sat down, as tired as the rest of them. Clearing his throat to put off the inevitable, he said, "Someone took the distraction of the earthquake as a chance to steal our suit of armor."

Michelle had been reaching for Leah, but now her head snapped up, and her eyes flashed. "What?"

Cord told her what they'd found. Annie threw in a few details.

Michelle shoved to her feet, but Zane caught her arm. Cord wondered if the brilliant, feisty woman had plans to saddle up and go running off after the thieves.

"We'll head for town first thing in the morning," Zane said. "Now sit down and eat. There's nothing we can do this time of day, and you haven't quit working since breakfast."

None of them had, but then they didn't have a baby to keep track of.

"The last suit of armor." Michelle's hands fisted, but she didn't run off. Instead, she took her seat at the table, and within seconds Annie had hot food in front of her and Zane.

"There are two suits of armor in town at the museum you opened with Tilda's pa."

Tilda, an orphan from her earliest memory, had only recently been reunited with her father, a wealthy New Yorker. He'd spent the winter trying to convince Tilda to forget her profound sense of abandonment and let him be her father. Toward that end he'd left New York City and assisted the Hart family in founding a museum in Dorada Rio to display their conquistador artifacts, a museum he now ran.

"Yes. I loaned one to the Crockers to display along with their growing California art collection, and one to the Archaeology Department at the University of the Pacific in San Jose."

The university was located near Sacramento, and they had a top music program. At one time, Cord had wanted to attend there badly, but Grandpa Westbrook wouldn't hear of it.

Cord finished chewing, then said, "Was it that hectic around here that some unknown person could have slipped in and stolen the armor we found?"

The artifacts had been buried in the wilderness east of their ranch three hundred years ago. Cord considered that as he ate. They'd found the five suits of armor by following

Graham MacKenzie's map, one sent to Brody's pa thirty years ago when he'd found treasure. Grandpa MacKenzie then died before he could move his family west. .

One of his cryptic notes was that he'd send a second map to Cord's Grandpa Westbrook. That second map would lead searchers on past the place they'd found the armor. Another note said Graham had gathered all the gold. That lack of gold—combined with the winter weather keeping them away from the area covered by the rest of the map—had calmed Thayne and Lock down enough that they were willing to spend the winter in Boston with their big brother, Brody.

Now they were back in California, the winter had passed, and the treasure hunt was back on—or soon would be once things had calmed down around the ranch. The absence so far of the gold hoard Thayne and Lock had conjured in their treasure-feverish imaginations wasn't enough to dampen the boys' enthusiasm. And they had found the suits of armor. True treasure if Tilda, Josh's historically wise wife, was to be believed.

Tilda and Michelle had created the museum in Dorada Rio. Michelle, who was well connected in the state, had approached some scholars of history at the University of the Pacific, where Ellie had gone to college shortly after the university had opened its doors to women.

Michelle had invited the scholars to come and research the armor and other things they'd found. Those men had been in and out of the museum in town and at the Two Harts all winter.

But they were well-respected scholars, not thieves. Professor Hardy, the most enthused of those scholars, was expected back anytime. He'd pushed hard to take all the armor back

46

to the university, and he was a gruff man on his best day. He wasn't going to like this news.

Yet the artifacts still belonged to Brody and his family, and since he'd married into the Hart family, the Harts had been included in that ownership.

The family had been well paid for the loan. They'd kept the fifth and final suit of armor because Tilda, a history fanatic, and Michelle, who was curious about everything, said they wanted to study the suit themselves.

Michelle chewed, swallowed, and said, "It was absolute chaos around here with the earthquake, but no one could have planned to take advantage of that. It was either a crime of opportunity—someone from our ranch realized in the middle of the turmoil that they could get away with the armor—or it was a preplanned crime by an outsider or one of our own that was made infinitely easier because of the earthquake."

"If it's a stranger," Annie said, "we should have noticed him. If it's one of our own, wouldn't they have taken the armor and run? In which case someone should be missing."

"Or," Michelle said with narrowed eyes, "they stole the armor and hid it with plans to get it later when their absence wouldn't be so noticeable."

Cord sighed. "That's a lot of possible scenarios. And we don't have any clear suspects. How are we going to find that armor?"

He wished Brody and Tilda were there, but they had turned in for the night. He didn't think anyone would be more upset about what had happened than Thayne and Lock. The thought that they might be harboring a thief right here at the ranch would have stopped Cord from eating altogether if he hadn't been outright starving.

"Does Brody know?" Zane asked between bites of the savory stew.

"No," Cord replied. "I inspected the laboratory last because no one needs it for shelter, so I wasn't too worried about it structurally. I wouldn't have gone in if the door hadn't been standing ajar in a way that struck me as . . . well, as not caused by the earthquake. I decided to take a quick look inside, then lock the door and look closer tomorrow. I noticed right away that the suit of armor wasn't there."

Annie finally had everyone a plate of food and sat down with her own. "The lock on the front door was broken."

Zane had finished his first plate of food and got up to refill it from the pot kept warm on the stove. Normally Annie would have put a bowl of the stew on the table, but everything was very informal tonight. "I'd shake everyone out of bed to search around the place in case it's hidden nearby, but no one's got the energy after today." He sat back at the table and looked at his wife. "I'm sorry about that, but I don't think I could find anyone awake to help us."

Michelle nodded. "You're right. Even I can't muster the strength to do anything but sit here and seethe. Besides, it's full dark. It's not as if we could look for tracks."

Zane rested his hand on top of Michelle's. Cord marveled at these two. Both were highly skilled, intelligent, if not a little stubborn. But they loved each other. They didn't bicker when they disagreed; they talked it out. They used the common sense they'd been richly endowed with, and they found a way to proceed. That was the strength and the depth of their love for each other.

"We've got some skilled trackers among the cowhands who could help me and Josh." Zane glanced over his shoulder as he volunteered his sleeping brother. "Though none is better than you, Annie."

Cord turned to her, and she shrugged. "It's true. I'm a hand at it."

"It's branding time, and everyone is busy," Zane went on. "Still, we'll take a few of our best trackers away from the cattle crews and get started at first light."

Cord nodded. "I know I'm no skilled tracker, Zane, but I've been working on it. And that suit of armor being stolen hits me pretty close to home."

A note found with the long-dead body of Graham MacKenzie had left half of his supposed treasure to Cord's grandpa, Mayhew Westbrook, who had loaned Graham money to purchase land and bring his family west. While the artifacts might not have been the treasure Graham promised, Mayhew—and Cord—still had an interest in this.

"I appreciate that, Cord. I was going to ask for your help with the search."

Cord lived in the bunkhouse with the other cowhands, but he had a cordial relationship with the Hart family, who regularly invited him to eat with them. He was grateful for their company, although tonight Cord had a deep need to find out how his family was doing. Had the quake hit Sacramento hard, too?

Michelle must have noticed the concern in his expression because she said, "Before I go up to bed, let's send a telegraph to your family, Cord. I've got a few I want to send myself. I want to find out what happened outside this area. Brody spent some time in Dorada Rio this afternoon with Ellie and his brothers to see if they needed more care than the single doctor in town could provide. But they're all back,

49

and Gretel left them a meal in their rooms over the doctor's office. He didn't report much, just said there were injuries and some damage."

Cord looked down and saw that Leah had fallen asleep in his arms, just as Caroline had done earlier today. Maybe he was good with little ones after all.

"Cord, bring Leah along, if you don't mind." Michelle finished her meal. "Let's go send those wires."

"I'll keep it short. We all need to get some sleep." Cord ate the last of his supper, then, cradling Leah in his arms, he followed Michelle to the study, where the family had a telegraph wire come right into the house.

He saw Annie start to clean up the kitchen and sped up a bit to send his wire. If he hurried, he could help tidy up and not leave it all to her. And spend a few more minutes with her besides.

Then he noticed Zane gathering up dirty plates and saw that Annie wasn't on her own. Regardless, Cord hurried anyway.

FIVE

"There are two sets of tracks." Josh jabbed a finger at the tracks they'd found just a bit back into a small grove of trees. "They hid their horses here and carried the armor out on foot."

Cord was riding with him in the early light of dawn. They'd taken the time to eat something, not knowing how long they might be searching for whoever had stolen the armor.

Zane had hung back to repair the lock on the door of Michelle's laboratory.

"I didn't see that spear tip last night." Cord had noticed the artifact just this morning, shoved up against the wall in the laboratory. Now he studied the tracks, knowing a good tracker could tell more than just that a horse had stood here . . . then walked on. They could judge the weight of the rider, the size of the horse, lots of things.

Josh was fond of saying that he could read a trail like the written word; he called it "reading sign." Cord couldn't see things quite that clearly, but then he wasn't done learning yet. And, he admitted, he probably never would be.

Josh paused to tug the kerchief off his neck and tied it around a branch. A signal to Zane that he wouldn't miss. "Zane should pick up the trail too, but this might speed things up some."

Josh set out then, and Cord fell in beside him. Michelle had taken a couple of cowhands and ridden to Dorada Rio to see if they'd had trouble at the museum in town. It seemed like it would be easier to snatch one of those suits of armor than to slink onto the Two Harts.

"Do the tracks tell you anything?" Cord asked.

"My first reaction is that it's not one of our horses. We have a mark on the bottom of all our horseshoes." Josh pulled up and pointed behind him.

Cord studied the track for a long while. Josh waited, not telling him what to look for. "It's your brand, the two hearts, lying on their side, touching at the point of the hearts like a sideways number eight."

"Yep, it's easy enough to mark the shoes when we make them. Pa started it up long ago. He said the horses sometimes wandered back when he was still building, and he'd let them out to graze like we do the cattle. The horses were branded, but we had neighbors whose horses wandered, too. And you couldn't see the brand until you saw the horse. This way you wouldn't spent time tracking your neighbor's horses."

"I like the idea. Is that common practice?"

Josh shrugged. "Around here I think we're the only ones who do it. But the horses are better trained these days and know where home is, so they're not as likely to wander off."

They rode along, the trail being easy enough to follow once Josh had found it.

Cord continued to study the tracks, trying to glean information.

Josh, his eyes fixed on the ground, said, "So you like our Annie some, then?"

Cord's head snapped up to look at Josh, who lifted his head and met Cord's eyes with his cold blue ones.

"Why? What did I do that brought on such a statement?" Cord's mind rabbited around. Josh hadn't seen him and Annie together yesterday, sitting out an aftershock . . . or had he? And anyway, nothing had happened. Even so, clearly something had drawn Josh's notice.

"No man would be fool enough to be around such a fine woman as my sister and not like her."

Cord narrowed his eyes. "She is a fine woman for a fact. And one whose heart seems to still be devoted to her husband. Nothing has gone on between us."

"I reckon not." Josh then flashed him a look that belied his words, as if Cord's defense of himself was some kind of insult. "I believe in my sister's honor too completely to think it was otherwise. Still, you've got eyes, and sometimes they linger on her for a bit too long."

It stung Cord a bit that Josh felt the need to warn him away from Annie. "You're saying I need to stay away from her?" he flat-out asked.

"Is that what I'm saying?" Josh gave a half smile, then went back to focusing on the tracks. A moment later, he urged his horse forward, ready to ride on.

Cord quick reached out and grabbed Josh's arm.

Josh twisted around in the saddle to face Cord, and the blazing blue glare was a reminder that Josh wasn't a man to be trifled with. He had the ironhard muscles of a seasoned rancher who'd wrestled a living by breaking wild horses, roping ornery cattle, and working the land in all manner of weather.

Cord swallowed hard, letting go of Josh's arm. "Josh, you should know that I'll be leaving here soon. My plan is to stay until we've come to the end of my half of the treasure map. But I want to go and live closer to my family. My life isn't here, and Annie's is. Add to that, when I look at her, I see love for another man in her eyes. I see grief there still. She needs time to get past that before she can think of another man. And when that time comes, I'll be long gone."

Josh nodded. "Did she ever tell you that her husband, Todd, was murdered?"

Cord had heard as much, yet he knew few details of what had happened exactly. "Who killed him?"

"Someone burned their place to the ground. Todd, Annie, and Caroline took off on horseback, riding from their ranch for the Two Harts, and while doing so Todd was shot. By the time they arrived here, he'd taken two bullets in his gut. Caroline was on Annie's lap, and she had bullets in her leg and arm. Michelle got the bullets out of Todd's body, but he'd already lost a lot of blood. He died soon after in Annie's arms."

Cord let out a low whistle and shook his head slowly.

Josh went on, "So you're right—a wife needs time to get over something like that. I hadn't yet returned home from the sea when it happened, but I was here not long after. And my lively, bright-eyed big sister was replaced by someone quieter, bitterly hurt, and saddened. I swear to you, Cord, I won't stand by and see her hurt again."

And that's the danger, isn't it? Cord thought. How could

a man promise not to hurt a woman when all of life seemed to end up hurting at one time or another? It was a mighty hard promise to make, and Cord was nowhere near ready to make it. There was only one honorable way to act.

"You've delivered your message, Josh." Cord looked away from him to the trail ahead. "How about we get back to tracking now?"

Though Josh didn't say anything, Cord could tell that their little talk was over. His boss kicked his horse, and they went back to searching for thieves.

—— ◇ ——

Annie ached to go along and help search for the stolen suit of armor. She also wanted to go on the next treasure hunt, which was coming up if the buzzing energy of Thayne and Lock MacKenzie was any clue.

Instead, she taught school.

They had four classrooms. In the mornings, they divided the school into four groups—older girls, older boys, younger girls, younger boys—teaching the different groups general subjects like reading, writing, and arithmetic.

In the afternoon, they focused on subjects beyond the basics. It had been Michelle's idea to bring out the strengths and interests of each child, orphans who'd led hard lives. Michelle wanted to prepare them for a future full of promise.

They offered several classes, including a history class taught by Tilda, who had a rare and fascinating way of talking about the past. Her classes were always crowded.

Annie usually taught writing skills, hoping she'd inspire the children to want to further their education. Being a skilled writer could help with that.

Michelle wanted their students to be prepared for the future and to find work that they'd enjoy. Work that suited their intelligence and temperament.

The Two Harts School for Orphans was an idea that they'd begun two years ago. The younger children had time to improve, but the older ones, many of whom had spent a good portion of their childhood running the streets, had serious gaps in their education. The teachers had worked together to identify the gaps, then addressed those gaps by educating the students, hopefully preparing them for life on their own someday. They'd already had a few children leave school, bound for work and independent living. They'd trained three teachers, two of whom had married each other and remained at the Two Harts school. The other had found a teaching job at Dorada Rio but came out to the ranch regularly to visit with her friends.

Two of the young men had been eager to learn cowboy skills and had taken a job on the ranch. Two others had been hired on at Stiles Lumber. One was a lumberjack, while the other got a job working at the sawmill. Since Michelle was a member of the Stiles family, she owned a third of the lumber dynasty her father had established. She was happy to send her former students to a place of work where they'd be treated right and paid well.

They had four more students itching to get out on their own, including one who'd gone off to college to study medicine.

The training for the students was geared toward practical careers, but not for the first time, Annie wondered if they shouldn't be teaching their students music too, especially with Cord, a skilled musician, being so close at hand.

Annie pondered this as the older girls filed out of the classroom for the noon meal.

Tilda came out of the classroom for the older boys. They all loved her to the point they'd considered having her teach the older boys and girls in the morning, then about half the school in the afternoon. But the older boys were the hardest, and each of the classes had around fifteen students in them right now. Giving her thirty students to teach all on her own would be too much for her to handle.

Tilda came and wrapped an arm around Annie's waist. "I've got two of my older girls asking about becoming teachers."

Annie smiled. "Can I work with one of them? The Sidleys are doing great in the other two classes."

The Sidleys were the young couple who'd met and married and stayed on to teach at the school. Jessica Sidley taught the younger girls, while her husband, Larry, taught the younger boys.

"Do you think they'll want to stay? You need someone to take over your class, especially the boys in the morning. I don't know if anyone can do what you do with history in the afternoon."

"Larry's got a talent for teaching and a love of history. I've had him sit in on my history classes. I don't know about him taking my older boys in the morning, though. They're friends of his, so he might have trouble controlling them."

Annie laughed. "Him and everyone else but you."

"We'll think of something." Tilda's smile faded, and she gave Annie a worried look. "But you don't want to claim one of them, Annie? I thought you loved teaching?"

"It's true I love doing it, but I'm not sure I want to keep on teaching for years. I didn't exactly choose it as a career. Like you, I got roped into this. One day I found myself standing too close to Michelle."

They both laughed as they walked to the ranch house for the noon meal.

"What would you rather do, Annie? We all depend on you so much. I guess I've never asked if you're happy doing it. I'm not sure if anyone has thanked you, and for certain no one pays you."

"Or you," Annie reminded her.

"Right, and we're going to have to pay the students who stay here to teach. We can't just dragoon them into working for us."

Annie couldn't hold back a smile at that. "One reason I'd like to find another teacher is because I sometimes feel as though I'm missing out on other things when I'm in the classroom. Take last fall, for instance. Everyone went on the treasure hunt but me." She sighed wistfully. "Although I don't suppose a treasure hunt in the wilderness is any place for a five-year-old."

Tilda said, "Why not? Children have walked with their kin across the country following wagon trains. They're a tough lot. Caroline can ride a horse, can't she?"

"With close supervision." Annie felt a spark of excitement at the thought of riding out into the wilderness. "But riding a horse is one thing. Some of our treasure hunters have ended up getting shot."

Tilda waved a hand as the two of them approached the ranch house. "That only happened once." Her brow furrowed. "Of course, there's the time Cord cracked his head on a shield, and his wits were almost knocked out of him when a skull rolled out of that helmet. Still, that isn't the same as dangerous outlaws trying to overpower us to steal gold doubloons."

"Cord hit his head?"

"That's right. He bled all over, and Josh was worried because rusty iron isn't anything you want to mess with. He had to let it bleed a while to clean out the cut so it wouldn't become infected."

"I don't remember that."

Tilda gave her a long look. "No reason you should remember. He was mostly over it by the time we got back to the ranch."

Annie wanted to ask Tilda what that look meant. Instead, she reached for the door handle and let Tilda lead the way inside.

Michelle was busy setting the table with Leah on her hip. Gretel was working over the stove with her toddler dancing around the hot metal. Gretel was a master at blocking her attempts to get too close while still getting her work done. Her baby was in a little playpen Zane had built. Sometimes Leah went in there with her.

Tilda took the plates Michelle had in one hand. "I'll finish setting the table. Tell us what you found in your workshop. Are the men back from visiting the museum in town, and did Josh come back?"

As usual, Annie had been busy teaching and, not counting yesterday's earthquake, had missed all the excitement.

"None of the men are back yet." Michelle sat and bounced her little girl on her knee. "The big development this morning is that I found the missing shield."

"Where was it?" Annie slid biscuits out of the oven, off a

baking sheet, and into a basket. "Was it hidden somewhere in the woods?"

"No, it must have been overlooked. It was lying flat on the floor and shoved under the table where I mix chemicals."

Annie frowned as she helped Gretel get the meal on. "I didn't notice it there last night."

"I didn't see it right away either. There wasn't a lot of light, and it was pushed way back in the shadows under the table. I expect those no-good thieves just didn't notice it. I wonder if the earthquake knocked it off the table. Depending on how it landed, it could have rolled before it tipped over."

"Did you look to see if there were more pieces still there?" Tilda loved that suit of armor. Of all of them, she'd been the most involved in researching the historic pieces and studying the conquistadors and especially Captain Cabrillo, whose armada of Spanish ships had explored the California coast some three hundred years ago. And anything she found, she wove into her history class.

"I scoured the place, believe me," said Michelle.

And Annie did believe her. Michelle wasn't a careless woman.

"Do we have a list of all that was kept in there, so we know what exactly got stolen?" Annie thought between Tilda and Michelle they could remember, but there were many small pieces to the suit of armor plus the weapons.

"Yes, we have a thorough list. Besides the full suit of armor, we kept one of every type of weapon: a spear tip, a shield, a sword, a halberd, a dagger, plus the helmet."

"What's a halberd?" Annie asked.

Tilda answered, "It was that thing that looks like an ax with a spike at the top. It normally would have been on a wooden handle about six feet long. Nasty weapon. But the handle had rotted away—three hundred years will do that to wood."

"I remember it now. Did we have any one-of-a-kind weapons or pieces of armor, or was everything like the other artifacts we've loaned out?"

"None that I can think of," Michelle said.

"Well, I doubt the Crockers or your pa, Tilda, would steal from us. But those men from the university might," Annie suggested.

Michelle snorted as she bounced the baby on her knee. "Those men are highly respected scholars. They wouldn't do such a thing."

"Someone sure did."

Tilda came to the table with a bowl of chicken and noodles. "Gretel, you're welcome to stay and eat with us. Rick can eat with the cowhands. It's a big job for you to haul food and your children all the way home."

"No, thank you. Rick will come and help me. He likes seeing me and the children and joining us for meals."

A knock on the back door told them he'd come just like Gretel said. "That's Rick now," she laughed.

Rick didn't wait to be invited in. Walking home with his family to eat together was routine. Soon Annie, Michelle, and Tilda were alone. As for Caroline, she preferred sharing the midday meal with her friends at school.

"What did you find out in town?" Annie asked Michelle. "And didn't Zane ride with you? Where is he?"

"He went back to branding. He says two more long days and they'll be done. The remaining chuck wagon—the one left after the other sank into the ground yesterday—was just

heading out when we got home, so he's eating with the men."
Michelle scooped up chicken and noodles onto her plate and
dug in, chewing thoughtfully.

"We talked to your pa, Tilda. He hasn't had anything
go missing. He said the men we brought in have been there
studying the armor, and they're fascinated by it. Professor
Hardy is around the most. But Carl didn't think they'd done
anything suspicious. So far he isn't seeing many folks interested in visiting the museum. We talked about maybe moving
it either to Sacramento or San Francisco. We liked the idea of
keeping the museum here, luring tourists into town, but we
haven't had much luck with it. I think he'd push for moving
it, that is, if he didn't want to stay close to you."

Carl Cabril seemed to enjoy sitting in on his daughter's
classes and would sometimes add to the discussion in fascinating ways. Tilda was still adjusting to having a father
after her years of living as an orphan. She'd also discovered
that she had an older brother and a twin sister, Maddie, who
had become a true sister to her.

"Josh told me he was riding out with Cord today in hopes
of finding and following any tracks."

"Zane might throw in with them after he works a few
hours. Josh promised to leave a trail."

Annie helped herself to a second biscuit, along with more
chicken and noodles. This was her favorite meal that Gretel
made, and it seemed like she was still hungry after a sparse
day of eating yesterday.

"We'll be to the end of the school term in a couple of
weeks. We need to figure out how to give the children a fun
summer. It's not like they can just go home. And the baby
will be here before school resumes, so I'll need to quit teach-

ing." Tilda and Josh's baby was expected to arrive by the end of summer.

Michelle nodded. "Even with a baby, you can keep teaching the history class. You realize you have a rare talent for it."

The small tip of Tilda's head, almost like a little shrug, was in Annie's opinion a long way from agreement. Annie wondered if her father or Maddie might step in to teach Tilda's classes. They were always on the lookout for teachers at the Two Harts.

Some of the archeologists who'd come to study the armor were professors. The one who came most often, Professor Oswald Hardy, had brought students out with him, and his assistant, Walter Rombauer, had been a constant at his side. And he was not at all pleased about how they'd brought in the armor. He'd insisted they should have contacted him. They should have allowed him to dig up that graveyard in a correct manner. In fact, he thought they should have given him and the university all the artifacts they'd found.

Hardy was big on issuing orders and pointing out mistakes. That might work with his students, but no one at the Two Harts Ranch was overly impressed with his bossy behavior, nor were they interested in earning a good grade from the man.

"Maybe Professor Hardy would volunteer to teach a class," Tilda said. "He could share with our students what he does for a living. It might pique their curiosity. Of course, the professor seems to think teaching young children is beneath him." Tilda's frustration was evident in her tone.

Annie pushed herself to her feet, feeling the burden of

responsibility for those young lives who'd started out in such a harsh way. She wished to help them find a path that would give them a good life. That conflicted with her often hard-to-control wish that it might well be someone else's job to see that task through.

SIX

"Josh, over there." Cord wasn't sure what he was seeing, but he thought maybe it was . . .

"That's part of the armor," Josh said, then pulled back on the reins and dismounted.

Cord, only a few seconds behind him, headed into the brush that edged the trail. They'd been searching for hours, although Cord had given up long ago and stopped pretending that he could spot any tracks on the sometimes grassy, sometimes rocky trail. Instead, he just kept an eye out as he followed Josh, who seemed to be following something with determination.

His distraction might've saved the day. And since Josh had ridden past the dull gray object, Cord happened to be closer. He pushed the scrub juniper aside and stared down at a helmet.

"Who did this?" Josh crouched down and picked up the helmet. "Look behind it. This could be everything that's missing."

Shaking his head in disgust, Cord said, "It's all just been tossed here. It doesn't look as though someone hid these things to collect later either. No, it looks like they just threw them into the underbrush and rode off."

Josh pivoted on the toes of his boots. "We can figure out why later. For now, we've got the artifacts back in our hands. Wait, you don't think . . . ?"

Josh's hesitation worried Cord. "What don't I think?"

Dragging in a ragged breath, Josh said, "To me this looks like some kind of prank, like the work of vandals. Something a bunch of kids might do."

Cord, who'd pushed deeper into the underbrush to gather up the armor, stopped and turned to face Josh. "You think some of the youngsters we've taken in at the ranch might've done this?"

Josh's jaw tightened until Cord thought his teeth might crack. "I hate thinking it. Anyway, how would they get this armor out here? How could they carry it this far? They must've stolen . . . or borrowed horses since we don't have any missing." He hesitated at the word *stolen*, knowing a horse thief could be hung. Accusing someone of such a thing was serious business in the West.

"We can talk it over later," said Cord. "Now, do we need a travois, or can we split these pieces of armor between us and the horses?"

Josh looked back at the armor. A smile quirked his lips. "You know, we could get all the pieces back home if we wore them."

Cord, still shocked by the idea that one or more of the orphans might be to blame, chuckled at the thought of their riding to the ranch wearing centuries-old armor. "It's all very old and delicate, but if we're careful, it should be all right, don't you think?"

"Then we'll be careful," said Josh.

Cord grinned. "I get the helmet."

—— ✧ ——

Annie caught Tilda's arm. "Looks like they found the missing artifacts."

They were on their way home from school. The students were acting subdued today. She blamed yesterday's earthquake for that. There was something very powerful, almost biblical about a *condition* that could shake the whole earth.

Now she watched Cord as he rode toward the ranch house, wearing a breastplate and helmet. Other pieces of armor were tied down in front of him on the saddle. Josh, riding right behind Cord, carried a sword and that odd-looking ax Tilda called a "halberd." The pieces for protecting a man's legs and feet were among those stacked in front of both him and Cord.

Cord waved. The helmet had a little strip of metal coming down from the forehead, probably there to protect the wearer's nose when in battle. She saw a smile flash from the helmet.

"Cord, Josh, you found the armor!" Tilda ran toward him.

Now that the two had made their grand entrance, they rode for the laboratory.

The door to the ranch house opened, and Annie saw Michelle coming, her baby in her arms. She was joined by Zane, fresh from the barn, Brody, and the bunkhouse cook, who stepped outside, wiping his hands.

Several students poked their heads out of the schoolhouse.

Brody nodded his approval. "Josh, Cord, you got the armor back."

Brody's younger brothers shoved past him and ran toward Josh and Cord. Annie knew those boys mainly wanted gold, but they were still very protective of anything connected to their grandfather's treasure.

Apart from Brody, who probably had a patient and shouldn't desert his post right now, they all converged on the laboratory at the same time as the would-be conquistadors.

Cord swung down from his horse. "Get this thing off of me. Be very gentle with it. How did those Spaniards stand it? The helmet may be stuck on my head. I never should have put it on."

They all got very busy reclaiming the armor and bringing it inside the laboratory.

Michelle frowned and said, "You shouldn't play with these things." Yet she didn't sound all that angry.

"It's the only way we could carry all the armor home without having to build a travois. And we were in a hurry to get it back here."

"I want to lay it all out." Michelle glanced at Tilda. "Can you help me decide where all the pieces go? Once that's done, we'll check for any damage?"

Annie took Leah and stayed back as they laid the armor out on the table. Some of the pieces weren't easy to identify. The iron that protected the shins looked a lot like the steel that guarded the arms.

Thayne and Lock got busy helping put the armor together like a puzzle they were eager to play with.

"Tell us how you discovered it, Josh," Zane asked.

Taking turns, Josh and Cord told everyone how they'd

found the pieces of armor tossed into the underbrush as if they were worthless.

Michelle, who was looking over the armor with a notebook in her hand, occasionally paused to listen to the details while the suit of armor came together. Annie bounced Leah, who reached for the armor as if wanting to play with the fun puzzle, too.

"That right there is a dent that wasn't there before." Tilda pointed at a piece that protected the knee.

"I don't see the dagger," Michelle said. "Could you have missed it when you gathered up the rest of the armor?" Her eyes shifted between Josh and Cord.

Cord shook his head. "We scoured the place, Michelle," he answered, and Josh voiced his agreement. "Of course, the dagger may have gotten thrown unusually far from the other pieces. I suppose we could ride out there and check around some more."

Michelle had a doubtful look on her face. "You didn't by chance drop it while riding here?"

Josh and Cord exchanged a glance.

"I would have remembered a dagger," said Josh, "and I sure didn't see one. We picked up a bunch of pieces of steel we couldn't identify, but—"

"It's all here." Michelle waved her notebook. It showed a complete sketch of the armor, assembled and in pieces. Each individual element had been numbered and identified. "The only thing missing is the dagger."

"We'll ride back there tomorrow," Cord volunteered. "Maybe whoever took the dagger was up to mischief and thought it was interesting enough they decided to keep it."

"Mischief? What makes you say that?" Annie asked.

"Nothing much mischievous about stealing something this valuable."

Annie took a turn looking between the two men. Josh shoved his hands into the back pockets of his denim britches. Cord rubbed the back of his neck.

The silence was thick, and no one broke it as they waited for one of them to explain.

Cord broke first. "It seemed to us that there was no good reason for someone to take the armor, then ride off and just toss it. Our first thought was theft—that armor is valuable—but why go to the trouble of breaking into a building, gathering up all those pieces of armor, only to ride a few hours away and toss it into the underbrush somewhere? Makes no sense. It seems like the kind of thing that, well . . ." He cleared his throat, clearly not wanting to finish his sentence.

Josh finished it for him. "The kind of thing a kid might do."

"Are you accusing our orphans of stealing the suit of armor?" Tilda crossed her arms, looking indignant on behalf of all the orphans in the world.

As if an orphan was above stealing. People were people, after all. Still, none of their youngsters would do such a senseless thing.

"Hey," said Lock, "those kids are our friends. And they like having that armor here; they've been excited about studying it." He was red in the face, ready to fight for the honor of his fellow students.

Michelle remained silent. She had that strange look in her eyes, a look that said she was thinking real hard on something.

Then Annie chimed in, adding, "I think I can account for

the whereabouts of every one of my students. I have the older boys. It would have to be one of them, don't you think? I'm not one to underestimate a woman, but it stands to reason. I was out on the range for a while after the earthquake hit, but not so long that anyone could have stolen the armor and run for the hills and then gotten back. The older boys were all here."

Tilda nodded. "The quake struck right when we were finishing with lunch. All the older students were in my history class."

"All of them, you're sure?" Annie knew Tilda had nearly thirty students in her class.

"Not Thayne and Lock—they'd just gotten back—but I was going to talk about Sutter's Mill and how the gold rush started." Tilda paused for a moment. "Yes, everyone was there. We brought in desks from the other classroom. The place was packed. There were kids standing up and sitting on the floor."

Like most people, the students were fascinated by stories of instant wealth.

"And I got back right after you'd herded everyone outside," Annie said. "We counted them. Remember, Tilda? We made all the students get into groups by age because it was hard to be sure we got everyone out, and they were all milling around. You had that mostly done by the time I got there. But to double-check we counted again, and the students were accounted for."

Annie, who happened to be closer to Cord than Josh, backhanded Cord in the belly. "None of my students would be party to such nonsense as vandalism or theft."

Which she knew hadn't honestly always been true, not

when they'd been running free on the streets. But since they'd moved to the Two Harts, she hadn't seen any of them get in too much trouble.

Cord nodded as he rubbed his belly. "I'm glad to hear it. We didn't want to believe it was one of them, but it was all that made sense. And now with the dagger still missing . . . well, it seems like something that might tempt a youngster to keep as his own."

"There goes the easy solution." Josh sounded relieved and frustrated at the same time. "So if it wasn't one of our noble students, then who else might it be? How do we get to the bottom of this?"

"First, let's find a way to lock up the laboratory more securely," Annie said, "so this doesn't happen again."

"Lock the laboratory door *after* the armor's been stolen, you mean?" Michelle said dryly.

Annie controlled a smirk.

Zane shrugged. "Then tomorrow, Josh, you and Cord ride back out there and search for the dagger."

"The dagger . . ." Cord said thoughtfully, "Is there any reason someone would steal just the dagger? You've all convinced me it's not the students here."

"It's not," Annie said firmly. "I say that not because I don't want to believe ill of them or have an idealistic belief in their honesty. They simply couldn't have done it. They have me and Tilda and Brody and Ellie as witnesses to their presence here all day."

"It seems to me someone went to some lengths to make the theft look sloppy and strange and, well, childish." Cord tapped on the table. "If that's true, then we need to at least consider that the theft and disposal of the armor is a distraction, so whoever took it will *hope* we blame the students and with some great regret give up the dagger as lost in the woods or swiped by someone because it's interesting."

That silenced the room. Michelle was the first one to talk. "But why would someone want that dagger anyway? It's no more valuable than, say, the sword or shield or helmet."

"Yes," Annie said, nodding. "Why would they want the dagger?"

"There's only one thing we can do about it." Cord kept tapping.

That got everyone's attention. Annie couldn't think of a single thing they could do about it. "What's that?"

Cord arched his eyebrows. "We've put it off long enough. It's time to finish the treasure hunt."

Annie didn't see how that made sense. Why did Cord want to get out of here?

SEVEN

School was out for the summer. It was the middle of May, and they let the children have some freedom for a stretch.

And Annie was finally going on a treasure hunt. She was giddy at the thought of not teaching for a while, and grateful to Michelle for offering to care for Caroline since she and Zane were staying behind.

"Remember now, when you find whatever is at the end of Cord's map"—Michelle spoke loud enough to reach the front of the line of riders just as they rode out—"none of you are doing the digging."

Annie thought Lock's shoulders almost trembled. That boy wanted to dig and that was that.

"Agreed?" Michelle put her most threatening tone into the single word.

They all rode away, soundly scolded. Professor Hardy had been infuriated about the armor being dug up by amateurs. He'd impressed them all with his scolding.

Michelle, apparently, took it to heart. The rest of them probably weren't quite so willing to be obedient.

Annie said, "Professor Hardy's scolding is clear in my

ears still even after he's been gone for weeks. You should not have dug up the armor. He wants to go over the site himself."

"We dug it up because I knelt on something sharp and found the helmet. We didn't know what it was at the time. He can't fault us for that." Josh glanced over his shoulder and grinned. He was enjoying arguing with her. "Besides, Professor Hardy hadn't had a chance to scold us yet." Josh seemed to be glad he'd annoyed the arrogant archeologist.

"I think he was just mad that we didn't leave things alone, so he could dig them up himself and claim he'd found the treasure," Thayne said. "He'd've probably tried to keep it for himself, too. We made some money on those suits of armor, and Hardy wanted that money for himself."

Annie considered that and wondered if Thayne had the right idea.

"I don't think he needs money, though some never think they have enough," said Cord. He brought up the rear, with their horses strung out five in a row. "I'd guess there is fame to be gained by finding things like that armor, at least in academic circles. It struck me that he was maybe hoping to go back to teaching in the fall with his name attached to a big find like the armor."

Hardy was a professor at the University of the Pacific, where Ellie had gone to college. He ran the History Department. But when Tilda wanted to talk about California history, especially Captain Cabrillo, her ancestor, Hardy had rolled his eyes and turned up his nose at her. And when it came out that her background included being an orphan, one who hadn't much formal education, he was outright rude.

He'd been lucky that Josh hadn't kicked him off the ranch.

Michelle had noticed his arrogance and muttered under her breath about education being wasted on the man.

All in all, it amounted to Annie wondering if they should trust the professor. Was he interested in history and research, or was he interested in his own fame and fortune? They'd decide how to handle him once they found what they were looking for.

Josh was leading the group. He didn't like leaving Tilda behind, who was dealing with morning sickness, but Brody promised he'd watch over her. Brody himself had to remain behind to watch over Harriet, and Gretel was getting close to delivering her own baby. As for Ellie, who had three months to go before her baby was to be born, she'd had labor pains last night. Brody had her tucked into bed and ordered her to stay there.

Annie figured herself to be good at reading a trail. Thayne, Lock, and Cord had gone on earlier hunts, yet no one thought they could find their way along the mapped-out trail without Josh.

He had led every hunt so far, but he'd refused to go until Tilda said Josh's nervous hovering made her nausea worse, so he agreed to join the hunt. He was a little moody, though.

Lock, then Thayne followed Josh. Nothing could have stopped them from being as near to the front of the line as they were.

Annie and then Cord came next.

Annie figured she was better in the wilderness than he was, but she worried it'd pinch his manly pride to insist on being last, and no danger was obvious. Of course, it hadn't been obvious on previous excursions, but she hoped it was safe enough. She still wasn't sure why Cord had decided it was time to go on this hunt, except maybe it just was. She looked over her shoulder at him. "What made you say it was time for the treasure hunt?"

"Whoever stole the armor and discarded it in the brush, but kept the dagger, well, it struck me that too many people are aware of our treasure hunt. We need to get this over with. It's spring now, which is what we were waiting for. I'm hoping this one last trip will uncover everything. We'll get it all situated in the museum or on loan to private collections, and then there'll be no more danger. No more gold fever. Life can finally return to normal."

Annie thought he had it exactly right. So here they were, working their way into the mountains and forests. She was fascinated by the green pool they'd come across on the first leg of the search. They'd paused and talked in solemn tones about Graham MacKenzie, lying there dead in a cave. As for taking his body back to the Two Harts to bury him, the timing never seemed to be right.

Before long they rode through a beautiful stone arch and reached the burial place where they'd found the armor—the location where Cord's map started. By then it was time to camp for the night.

"I hope tomorrow we can ride straight for the end of that map." Josh had a fire going and coffee boiling while Annie cut up jerky and potatoes and onions to make stew.

"So there are just the five graves here?" Annie looked around. The last group searching the area had placed a good-sized stone over each grave.

"That's right," Thayne said. "Grandpa's map led us here. But what were five men doing out here? And what does it mean that Grandpa drew a map, too?"

77

"We left the bones behind and just took the armor," Lock said.

Annie thought the boy showed a serious lack of sensitivity. "I wonder what Professor Hardy thinks he could have found here that you didn't." She meant that sincerely, but the men nodded without seeming to give it much thought, then quickly turned their attention back to the map Thayne and Lock had been studying.

"We know exactly where Grandpa Graham made a mining claim," Lock said.

"And Josh studied up on those lines of . . . well, whatever they are." Thayne turned the map he held sideways, then upside down.

"Latitude and longitude. It's something we use in sailing, but they help to find your way on land too, if you know how to use them."

"Can you teach us how to figure those things, Uncle Josh?" Lock poked sticks into the fire beneath Annie's stewpot.

"Sure I can," he replied. "Maybe the other youngsters in school would like to learn about latitude and longitude as well. It's a mighty useful skill to have."

"We grown-ups should probably think more about what knowledge we can pass on to those coming up behind us," Annie said.

"Michelle told me today she's ordered a piano. It's to be shipped here by train in the next few weeks. She thinks I should teach piano lessons." Cord shrugged. "I can play the piano all right, though I've never tried teaching it to someone else."

"You also worked at a bank, Cord." Annie began scooping stew onto plates and handing them around. "You could teach our students about keeping account books and balancing totals. And maybe if you find a child sufficiently interested, you could help them get a job someday at your grandpa's bank. Michelle's going to teach them Morse code." She hesitated, then added more quietly, "I myself am going to quit teaching." But everyone heard her just fine, and they jerked their heads around to stare at her.

"You are?" Lock's dismay was sweet. "But I've got a few years left still, Aunt Annie. Can't you keep teaching a little longer?"

Thayne said, "I'm done with school, I think. Brody found a doctor college near San Jose. I can start going there in the fall."

"Look what that did for Ellie when she went to school there for a while." Lock sounded as if he was hunting for a reason for his brother to stay with him. "She quit to get married, and then her fiancé broke her heart and tried to kill all of us."

"If he was that upset about losing her, he shouldn't have broken her heart." Thayne shook his head. They all knew Loyal Kelton, locked up now in San Quentin Prison. Only the gold coins in Brody's pocket had shielded his heart from what would have been a fatal gunshot.

"I wanted to go to the music conservatory there," Cord said thoughtfully. "The University of the Pacific was close to Sacramento. But Grandpa said no."

"I'm not sure what college could have done for you, Cord." Josh moved back just a bit from the warmth of the fire. "You're the best piano player I've ever heard. Not that I've heard many, but you're really good. It's hard to imagine you getting much better at it."

"Are you sure you're ready for college, Thayne? You didn't go to school all that much when you were growing up." Annie had done her best to fill in the gaps of his spotty education. She reminded herself that he'd gone to school in Boston through the winter, so maybe he was caught up now. Still, he was seventeen years old—a little young to start college.

"You may want to quit being a teacher, Annie," Cord said, "but you're a natural at it. Anyone here can tell that you're worried about Thayne and Lock's education." He then smiled at her in a way that confused and warmed her heart at the same time.

Annie sighed. "That may be true, Cord, but I'd like to spend more time running the house. Gretel, though she never complains, is severely overworked. Ellie's busy assisting Brody and will have her baby soon. And while Michelle is besotted with Leah, if she had a little help, I think she'd enjoy a little time with her inventions."

Josh looked up at the lowering sun. "We rode a long way today. When we first started hunting treasure, it took us three different searches to get this far—the first time to the green pond."

"That's when I fell over the cliff." Lock rubbed his ribs as if recalling the pain of his fall.

"And the second time," Thayne said, "was when Brody got shot."

Lock shook his head at the memory.

"The third time I joined you, and we found the armor," Cord said. "Maybe this time we'll finally get to the end of that map."

"Have you all got a copy of Cord's map?" Annie asked.

She kept hers close at hand and pored over it almost every night. "Do you all know where to go from here?"

The menfolk looked between each other, nodding, but they didn't seem all that confident to Annie.

"It didn't take long this time to get where we are because we knew where we were going," Josh said, setting aside his now-empty tin plate. "But we did a lot of searching to uncover the trail we hurried down today. I think a lot of tomorrow's trip should go fast, too. Even though it's not easy to be exact with longitude and latitude, we know where to find the large claim Graham MacKenzie staked. And I've figured out how to find the dried-up riverbed that runs through this area. That'll get us close. From there, the strange drawings on the map should point us to the last leg of the trail . . . I hope."

Annie looked around the circle of men, sitting around the crackling fire, sharing a meal together. She breathed in the smell of woodsmoke, the savory aroma of the stew, all of it flavored with talk of treasure and the adventure lying ahead.

"When we set out before," said Cord, "we told your family we wouldn't be back until we reached the end of the trail. And then we found the armor, and it was all we could do to haul it home. We didn't even start on my half of the map. I make no such bold claim this time, yet I surely do hope we find whatever is hidden out there."

"So do I!" Lock said.

He sounded so fervent that Annie worried about him. But then she'd always worried about the MacKenzie boys, who leaned toward recklessness—especially Lock. They had such a headlong desire to find their treasure that for all their intelligence, they had a dearth of common sense.

"Is your Grandfather Westbrook coming to the Two

Harts?" Annie asked Cord. "You know he's welcome to stay with us."

"I sent him a long letter, and Josh included his own letter telling him he was welcome. I hope he does. I'd like to see him get far away from that bank of his. It seems he has trouble leaving his managers on their own. Doesn't fully trust 'em."

Josh put on a pair of cowhide gloves and grabbed the pot of hot water from the campfire. He filled a basin and shaved soap into it, then removed the gloves and started in with washing the dishes.

Annie dried while the boys put away the plates, cups, and utensils.

"I'm going to build up the fire." Cord set to work. "It still gets cool at night up in these hills."

They all worked together to ready the camp for the night. That done, Annie settled under her blankets, already missing Caroline. It was strange to be away from her and away from the ranch. It occurred to her then that she'd been very much a hermit since her husband, Todd, had died. She rode into Dorada Rio on occasion, and the family attended church most Sundays, unless the weather prevented them from doing so. But she rarely went anywhere else, not even when the family had invited her along on a trip to San Francisco, where Michelle's family lived part of the year, depending on the lumber season.

And she'd never gone back to the ranch she once lived on, where her husband had been shot, their house burned down. She'd gotten the ranch back plus a lot more by the time the man who'd ordered Todd's killing was done paying for his crime. Now Josh and Zane ran the ranch for her.

She was afraid of that ranch. She was afraid of pretty much everything.

Maybe her restlessness wasn't just about teaching school. Maybe she should travel a bit, go somewhere else. She shifted under her blankets as fear welled up inside her at the very thought.

She realized she'd built up the outside world as a frightening place.

Her head felt the gentle, drowsy buzzing that preceded sleep, and she slipped into a dream of fire and gunshots, of her husband bleeding to death. She felt the searing pain of her own gunshot wounds, and in her arms her daughter wept.

Shaking woke her. Another earthquake?

Her eyes fluttered open to see Cord hovering over her, his hand rocking her shoulder. He was silent, and since everyone else in the camp was sleeping, that was wise.

In a whisper that barely reached her ears, he said, "Bad dream?"

She nodded as the worst of it faded, unable to speak quite yet. She'd had this same dream many times before, usually after having a really long day. It seemed exhaustion and stress brought the nightmares on.

Cord, his face visible in the firelight, said, "Maybe soon you'll sleep without them, peacefully . . ."

Annie reached up to rest her hand on his face. A handsome face. A kind man. Todd had been handsome and kind, too. She dropped her hand. "Thank you, Cord."

She wasn't sure what he saw in her expression, but it wasn't good. He looked as though he was about to move away, but before he could, Josh's voice sounded in the night.

"Morning comes mighty early, Cord. Best to get some sleep."

Cord stiffened as if the words were a blow. Then he looked at her as if he'd taken two blows: Josh's words, and whatever he'd seen in her eyes when she'd stopped touching him.

"Sweet dreams, Annie." Cord rose from where he crouched and went back to his spot on the other side of the campfire.

Moments later, Annie drifted off to sleep again, and this time the dream stayed away.

EIGHT

"You can really see an old riverbed here?" Cord had to admit, using every speck of his imagination, he just couldn't quite make a river take shape, particularly one that'd dried up three hundred years ago. Then he had a thought. "That letter from your grandpa, didn't he use the words '*a donde la río está muerto*'?"

"Sure, but Grandpa didn't speak Spanish, so he must've copied those words from something else." Lock looked half asleep in his saddle. Maybe Annie wasn't the only one who'd had a rough night.

Cord thought of his waking Annie from a bad dream last night, then seeing her look at him like she didn't want him touching her. He'd rather not remember that moment.

"We did a poor job of translation and came up with 'river of death,' which sounds like a terrible danger. But Michelle said it means 'to where the river is dead.'"

"But what if," Cord said, "it's talking about the bed of a dead river, like the one we're supposedly riding along right now."

Lock perked up.

"Better than *river of death*." Thayne shuddered.

Josh twisted in the saddle, looking interested. Which was a nice change from him glaring at Cord since they woke up this morning. "We're worried about whether we can find what we're looking for using only latitude and longitude on the eighty acres of Graham MacKenzie's claim. Eighty acres is a large parcel of land, and Graham's claim isn't a typical mining claim. It's more the size of a homestead claim, though he secured it before the Homestead Act. But following this riverbed could help us pinpoint the right spot, if we're right about a boat coming inland and possibly running aground in a storm. The folks on board might have explored the area by way of what used to be a river—maybe because they were curious, or maybe because they couldn't get back to the ocean. If that's the case, it stands to reason we'd find their boat on the land that was once a riverbed."

"We studied earthquakes a bit in school." Annie's eyes sparked with interest. "An earthquake can change the course of a river or even make it run underground. What if those sailors followed the river inland, but then an earthquake struck? The river could have vanished, and there they were, stranded in the wilderness with nobody knowing where they'd gone to, likely believing they'd all perished, whether in a storm or in the quake."

"Reckon that could be the truth of what happened back then," Josh said. "Hard to believe this was ever a river, what with these trees growing here for hundreds of years now. There's no sign that water once ran through this area. At this point, it's more about the lay of the land with this spot being the lowest point. Keeping that in mind, I'm pretty sure it was indeed a river at one time long ago. I say we keep following its path."

"I agree with Josh," said Cord, and the others nodded. "We should keep searching along this old riverbed, and hopefully that'll lead us to the MacKenzie claim."

The day had grown long, the way forward slowgoing. Annie was scratched up by pine branches, itchy from brambles, hungry and tired and bored. And she missed her little girl.

Treasure hunting had lost its shine.

They weren't following a trail anymore. Instead, they were picking their way through unsettled land, following the dried-up riverbed. Or rather, they were *attempting* to follow it.

Annie couldn't see much of anything. She didn't think Josh could either. He just knew where Graham MacKenzie's claim was and kept riding toward it. The old river was mostly something he was imagining.

Josh was in the lead still, and as usual they were riding single file: Lock, Thayne, Annie, with Cord at the back of the group.

Annie had grown up with Zane, Josh, and Ellie among the hills and forests surrounding the Two Harts Ranch. She'd learned to track wild animals. She was a good shot and knew how to bring in supper with a rifle. In short, she was annoyed that she wasn't bringing up the rear. She deserved acknowledgment at least that she was the better hand at watching their back, at keeping an eye out for potential threats.

The riverbed ahead widened just a bit, and Thayne trotted

up to Lock, who remained just behind Josh at the front. At the same time, Cord caught up to her on the right. They were back far enough they could talk. When he smiled at her, she quickly forgot her annoyance and smiled back at him.

With their horses walking along side by side, Cord reached across and ran his finger down her scratched-up cheek, then pulled it away with it tipped in blood.

She flinched, then said, "You have to look worse for wear than I do."

He lifted his hat, a fine new Stetson, and swiped his shirt-sleeve across his forehead. "I take that as a compliment, Annie, because you look beautiful today. I can look a lot worse than you and still be a fine figure of a man."

Annie chuckled. She glanced ahead and noticed Josh looking over his shoulder at them, his eyes narrowed.

"You can't blame the man," Cord said. "You mean so much to him. He told me about your husband dying in your arms, and you getting shot as well. He doesn't want you to ever grieve like that again or be hurt by some lummox cowpoke. And based on the way you looked at me last night, I'd say you agree with Josh."

"I don't think there's a thing wrong with you, Cord. But I'm afraid. I barely survived losing Todd. I fear my heart has hardened a bit. When I look at you and . . . feel something, it's a pain I can't bear. Please don't let that hurt you. It's my own broken heart that won't let anyone else in."

He nodded. "Your life hasn't been easy. I see that, Annie. Yet your devotion to Caroline and to your family is admirable. And you've done so much to help the students with their learning. Now you're talking of quitting teaching. I'm not sure I understand."

"We're asking too much of Gretel. She's become a good and loyal friend, and she needs for me to take the load off her shoulders or at least share a greater part of it."

Cord eyed her intently as she spoke, and it made her think of the times Michelle had brought her microscope to the classroom. How you could see tiny new details of something you thought you knew everything about. What was Cord looking for in her? What details could he see?

"Annie, w-would you consider spending time with me, just the two of us? I'd like to get to know you better. As you've probably guessed, I have feelings for you. And I believe . . . I mean, I *hope* you have feelings for me. But it's not easy to explore those feelings when we're never alone together. Let me take you out for dinner? Give us a chance to find out if what we feel is enough for you to take a risk."

Annie hadn't courted a man since Todd, and she'd barely done so with him before they decided to marry. He was running his ranch with his father. She and Todd had been childhood friends who'd just always known they were meant for each other. They'd gone for a walk around the Two Harts when his parents came to share Sunday dinner.

His family would visit her ranch most Sundays. They'd all worship together, then share a meal and spend the afternoon enjoying each other's company. She and Todd were seventeen when he proposed. She'd said yes without a moment's hesitation. He kissed her then for the very first time, and then they ran into the house to tell their families the happy news.

Caroline was born less than a year later. And Annie was all set for a bigger family and a life of love when Todd had been shot and killed, their ranch destroyed. With their home in ruins, her life was forever altered as she moved back to the Two Harts. Zane now kept a bunkhouse full of men at Lane Valley, her former ranch. Since losing Todd, Annie had never gone back there.

So Zane took over the management of Lane Valley. He paid the cowhands and covered all expenses out of the earnings made from raising high-quality livestock. Then her ranch expanded when Zane had demanded through the courts a disbursement of money from the man who'd arranged for Todd to be killed. After the dust settled, Annie became probably one of the richest women in California.

And she'd barely spent a penny of it.

She really ought to make the trip to go see her ranch again. Having her house reduced to ashes had made it easy to stay away. She weighed whether it was maybe time for her to move back home. Yet deep in her heart, she knew she probably never would.

All of this ran through her mind in the seconds since Cord had suggested he take her out for dinner. She was tempted by his offer. She turned her head and looked at him, wondering, afraid, but interested. "I'm not so sure about courting a man again . . . but yes, Cord, I'll go to dinner with you. Or how about a noon meal in Dorada Rio? That way we won't be riding home in the dark."

Cord nodded as if afraid to make any suggestions for fear she'd change her mind. "We'll do it the first Saturday after we get back."

"That sounds nice, although I still feel uncertain about seeing another man. I'll need time to get used to the idea." She thought saying yes to their sharing a meal together might be all she was capable of, but then that was all he'd

90

asked for. She decided then she'd take all this one step at a time.

"This might be it!" Josh hollered back. "I think we're on the right land. And would you look at that—your grandpa built himself a cabin."

The building was derelict after thirty years of sitting empty, trees having grown up around it on all sides, but sure enough, there was a small house there. Not a one-room shack, but a bona fide house.

"Do you think he built the house near where the treasure's hidden?" Lock asked. He was already pulling out his map, no doubt looking for landmarks and other clues. "I think this little triangle here marks the cabin's location."

"Let's get the horses staked out to graze and then start looking around." Josh always took care of his horse first.

Annie was exhausted from a long day in the saddle, and she needed to tend to the scrapes and scratches she'd collected along the way. She suspected everyone else was just as tired as she was. But as she swung down from her horse, suddenly she got a burst of energy just thinking about the treasure.

They all got out their maps. They'd had all winter to make up copies.

"How far from that cabin is the X, do you think?" Annie studied the odd little drawings, which to her looked to be made mysterious on purpose.

They figured Grandpa didn't want the map to make sense easily if it fell into the wrong hands. In fact, he'd been so cryptic about it that his son, Frasier—Brody, Thayne, and Lock's father—had ruined his life chasing after the treasure the map supposedly pointed to.

"The X is off to the west." Josh turned to face the land beyond the cabin. "It feels as if we're still on the dry riverbed. I'd say your grandpa built the cabin where he did because the land is more level here. He probably didn't even know this area was once a riverbed."

The cabin had no windows or doors, just gaping open spaces. The roof seemed to be mostly intact, which was surprising. Annie went and glanced inside. Years and years of debris had blown inside the cabin. Leaves, broken branches, evidence of animals burrowing in the dirt floor. Inside, it was clear that one of the main walls had been badly damaged, caused by a fallen tree.

Hearing rustling behind her, Annie turned to see Cord poking his head into the cabin. "We found where Graham died. Now we see where he lived. There are extra rooms, which means he built this place with his family in mind. Seems Graham MacKenzie did everything with his family in mind."

Annie smiled at him. "Let's go treasure hunting."

Cord rested a hand on her back and nodded.

Josh, Thayne, and Lock had already gone in search of the treasure. Looking around a derelict house didn't interest them one bit. Well, it didn't interest Annie for long either.

She and Cord rounded the cabin to see Josh walking slowly down a path he must believe was that "river of death" written about in the journal. But Grandpa Graham had been here before them. Even thirty years later, there was no mistaking the spot.

"He hung a shield from a tree." Josh pointed to a rusted piece of steel about fifty feet west of the cabin. "Just like he did where we found the armor."

They all walked through the underbrush, weaving around trees to where the rusted-out shield hung.

"I thought you said this shield was hung by the conquistadors," Thayne said as he made his way across the rugged terrain.

"We thought that at first, but the archeologists who studied the armor said it couldn't have been hanging there for that long a time."

"I wonder what in the world brought Grandpa this far into the wilderness," Thayne said. "And I wonder what he saw that stopped him here in this spot. He wrote that the mountains around here called to him like the Scottish Highlands, but I wish he'd've written his reasons down."

Annie glanced to the west and said, "The sun's getting low in the sky. We don't have much daylight left for hunting treasure, and we've had nothing to eat all day but beef jerky and bread. I think it's about time we set up camp. We all could use some sleep."

The men turned toward her, by turns looking horrified, dismayed, and annoyed, all such expressions directed right at her.

She fought down a smile, then walked over to the hanging shield. "For now, though, let's search for treasure while we have the light."

NINE

"Last time, that treasure was found right under the shield, wasn't it?" Annie stared at the ground near where the shield hung.

Thayne was already on his hands and knees, studying every grain of dirt in the patch of earth surrounding the shield. Josh, meanwhile, had grabbed one of the shovels they'd brought along and was busy digging random holes, something that cranky Professor Hardy would surely not approve of.

Cord paced back and forth. He'd been looking a bit farther afield. "I don't get it. It should be right here." He sounded puzzled. "Why would Graham mark the treasure to be in a spot that's different from before?" Cord pulled the map from his pocket; he'd taken his map out five times in as many minutes. "Maybe we are missing something because we're making too many assumptions."

"Well, I'm going to start a fire and get a meal on," Annie said. She was clearly spent, ready to call it a day. For her, the treasure hunt would have to wait till morning.

The horses were tied close by, grazing, their saddles removed. Annie went to one of the saddlebags and fished out a tin of matches. Using a shovel, she began clearing a spot in which to build a campfire.

Cord nodded, tucked the map away, and began gathering firewood. Josh helped him. The boys weren't quite so practical, as they continued with the searching.

Before long, all but Thayne and Lock were seated around a crackling fire, drinking coffee while Annie's beef-jerky stew started to bubble.

Dragging his map out yet again, Cord said, "I wonder, did we copy the map in Grandpa Westbrook's journal correctly?"

After taking a sip of coffee, Annie answered, "We can compare our maps to see if there are any notable differences, but I helped with the copying, and we were painfully careful."

The three of them sat and drank coffee as Thayne and Lock searched on. Then Annie asked, "Do you think he found the gold coins buried with each man, or didn't the conquistadors do such a thing? You know, like the Egyptian pharaohs did who wanted certain items buried with them."

Not knowing much about Egyptians or pharaohs or conquistadors, Cord didn't respond.

"Graham drew the map in a way that led us to this very spot." Josh looked around impatiently, as if to demand the forest give up its secrets. "He had a reason for doing so. I'm guessing he didn't remove the gold from those graves, but he obviously got it from somewhere. Anyway, why would they bury gold with regular sailors, as I'm sure these men were. No, he likely found the shields and such and brought one of them here." Josh shook his head. "I wish we knew what the X on that map stands for right beside the shield."

"We're close—I can feel it." Cord glanced down at the map. An odd little triangle caught his eye once more, indicating something he hadn't yet figured out. He looked up at the cabin. "I wonder . . ." He stood and headed for the ramshackle building, Josh right behind him. Annie came along, too.

"What are you all up to?" Lock called from behind them.

"I'm just wondering," Cord began. "Your grandpa, he didn't come out west just to search for treasure, did he? He came out here for the land. He bought farmland along with a mining claim. What if he built this cabin—" Cord paused as his eyes landed on a heap of stones with trees growing around it—"and then he dug himself a well?"

"Everything he did was to get this place ready for his family to come here and join him," Annie said. "One day he was digging and found the treasure."

Cord charged straight for the jumble of stones. Annie was only a few paces behind him, along with the MacKenzies and Josh. Only Josh had a shovel with him. "We're gonna need every one of the shovels we brought," he said.

Annie shook her head. "No, Josh. You can't just tear up the ground and haul whatever you find home like last time."

"But we're hunting treasure," said Lock, jumping in. "And we can't do that without digging!" He looked visibly upset.

"Let's not forget how red-faced Professor Hardy got when he learned you'd dug up the armor."

Cord flinched. "Hard to forget a lecture that about peeled the skin off my ears."

"Let's just see what we can uncover," Lock said, acting eager as a child on Christmas morning. "We'll be extra careful with the shovels. Besides, we can't stop to bring those archaeology folks out into the wilderness. What if there's nothing to find here? We'd be making fools of ourselves and wasting their time."

It was extremely likely that Lock wasn't one speck worried about wasting a professor's time. And considering the way he carried on, he probably didn't care much about looking foolish either. But it seemed those were the first two excuses that popped into his head, so he used them.

Thayne, ignoring his brother, said, "Grandpa dug up the armor and then reburied it, remember? Then later he left clues for it to be found again someday."

"I think he marked the spot for himself to come back later," Josh said. "Pretty sure he didn't figure on dying the way he did."

"Point is," Thayne went on, "that archeologist wanted to study the landscape more than anything else. He wants to measure and sift dirt and . . . well, do all sorts of strange things. He said his aim was to dig up the story of the past around these parts."

Annie said, "I remember that. Archeological sites tell the story of the past. He seemed to care most about learning the history of this place. It's an interesting way to look at our treasure hunt."

Cord remained skeptical. To him, Thayne, like his brother Lock, was just looking for an excuse to start digging.

Sure enough, Cord walked over to where the shovels were, grabbed three, and came back with them. "I'm almost certain your grandpa hit upon the treasure while digging this well. I can understand the professor's way of thinking if this area was undisturbed for the last three hundred years, but this is your grandpa's well from *thirty* years ago. If there's any history to learn here, well, your grandpa already disturbed it."

"How about we dig a while," suggested Annie, "at least until we learn if we're right or not? If we find anything, we can decide then if it's something your grandpa dug up and reburied. And if that be the case, then we'll gather what he found. But if it looks like what we're finding has been here for three hundred years, we'll stop what we're doing and ride back to the ranch. Then wait for Professor Hardy and his crew to make the trip back here. We'll lead them to this spot to dig up the history the way they see fit."

That suggestion made a lot of sense to Cord, but then he was itching to see if they were right about what Graham had found.

He looked at Annie. She was the only one who hadn't gone on the last treasure hunt. She was the teacher, the sensible one, and the telling gleam in her eyes told him she badly wanted to see what was down there in the well. "What do you say, Annie?" Cord asked.

"I don't think it would do any harm for us to very carefully dig down a ways. We should stop if we find an artifact and measure how deep we dug. Then we'll try to judge if what we've found has been moved in the last thirty years." She hesitated for a moment, then added, "I don't think it's going to be easy, though, judging what's really old and what's more recent."

"So let's get started already," Lock said, a little whiny.

"All right then. We'll begin by digging down to see if we're right or not." Her spine bent before the pressure of everyone else's hopes and her own fascination for treasure hunting.

"Here you go, Thayne, Lock," Cord said as he handed

them each a shovel." The two brothers could hardly contain their excitement.

Cord was excited himself. This was his half of the map, after all. He considered goading them about whatever they found belonging to him—which it most certainly didn't— just to torment the gold-crazed boys. Instead, he kept quiet and went to where they'd stripped the horses of their leather, reaching for the saddlebag that held his cowskin gloves. He gave the horses a quick check and was startled. "Josh," he called, "any reason you picked this spot to picket the horses?"

Josh and Annie walked toward him, Josh handing his shovel to Thayne.

"What's the matter?" Josh said.

"Look at this patch of land," Cord said. "It's studded with young trees, but it's more level here, and the grass is thicker for some reason."

"Maybe because the trees aren't so big." Josh pointed to the area around them. "I didn't notice anything different at the time. I saw the cabin, dismounted, and staked out my horse near the good grass."

Cord gestured to his right. "The stream that ran through here, I think it started at the spring there, still bubbling up from between the rocks."

"What're you saying?" Josh asked.

"I'm saying Graham MacKenzie picked this spot for a very good reason." Cord's jaw flexed as he imagined it. "He was drawn here by the mountains, which made him think of Scotland and the Old World. His home. Then, exploring the area, for the pleasure of it and because gold hunting was proving to be more of a nuisance than he'd expected, he saw good land all around him—both for farming and for grazing."

"Why did he bother digging a well if there was water already available, a spring not far away?" Annie looked back at the pile of stones that were once part of the well, then back at the cabin.

Cord looked at Annie and shrugged. "Every time I think I've figured out what he was up to, I find there are more questions to ask. Maybe the sunlight or soil back then were just right for building a house there. Still, it's a hike to the spring to gather fresh water, especially in winter. Or maybe he figured if the water was this close to the surface, a well might only be ten feet deep. Could be he was thinking of his daughter-in-law and her comfort by wanting the house where he built it, with a well right out back."

Annie beamed at Cord. "That's it."

Her smile felt like sunlight shining down on Cord on a cool spring day. "Considering the rough country we rode through to get here, this area would have looked like an oasis in the desert to Graham. His aim was to build a house, get a farm started on a decent piece of land, then send for his family—not go looking for some treasure."

"Maybe this area was the floodplain of that old dried-up river. That's why it's level here and why the grass is so rich." Josh pointed at the young trees growing nearby. "I'll bet those trees have grown up since the time Graham MacKenzie chopped down what was here to build his cabin. The trees here look to be around thirty years old."

Cord nodded. "I wonder if a dry riverbed—"

"Better to call it that than the 'river of death,'" said Annie.

Cord conceded the point. "But I wonder . . . if it's true an earthquake long ago stopped or *killed* the river dead, could another earthquake bring it back to life?"

Josh scowled.

Annie looked around nervously. Then she gave him a swat against the belly with the back of her hand. "Thanks, Cord. We needed more to worry about."

"Are we gonna start digging or what?" Lock called out, breaking into their attempts at figuring out what Graham MacKenzie was thinking when he'd homesteaded this piece of land.

Near the well, Lock held up a triangular metal object with some elaborate detail amidst all the dirt and rust. "A spear tip, I think."

Thayne stopped digging to look at it. "We found a spear tip like this in each of those graves, along with the armor. It was the archeologists who identified them as spear tips. They said they once would've been mounted on a six-foot wooden handle or shaft."

Cord brought a dagger out of the hole he was digging. "Isn't this like the dagger we had stolen?"

Everyone turned to stare at it. Unlike the spear tip, it was in much better shape. Cord used his thumb to wipe away the dirt that caked the dagger. The weapon was completely intact, just as the other dagger had been. Steel all over, with no wood there to decay.

Cord said, "I'm glad we found one to replace the one that was stolen. I liked the feel of that dagger in my hand."

Lock gasped. "Did you try and use it, Cord? I admit I picked it up a few times and pretended to do some, well . . ."

Annie saw his cheeks turn pink and thought she knew the reason why. In fact, they'd both just admitted to it, even if accidentally. "Lock, did you get caught up in playacting with that dagger, taking on the part of a swashbuckler maybe?" Her eyes shifted to Cord. "What about you?"

Josh cleared his throat. "The swords looked a bit fragile. They're heavy too, and I didn't want to risk it by swinging one around. But the dagger?" He shrugged sheepishly, yet he was fighting back a smile.

"I might've tried a sword once," Thayne admitted. "But you're right—it was heavy and seemed like it'd be more apt to snap in half. The dagger wasn't like that."

"I waved the dagger around myself, even wore a helmet while doing so." Annie figured she might as well come clean. "I couldn't lift the shield or the sword well enough to do much with them, though I tried. But the dagger . . ."

Josh scratched his chin. "You don't suppose someone stole it because they were having fun fighting invisible pirates and couldn't stand to give it back?"

Cord looked at Annie with smiling eyes. "I reckon we all have a tiny place in our hearts that wonders what it would've been like to be a pirate back in the 1700s."

All five of them burst into laughter. After everyone quieted down, Annie said, "I say we stop now. In fact, I think we've dug deeper than we should have."

It was no surprise when Lock argued, "I say we don't stop, not until we've dug up everything that's down there."

Suddenly, Annie no longer felt like a treasure hunter but like a mother and teacher combined. "I think the honorable thing to do is to go fetch the archeologists. We agreed to dig until we were sure something was here to be found. Each of us has unearthed something now, and we were careful in how we went about it. It's clear there's more to be found, so it's time to pack up and ride home and come back here another day. Everyone agreed to let me decide when to stop, and I'm deciding. Besides, I'm too tired to keep going. Let's all eat something—I'll heat up the rest of the stew."

Cord dropped his shovel and headed for the fire. He began building it up from embers. "Lock, help me gather up some firewood."

Josh turned to Thayne. "And I could use help leading the horses to water."

Annie was glad to see them all set aside their shovels and pitch in to get dinner ready. They all needed a hot meal and a good night's rest.

Soon they were sitting around the campfire again, eating and talking about the pieces of metal they'd dug up out of the earth. No suit of armor this time. Instead, they'd found a dagger and a spear tip and two other bits of iron they couldn't identify. Apparently, somewhere near their campsite long, long ago, a ship had run aground when the river drained away during a terrible earthquake.

Annie smiled to herself as they talked. A ship this far inland from the ocean? That would have had to be some river. It was possible, but of course they didn't really know.

With the stew all eaten, they settled in for the night. It was time to give up on the treasure hunt and, at first light, set off for home.

TEN

They rode out the next morning with Josh leading, Lock and Thayne begrudgingly following. Just as before, Annie with Cord brought up the rear, each carrying an artifact. Though it was a small treasure find, it came with the tantalizing prospect that there was likely more to be found.

"As soon as we get home," said Annie, "we'll send for the archeologists. Professor Hardy is sure to hop on the next train and head straight to the Two Harts."

"Last time Hardy visited, he ate us out of house and home, and that assistant of his was worse than him," Josh said as he lifted the iron disk he'd found. He turned it back and forth in one hand while guiding his horse with the other.

A plate maybe? Annie found herself as curious about the strange disk in his hand as she'd been when studying the armor.

"What was the assistant's name? He's an odd duck." Cord remembered he was a big man—not fat, but solid. He seemed too old to still be someone's assistant, probably in his forties or fifties. The man wasn't a professor himself. It appeared that mostly he was there to carry things for Professor Hardy.

"It was 'Rumbum' something or other, I think." Cord had had a tough time deciphering the man's heavy accent. "He spoke to Gretel in German, remember? She might remember his name."

"Professor Hardy isn't going to be happy with us," Annie said.

Josh chuckled. "I'm not looking forward to being scolded again, especially by a man I wouldn't trust to watch my cows." He held up an oddly shaped bit of steel, the artifact he'd dug up, staring at the thing as if trying to make sense of it.

"Josh, are you leading us down a different trail than the one we rode in on?" Cord asked. Much as he disliked admitting it, he felt as though they'd somehow gotten turned around in the woods.

"Yep, we're riding straight to Cornerstone, where Ellie, Brody, and your grandpa Mayhew found the paperwork for Graham's land claim. It took a little time finding this trail from the direction we came, but once I found it, I realized we were closer to town this way. We'll get home fast now that we're on a better trail. My guess is, Graham rode into the area from this same direction. He must've found something along the way that led him to those graves. Remember the words etched on the back of that first shield we found? Anyway, we're gonna cut a full day off our trip home."

"Do you think if we dug deep enough, we might find what remains of that ship?" Lock asked, looking back longingly.

"Dunno. But don't worry, Lock—we'll go back there as soon as we can." With that, Josh picked up the pace, guiding them along the narrow trail.

A trail Cord could hardly make out.

"What we found back there is just the beginning of a job that could take years," Annie said. "If there is a ship down there, we'll have to dig for a long time to reach it. And to do it right is a painstaking business. Best to leave it to the archeologists. It's about more than just finding artifacts. Hardy wants to study the people who first came here, to learn more about them and the time they lived in."

Cord looked at Annie, then at Josh. "Remember how the chuck wagon fell into that crack when the earthquake rocked us?"

They both nodded.

"Did you try to haul the wagon back up, Josh? Have you gotten a good look at the crack?"

"No, I haven't," Josh replied.

"I wonder how far down it fell. Is the wagon visible? Is the crack still open, or did the ground swallow the chuck wagon whole and then close up? Because maybe the ground did the same to that ship."

"I've had the same thought myself." Annie looked over her shoulder and smiled at him.

"If that's the case, who knows how far down into the earth the ship might've fallen?" Cord sighed. "Hunting treasure is an adventure, but I can't give years of my life to this. None of us can."

Annie nodded. "It's clear that people who know what they're doing should be the ones to dig up that site . . . and that's not us."

Josh urged his horse along a little faster. "If I'm gonna work this hard, I'd as soon be branding calves back on the ranch."

———— ✧ ————

They'd arrived home from a different direction. They usually rode to the ranch from the east, but they'd ridden so far north and west, they'd ended up passing through Dorada Rio. It turned out the Cornerstone trail was easy to follow, the going smooth enough that Josh had decided to stick to it. That cut a full day off their painstaking trek through the wilderness.

"Uh-oh, looks like Professor Hardy is already here and waiting for us." The professor's shiny buggy sat unhitched outside the barn. Annie resisted the urge to act like a naughty schoolgirl and hide somewhere. "We probably shouldn't have done any digging."

"Michelle must have mentioned in a wire to him that we were out searching for treasure. Or maybe she told him about the suit of armor that was stolen."

Cord added, "I'll bet anything he plays with the dagger and swords, too."

Annie narrowed her eyes at the cranky old coot. "He'd die before he'd admit it, though."

They rode into the ranch yard just as the sun dipped toward the horizon. She doubted they'd planned on having extra mouths to feed, but they'd come up with something.

"Aunt Annie"—Lock tended to use kinship words like *Aunt* and *Uncle* when he was trying to get his way or dodge trouble—"you know we were only guessing about the well. We *had* to do some digging before we were ready to come back for help. We all talked it over, remember? And we quit digging a whole lot earlier than I wanted to."

"It was a good guess, wasn't it?" Annie straightened her

spine. Yes, they'd needed to be sure. True enough, they discussed it, and she agreed to what they'd decided together. And now she'd stand up and face whatever scolding came her way. She wasn't in the mood for this. It'd been a long day, one spent on horseback. She was exhausted with little patience left. She might just scold back this time.

"Why is he here?" Lock sounded annoyed, as if he might just do some scolding of his own.

"He's been around the ranch plenty lately." Josh led the way toward the barn.

"I'm hiding the dagger inside my shirt." Lock looked around. "We lost the other one; we need to be careful about flashing this one around."

"Good idea," Josh said. "We've got a few other objects we found to show Professor Hardy. He doesn't need to see everything."

They all dismounted and saw to their own horses. Annie noted that Thayne and Lock did their fair share. Those two were growing up.

Josh clapped Lock on the back. "Come to the house for supper. Brody and Ellie are probably asleep by now. No sense waking them."

As they headed for the house, Josh muttered, "Hardy is going to want to turn right around and head back to the site of the treasure. Which means I'll have to lead another treasure hunt. None of you could find that spot."

"I could." Annie locked eyes with Josh. "I'm sure now that I could ride straight to it."

He nodded, then said, "I wonder how Tilda is feeling?" He hadn't liked leaving her before. Now he seemed to be considering letting Annie be the trail guide.

She was a little bit sorry she'd offered. It flickered through Annie's mind that Josh was tougher than anyone else in their group. She didn't like the idea of riding into the wilderness without him.

"I hope she's resting. I shouldn't have left her for so long." Josh strode toward Professor Hardy, who was pacing outside the back door.

The man had rather thick white hair. He wasn't a big man, but he looked like he was in decent shape. He had on a white shirt with its sleeves rolled up to his elbows. He wore round glasses with gold rims, and he had his arms crossed. Suddenly the professor stopped his pacing to focus on what they all carried. Each of them had an artifact in hand, all except Lock who'd hidden his dagger.

"I told you not to dig. I told you—"

Josh walked right past Hardy and through the back door, intent on finding Tilda.

The finicky professor sputtered, then turned his eyes on Lock. "I could have learned a lot from—"

"Stop scolding us like we're your students who need a good grade, Professor," Cord snapped. "It's our treasure, the MacKenzie family, and we handled it as we saw fit."

Lock and Thayne walked on past the man, who had his jaw clamped shut now.

Annie couldn't hold back a grin. "We found the way to the end of the Westbrook half of the map. We didn't know if we would find anything there, but we dug very carefully just in case. After we found a couple of things, we stopped digging and rode back home to get your assistance. So are you gonna stand there and fuss like a mama hen whose chicks won't stay put, or are you gonna stay calm and let us tell you about it?"

Professor Hardy got a rueful look on his face. "I much prefer dealing with students who do what I ask in exchange for a good grade. It's entirely possible I treat all people like that."

It was the closest to humble he was likely to get.

"We're starving, Professor. Come on inside and we'll scrounge up a meal while we tell you about what we found." Cord patted Hardy on the shoulder by way of turning him toward the back door of the house.

They spent the next half hour eating and telling their story of the treasure hunt. Much to Hardy's disapproval, Josh didn't share much of anything. Instead, he'd scarfed down his food, and then he and Tilda got up and went to their room in the house.

"I want to head back out to the dig site early tomorrow morning." The professor fidgeted at the table, tapping his fingers, his knee bouncing. "There's more to be unearthed in that spot, I'm sure of it."

Cord shook his head. "Tomorrow's out of the question." He stood from the table. "We need to wait a day or two. We're all exhausted, and we're behind on the ranch work. Give us time to rest up a bit and prepare."

"No!" Professor Hardy shot back. "I insist—"

The back door closing behind Cord shut Hardy right up. He quickly shifted his attention to Annie. She and the boys were the only ones left at the table.

"I'm ready to hunt for treasure again," said Lock. "Tomorrow suits me fine."

Thayne said, "Lock, we'd better talk to Brody first. We haven't even told him we're back yet. Good night, Aunt Annie. Professor." With that, he and Lock got up and disappeared out the back, the door shutting solidly behind them.

Annie sat at her usual spot at the table, Professor Hardy sitting to her right.

The professor gave a sigh and said, "Are you going to walk out on me too, Mrs. Lane?"

She stared at him, one teacher to another. The arrogant man most likely didn't consider a woman teaching youngsters an equal in any way. Still, she had a talent for taking charge of a situation. "I assume you're staying here in the ranch house." It occurred to her then that the next thing they needed to add to the ranch was a guesthouse—one room with a dozen bunk beds. She wasn't interested in making unwelcome guests too comfortable.

"Yes, I've been shown to a room upstairs, along with my assistant, Otto Rombauer."

Rombauer, that was it. Yet she was so tired, she figured by morning she'd forget the man's name all over again. She didn't like having two strange men sleeping upstairs near her and Caroline, despite the presence of Zane and Michelle up there, and Josh and Tilda downstairs.

They definitely needed a guesthouse, and soon.

"I've been gone for days, sir. I haven't seen my daughter in all that time, and now she's tucked up in bed before I could even speak with her. I am *not* leaving the ranch tomorrow."

"But I—"

"Enough," Annie said, one hand raised to silence him. He stopped talking so completely she was impressed with herself. She lowered her hand. "Spend the next few days studying the artifacts we just handed you while we rest up and prepare for the next trip. It was a hard journey through rugged terrain, and we had a large area to cover. But on the way home, Josh found us a better trail that'll save us time. We can get out there in a single day's ride now."

Professor Hardy gave her a look that bordered on approval and might even have held a little bit of respect.

"Go on up to bed, Professor. I'll tidy the kitchen, and then I need to get some sleep."

He gave her a firm nod, stood, and left the room.

After cleaning up, Annie headed upstairs. This floor of the large ranch house had a lot of space. Michelle and Zane stayed in the room he'd slept in all his life. They kept their little one, Leah, right there with them. Professor Hardy and Mr. Rombauer each had their own rooms. Annie slept in the fourth room with Caroline. She moved to open her door and felt the dull thud of it hitting something, then heard the low moan of someone stirring. It was Zane, who slowly got to his feet and swung the door open fully. While remaining dressed, he'd been sleeping on the floor in front of the door.

Annie peeked into the room and saw Caroline, asleep in the small cot they'd squeezed into the room next to Annie's bed.

Zane whispered, "I didn't like her being here alone with strangers in the house. Michelle stayed with Caroline until she fell asleep, and I took over while Michelle tucked Leah in. I decided to stay up here until you came."

"We need to build a guesthouse."

Zane nodded his agreement. "We're already rebuilding Harriet and Bo's house. We can put up another while we're at it."

Annie leaned close. "Don't bother making it overly comfortable."

Grinning, he said, "I get your meaning."

"Good night, Zane."

"One more thing. Because we've had so many guests lately, I've put locks on all the bedroom doors. But I didn't want to lock Caroline in alone." He pulled a key from his pants pocket, handed it to Annie, then said good night and left the room.

She saw Zane unlock his own bedroom door before she closed and locked hers. Their two guests had been no trouble, so Annie didn't think there was anything to fear. Even so, they were strangers. She wasn't completely comfortable with their spending the night in the house and being so near.

She hadn't felt this way when Cord's grandfather stayed with them. To her own shame, she hadn't felt this way when Tilda's brother stayed either, someone who'd ended up being untrustworthy. She'd certainly never felt this way when Cord stayed in the house for a while before moving to the bunkhouse.

Annie felt her cheeks flush as she thought of Cord. She'd agreed to go to dinner with him. He was the first man who'd been in her thoughts in any personal way since Todd.

But with the arrogant Professor Hardy and the rather hulking Mr. Rombauer, she wasn't comfortable. Zane clearly wasn't comfortable with the situation either. Nor was Michelle since no one needed to get Caroline ready for bed or sit with her until she fell asleep. Caroline was a very capable child who went to sleep quickly with no bedtime dramatics.

Guesthouse for a fact.

She checked the door lock one more time before moving to the bed.

———— ✧ ————

"Grandpa, I'm glad to see you! I didn't know you were coming." Cord strode toward his grandfather, who was being driven into the ranch yard by the hotel owner in Dorada Rio. The proprietor also ran a wagon-for-hire business in town.

His grandfather smiled. Cord noticed an ease in the man's demeanor. He hoped that meant Grandpa wasn't working as much these days. Cord had nagged him to quit or cut back for years. He had cut back some, but he'd never stepped away completely.

Or maybe his arthritis was feeling better since Brody had been doctoring him. Or maybe he was just glad to see his only grandson. Cord thought all those reasons were good ones.

Grandpa stepped down from the wagon with surprising agility. Cord hurried to the back of the wagon and pulled out the trunk Grandpa always traveled with. He mentally ran through the occupants of the house. There was one available bedroom upstairs; Grandpa would be happy there.

"Cordell, good to see you." Grandpa was the only one who called him that. "Your wanting to be a cowhand is nonsensical, but I have to admit—you look good. It appears you're making a fine job of it."

Cord almost dropped the trunk. When he thought of how fiercely his grandpa had fought with him over even a visit to his other grandparents, together with his grandpa's disregard for life in the country, he was amazed by the change of heart. Cord had to wonder if the old man was up to something. Or maybe he was feeling better, which had left him with an improved attitude.

"Zane and Michelle have bought a piano. It should be arriving soon. I can play for you in the evening," Cord offered.

"Excellent. I doubt it'll be as magnificent an instrument as my Steinway, but I'm sure you'll get wonderful music out of it anyway."

That was just the simple truth. There was no better sounding piano in the world than Grandpa's Steinway.

Professor Hardy picked this moment to emerge from the house. He grunted what might well have been a "good morning" to Cord and his grandfather, then headed for the laboratory where the artifacts were stored, not counting Lock's dagger.

Grandpa hadn't met the cranky professor before today. When Grandpa had heard they were coming, along with others interested in the artifacts, he'd returned home for the winter out of consideration for the Harts' crowded home. "Who's that?" he asked.

The back door opened again, and this time Mr. Rombauer stepped out and followed the archeologist to the laboratory. It was his designated place—never beside the professor but always following from behind. Cord wondered what the man got paid to be treated with such disrespect. Or maybe it just seemed disrespectful to Cord. He didn't know how the two men got along.

He and Grandpa reached the house, and the door swung open yet again. Annie appeared, a smile spreading across her face. "Mayhew, you're back. It's nice to see you."

"Nice to see you too, Annie. Is it an imposition for me to stay in the house? I didn't realize your archeologists were still here."

115

"We've got one empty room remaining." She rested a hand on his shoulder, urging him inside.

"Hi, Grandpa." Caroline was right behind her mama. She peeked out from behind her mother's skirts.

Caroline had heard Cord call him Grandpa enough that she'd fallen into the habit of doing the same. She had no grandparents in her life, and she and Grandpa Mayhew had learned to enjoy each other's company.

Grandpa reached into his pocket and drew out a small wooden horse about three inches long, beautifully carved.

Caroline gasped as he extended the toy to her.

Caroline came out from behind Annie's skirts. "For me?"

"That's right. And I brought a few other animals for you to share with Gretel's children—a cow, a pig, and a chicken. There's a little barn in my trunk, too. You can have your own ranch."

Caroline's eyes grew wide. "My own ranch, really?"

Annie invited Grandpa inside while he talked with Caroline. Cord couldn't remember his grandpa spending much time with him when he was little. He hadn't been a bad grandfather, just busy and a bit full of his own importance. Cord liked seeing this kinder side of him.

It wasn't all for Caroline either. He was going to church now, too. At least he had when here on the ranch last fall. The whole family and many of the cowhands had ridden into town to attend the weekly church service, where Cord played hymns on the piano for the congregation.

They all had coffee and did some catching up, Annie and Caroline with them, while Gretel and her youngsters worked on the noon meal. Grandpa produced a pocketful of wooden animals, promising to give them the barn later when he un-packed.

As the children sat together on the kitchen floor to play with the animal figurines, Cord turned to his grandpa and said, "We reached the end of our map."

Grandpa's eyes snapped up to meet Cord's. "You did? You really found it?"

"We're certain we've found the right spot. We brought home four . . . uh, that is, three artifacts. But we think there's more to find."

Grandpa's eyes narrowed. He might be old, but he was still sharp.

Cord leaned close and touched a finger to his lips. He didn't want Gretel or the children to overhear him; they might accidentally slip up and say something in front of the professor or his assistant. He whispered, "We kept one a secret from Professor Hardy. Lock was afraid he might abscond with the artifact. We had a suit of armor stolen. We got it all back except the dagger. We found a second dagger recently, and Lock is hanging on tight to it."

Grandpa nodded and asked about the theft and finding the armor, as well as about their trek out to Graham's claim.

"What we found out there is half yours." Annie patted Grandpa on the arm. "Just like Graham MacKenzie prom-ised when you loaned him money all those years ago."

"How did Sacramento fare from the earthquake?" Cord asked. "Any damage to your house or the bank? I wrote to Ma, but I haven't heard if she or Grandma and Grandpa Rivers had any trouble."

"They're fine. I took the train here like usual, and they're not on the route. But I sent a man on horseback to check on them and see if they were in need. He reported back that everything seemed to be all right. Of course, your stiff-necked grandpa wouldn't accept any help, though I offered."

Cord grinned. "Lots of stiff-necked grandparents in my life, and I love every one of you."

Grandpa laughed. "Now, when are we going after that treasure?"

Cord looked at Annie. She blinked, and they both looked at Grandpa. At the same exact time they said, "We?"

He grinned and rubbed his hands together with glee.

Apparently, Grandpa Mayhew was feeling better enough that he wanted in on the treasure hunt.

ELEVEN

Tilda's father and sister turned up later that same day. Annie hoped they had no plans to stay at the ranch. The house was full.

It turned out they were there to examine the latest find, hoping the artifacts could be added to the museum. Carl Cabril was a direct descendant of Captain Cabrillo, the Spanish ship captain who'd been among the first Europeans to explore the California coast.

It was believed that one of Cabrillo's ships had been blown off course into the fog surrounding San Francisco and had sailed inland by way of a river, now vanished. The explorers became stranded, lived out their lives in California, never to return to Mexico to be reunited with their fellow Spaniards who were busy rampaging through Mexico.

Annie liked to believe the explorers were happier not rampaging, but it was possible they'd just been stranded and died before they could go back south.

Tilda came out of the house. The whole ranch was much less regimented in the summer. The children, now playing, would need to be fed and cared for, but their lessons were halted this time of year.

With the school year ended, the three older children who wanted to be teachers were put in charge with only minor supervision. Another of the older teen girls planned to marry one of the Hart cowhands, and there would be a cabin available for them soon. Between rebuilding Harriet's house, a guesthouse, and a new cabin for the young couple, Annie couldn't help but wonder just how many houses they were going to have to build. The list kept getting longer, it seemed.

Tilda rushed up to Maddie, and the two hugged. Tilda whispered something into Maddie's ear. From Maddie's squeal and sudden tears, Annie was quite certain it was the news that she was expecting a baby. Tears seemed to be the poor sensitive woman's response to most things.

Despite the crying, Maddie had a big smile on her face when their father joined in with the chattering and crying. Annie was happy to see Tilda truly had a family beyond the Harts.

The threesome walked toward Michelle's laboratory.

Annie, curious about the objects that had been found most recently, went along to hear what Professor Hardy had determined regarding them.

Annie followed close behind Tilda. Her father got the door for her. Hardy, Rombauer, and Cord were studying the steel pieces, with Lock and Thayne close by and listening to every word.

Professor Hardy lifted a small hoop. "This appears to be the remains of a barrel."

Annie had wondered that exact thing.

"And this disk looks to be the lid to a kettle or a small pot.

The Spaniards of this particular era liked to drink coffee, so perhaps it's the lid to a coffeepot. Of course, coffee was still rare in Europe at the time and not greatly consumed. Coffee didn't come to the Americas until the seventeen hundreds. The conquistadors might have brought coffee beans along, but I'd say it's more likely the lid to a teakettle."

A lid. She thought Lock looked unimpressed, but then he wanted everything to be either gold or some kind of weapon.

Professor Hardy lifted a small piece of metal that Josh had carried on the ride home. It was irregularly shaped, reminding Annie of a sheriff's star. Yet she doubted that explained much as to what it really was.

"If you look close," Hardy said, running his thumb over the strange object, "it is etched with a picture. It could be a decorative badge or button to honor the king of Spain or perhaps Cortés himself." The professor's eyes glowed with excitement. "We'll compare this to pictures of Charles I, who ruled Spain during the time of Cabrillo's expedition. If it's not King Charles, it's very likely Cortés. We have pictures of Cortés in his later years, but none before his return to Spain. This could be a monumental find."

Annie was having a hard time getting excited about it, but she tried to let the archeologist's enthusiasm infect her.

Studying the object, Hardy continued, "The flat, curved steel reminds me of the protective shield worn around the wrist that we saw with the armor." He turned toward the reassembled suit of armor, his eyes alight.

Lock and Thayne stepped to the far side of the room and started whispering together. Annie thought that if a piece of armor was at the site by the well, it made sense for the dagger to be there. Lock didn't produce the dagger. He'd probably hidden it under his bed in his room over the doctor's office.

Annie moved to stand beside them. "Is Ellie all right? Brody didn't think she was in any danger when they stayed behind, but he wanted her resting instead of going on a hard ride for days."

"She's fine." Thayne's brow furrowed. "Brody is watching her close. He's not here right now because he has a cowpoke with a nasty cut on his arm that needs stitching up."

Professor Hardy took the curved steel to the laid-out suit of armor. He held it beside the wrist guard and compared the two pieces. Annie could see from where she was that they were the same.

"When can we go out there again, Aunt Annie?" Lock asked. "We're ready to ride."

"I was away from Caroline for three whole days. So I'm *not* ready to leave the ranch just yet."

"Is she upset?" Thayne gave her a very mature, concerned look.

"She seemed fine this morning. Michelle and Zane took good care of her while I was away. I think I missed her more than she missed me. I do want to go treasure hunting again, boys, but not quite so soon."

"It is not 'treasure hunting,' Mrs. Lane." Dr. Scold had overheard her. "It is a very important archeological research trip. Artifacts like this one"—he held up the steel wrist guard—"are more valuable than gold."

Annie couldn't miss the extremely skeptical look she saw on Lock's face.

"I don't suppose it would do to bring my daughter along next time? Caroline would enjoy digging in the dirt."

Dead silence filled the room. Even Professor Hardy looked up from the artifacts to stare at her.

With a shaky voice, Thayne said, "Honestly, Annie, if it hadn't been for Lock falling off a cliff on our first treasure hunt, and Brody getting shot on the one after that—"

"It'd probably be all right," Cord said, cutting Thayne off. "We're at the end of my map now, so we won't be riding through unknown wilderness with no trail, getting clawed at by brambles and scraggly pines. We found a much better route there."

"And as far as we know," Lock added, "no one's trying to kill us and steal the treasure anymore."

"No one is trying," Thayne said, "except someone *did* steal that armor only a few days ago. Whoever did that may still be around."

"Caroline is absolutely not allowed to go." Sweet-natured Tilda seemed to have no trouble finding her voice. "The wilderness is no place for a child."

Annie narrowed her eyes at her sister-in-law. Tilda had certainly gotten spunky since she'd married Josh. Or maybe she was simply right.

"I'll be staying right here on the ranch, Annie." Tilda cast a derisive look at the little hunks of steel they'd dug up on their last trip. "I'll watch her. The only thing is . . ."

Annie braced herself. "What?"

Tilda gave a little shrug, "I don't think Josh wants to go again. Not for another week at the very least. He didn't like leaving me alone when I was feeling poorly. Can you all wait a week or two?"

"No, we cannot." The professor plunked his hands on his hips.

"We're not waiting that long," Lock said firmly.

"We've *got* to finish this." Thayne's posture looked as immovable as a boulder.

Cord looked around the room until his eyes landed on Annie. "Do you think you can get us there?"

"I need a few more days to prepare, but, well . . ." Annie cleared her throat to force the words out. They were no more than the truth, but were they wise words? "Yes," she finally said, "I can get us there." Then her eyes landed on Hardy and his assistant, Rombauer. Could she trust them? Were they honorable men?

That remained to be seen.

Once they got to the site and started digging, bringing up more artifacts, how could she be sure that Hardy and Rombauer wouldn't just try to take the objects for themselves? Surely he couldn't make a reputation for himself, showing off three-hundred-year-old artifacts without talking about where they'd come from. And if he stole them and displayed them and talked about where they'd come from, that was as good as a confession, wasn't it?

Still, something about all of this didn't sit right with Annie. Which probably wasn't a good enough reason not to go. "We'll leave next Monday morning," she stated. "First light."

"That's half a week away," Hardy growled. "It's too long to wait."

"You teach at the University of the Pacific, is that right, Professor Hardy?"

His thick white brows lowered to the level of his gold-rimmed glasses. "You know I do."

"Go back there," said Annie. "You and Mr. Rombauer

are no longer welcome to stay on this ranch. I'm not listening to your complaints for one more minute. I don't want to see you and your assistant again until Monday morning. Understood?"

That shut him up good. He glowered at her, the color rising in his cheeks, but he didn't argue.

"You can travel to town with us, Professor Hardy," Carl Cabril said with a welcoming tone. Cabril had been a successful businessman back in New York City. It was clear he knew how to handle difficult situations. Carl went on. "Stay in the hotel and spend time in the museum. My daughter and I have been writing about what's been found so far. We've been living in the hotel while our new house is being built. We've written about the history of Cortés and Cabrillo, my ancestor, and these Spanish artifacts discovered in the wilderness of California. You would be a big help to us if you'd read what we've written and add your knowledge to ours."

Professor Hardy nodded at Carl, clearly appreciating someone who gave him such respect, even if everyone but Hardy knew Carl was just trying to get the man off the ranch before he was kicked off.

"Thank you, Mr. Cabril. I'd be interested in your opinion on this badge or button. I'd like to take these few pieces into town with me." Hardy now spoke exclusively to Cabril, maybe because his pride was being stroked. "Are you planning to add them to the museum collection? But first things first—this decorative badge needs to be researched."

Annie spoke up quickly. "No decision has been made yet as to the artifacts' permanent home. They were found on land owned by the MacKenzies, land legally purchased by their grandfather and left to their father and now passed down to them. So these artifacts are the MacKenzies' property, and the decision about what happens to them will be theirs." She turned to Thayne and Lock. "What do you want to do?"

Lock looked a bit confused, as if the idea that he owned the objects had never occurred to him. But then his focus was mainly on gold, of which there seemed to be none since the doubloons they'd found early on.

Thayne spoke up. "We'll need to talk to Brody first so he can see what all we have. He's been busy all morning. If he approves, I suppose you can take the pieces to the museum—for now anyway."

Annie nodded, then added, "I'd also like for Michelle to take a look at them before they leave the ranch."

"Maybe she'd ride along to town with us," Maddie suggested. "Tilda, would you want to come, too?"

Tilda gave her sister a one-armed hug. "I'd better not. My stomach isn't that steady. But I'll go find Michelle and tell her if she wants to see those objects, it'd better be now."

Tilda left the laboratory with Maddie tagging along.

"Thayne and Lock, would you go talk to Brody and Ellie?" Annie asked. "Tell them everything we've discussed just now."

"I'll stay here," said Cord. "I want a closer look at the new pieces, too." He gave Annie a strange look that seemed to imply he didn't want to leave Hardy and Rombauer alone with the artifacts.

That suspicion, which might only be in her head, sent a chill down her spine. She asked herself once again if she should lead this next expedition. If she did, she was definitely packing a gun just in case.

TWELVE

Cord rode in from moving the cattle to a new pasture. Josh had invited him to the ranch house for supper to talk about the return to Graham's claim with Hardy.

He caught Annie alone in the house making supper. Cord was surrounded by the fine smell of the chicken and the freshly baked biscuits she'd piled into a basket. A strudel sat cooling on the countertop.

"Where is everybody?" Cord said.

Annie turned and smiled, making Cord feel confused. Or maybe when it came to Annie, Cord was permanently confused no matter what her expression was.

"Michelle's in her lab, and Tilda's resting. Her stomach is still unsteady. Gretel went home. I'm determined to take some of the weight off her shoulders. Poor woman, cooking for all of us and her family and running two households . . . well, it's one of the reasons I need to stop teaching or at least cut back some. And while it was fun gallivanting off in search of treasure, it's been good to be back."

"Where's Caroline?" Cord asked, looking around.

"She's in the office, playing with your grandpa."

Cord glanced at the office door and smiled. Caroline could be heard singing quietly. Cord knew Annie kept a few playthings in there for the little girl.

"Caroline doesn't seem to have missed me overly," Annie went on. "But with her out of school for the summer, her routine has changed. I'll need to stay close by her for a while." Annie turned the chicken she was frying. Potatoes boiled away on the stovetop.

Dinner was almost ready, and Cord was the first of many she'd feed.

"I suppose Caroline hardly realizes I'm her mother these days, what with so many caretakers, and myself gone for a time." She'd started out saying that with some amusement, but as she talked, her tone turned more serious. Cord wondered if she thought it was true.

"She knows who her ma is," Cord reassured her. "She loves you. Whenever there's a commotion and she becomes frightened, she runs straight to you."

Annie locked eyes with him. "Commotion like an earthquake?"

Cord came to her side and rested his hand on her back. "I was thinking more about when company comes. We've had people invading the ranch regularly since we found that treasure . . . including me. I guess I'm an invader, too."

"No, Cord, you work here. If you're an invader, all our cowhands are." She smiled at him, and it appeared her uncertainty about Caroline had passed.

He'd enjoyed the few times they'd talked alone together. More than enjoyed. He'd come to have great respect for Annie Hart Lane. In truth, what he felt was considerably warmer than respect. Now here he was with questions that bubbled up from deep inside him. "Tell me about your late husband. Was he kind to you? Was he a skilled cattleman?"

Annie's smile remained, though it was a sadder version now. "I told you how we ended up married."

"You said you'd known him all your life and were good friends. It was the most natural thing in the world to get married." Unlike Cord. She'd met him only last year, and he'd spent most of the winter in the bunkhouse or out on the range. Even so, from the moment they met, he'd felt there was something special between them.

"Todd was a good rancher. He lost his ma when he was young, and his pa never remarried. When Pa Lane died from a fall off a horse, I didn't think Todd would ever smile again. At the time, Caroline was about one year old, and Todd spent a lot of time with her—almost like he wanted her to be as close to him as he'd been to his pa."

"So your husband had no brothers or sisters?"

"He lost an older brother in the war, and his two little sisters died in an outbreak of cholera. Then he lost his ma in childbirth, and the baby didn't make it either."

Cord shook his head slowly. It was a sad litany of death and grief. "When my pa died, it was a terrible blow. My ma has never really gotten over it."

Annie nodded. "So you were still young when you lost your pa?"

"Yep, and we all went to live in Sacramento, closer to Grandpa Westbrook. But Ma couldn't take it for very long, not without Pa there to soften Grandpa. Eventually she moved back home with her parents."

"Did you spend much time with your grandpa?"

"This was before the train came through and sped things

129

up, but we went to see him several times a year. Grandpa Westbrook lived in a mansion near Sacramento, not far from the bank he owned. Grandpa Rivers had homesteaded and owned a one-bedroom cabin. While it was more comfortable in town, I loved life on the farm and wanted that for myself someday. Because I needed to earn money to buy myself some farmland, I went to work at Grandpa's bank."

Cord spoke softly, aware that his grandfather was nearby playing with Caroline. His quiet voice drew Annie closer.

"Grandpa was hard to live with, so I found a place of my own. But with that little bit of space between us, we formed a good relationship. I went to see him often and played the piano for him."

"You do have an extraordinary gift for the piano."

"I've loved playing from my earliest memory. Grandpa let me take lessons from the man who played the organ at our church. I enjoyed that; no one had to scold me to practice my lessons. Grandpa grumbled about it being a waste of time, but then he bought me a Steinway piano. It seemed to soothe Grandpa's soul to hear me play on it." Cord smiled as he pondered those days with his grandpa with fondness.

Annie turned the chicken again, even though Cord thought she'd just done so. "Looks done to me," he said. "You've fried it up to a perfect, crispy brown." He inhaled deeply and couldn't help but catch the scent of Annie mixed in with all the other wonderful smells.

That was when he realized he'd been standing here talking to her all this time with his hand still on her back. He probably oughta step away from her now.

Using a fork, she removed the chicken from the cast-iron

skillet on the stove and placed it onto a serving platter, then set aside the fork.

When she'd finished, Cord turned her to face him. Not stepping away at all, not letting go. "Annie, I don't know when we'll find the time to get to town for a meal together. Do you think, maybe after we eat, we could go for a walk later this evening?"

Her cheeks turned a bit pink. She met his gaze, then dropped her eyes to where her hands were intertwined. Then she looked up again. "I'm glad the professor and his assistant went to town."

"They couldn't do much else when you as good as kicked them out."

Her cheeks pinked up even more. "The man is aggravating, and I . . . well, I didn't like him staying upstairs in the house, not with Caroline and I sleeping so close by."

Cord felt his temper rise. His hands tightened on her waist, and he drew her closer. "Did he do something to Caroline? If he has, I'll—"

"No." Annie touched her fingertips to his lips. "It's nothing like that. It's just awkward . . . although I never felt that way when your grandpa was staying in the house. Nor when you were."

Slowly, gently, Cord leaned down and kissed her on the lips. Really kissed her.

The seconds grew to a minute, with Cord losing track of the time. He came to his senses after a bit to find his hands sunk deep in the rich, dark silk of her hair. Her cheeks were even rosier, and her lips shone.

Only an inch away, he gathered his wits and said, "Will

you go on that walk with me, Annie? I'd love to stretch this time with you a bit longer."

She smiled. "I'd like that. And maybe soon we can get to town for a meal together. But for tonight, after I tuck Caroline into bed, I'd be honored to take a stroll with you."

He kissed her again. When the potatoes boiling over hissed on the stove, Annie pulled away from him reluctantly as if she were tearing herself free. Finally she turned back to the stove.

"Could you please set the table, Cord?" she asked, clearing her throat.

Cord got busy. He had to or he'd end up pulling Annie close again while their supper went up in flames.

— ✧ —

"Annie has agreed to go for a walk with me after supper." Cord spoke, and it was like a sudden deep freeze swept across the table.

Everyone sat there, motionless and silent. Josh and Zane exchanged a long look.

Michelle spoke first. "I'd be glad to get Caroline settled into bed for you, Annie."

Tilda was next. "And don't you worry about the dirty dishes. We can do the cleaning up."

Zane said, "You're going to do *what*?"

Josh looked at Cord with narrowed eyes.

Annie turned to look at her brother. She was older than him, so he didn't boss her around like he did most everyone else. But he sure tried. "We're going for a walk, Zane." She almost laughed at the stunned look on his face. The man truly had no idea.

Josh had said a thing or two that told her he'd noticed

something going on between her and Cord. He couldn't have noticed much, though. She thought of today's kisses and was glad neither brother had been there to witness her and Cord's intimate moment.

There'd been other moments, too. A connection that drew her to him. But those kisses had been serious . . .

Staring straight at Zane, she said, "Thank you, Cord. Yes, taking a walk with you would be real nice."

Caroline was busy finishing the strudel they'd served with whipped cream and didn't bother looking up. And she was the only one Annie worried about.

Zane's brow furrowed, and he looked from Annie to Cord, then back again. Then he stood from the table and said, "I'll wash, Tilda. Josh can dry."

Annie smiled at him. Standing, she proceeded to the back door, Cord right behind her. They stepped outside into a cool California evening.

"I thought there might be trouble there for a second." Cord spoke quietly as they started walking toward the west.

She gave a little laugh. "Zane looked surprised, but he adjusted soon enough."

Cord took her hand and hooked it through his elbow, and they strolled in silence for a while.

She realized then that the last time she'd gone on a walk with a man, she'd ended up marrying him.

Annie didn't say that out loud, yet it all felt so strange to her.

It was late spring, the days growing longer now, and the sun was setting as they followed the trail that led to Dorada Rio. They had no destination in mind but just enjoyed being alone together.

"I want us to spend time getting to know each other, but I can't think of a word to say or a question to ask." Cord patted her hand where it rested on his elbow.

She chuckled quietly. "Maybe that means we already know each other."

"I do know you, Annie. Not all the details, of course, but I know you're an intelligent, hardworking, honorable woman. I know you're a fine mother and a talented teacher. All that brought us here are details we can learn with time."

She squeezed his arm, nodding in agreement.

"Sometime soon," Cord rushed on, "I'd like to ride with you to where the ground cracked during the earthquake. I want to see what it looks like now. That chuck wagon might not have fallen far into the crack. Maybe we can haul the wagon to level ground and repair it to be used again."

"Maybe so," she said. "I'll never forget the sight of the earth cracking like that and the wagon falling into it. It reminds me of what may have happened to that ship long ago. How shocking would it be for a river to suddenly dry up, its water source cut off? Could the ship have fallen into a crack like the chuck wagon? I wonder how many of the crew there were besides the five graves we found in the wilderness? Did they die when the ship disappeared into the cracked earth as the river it floated on was forced underground?"

"The ship could have run aground when the river was diverted. Five of the crew at least were able to walk away. Probably a sixth as well, as someone had to be there to bury the five. After three hundred years, armor and weapons, gold . . . and bones would be all that was left. Maybe Professor Hardy could tell us more about what happened back then.

134

Would an archeologist know about earthquakes, or is that a different kind of professor?"

She smiled up at him. He wasn't an overly tall man—six feet, maybe a little less. Being a woman of decent height, she only had to look up a bit.

He drew her to a stop, turned, and kissed her. The kiss drew out. It baffled her honestly. He'd kissed her in the kitchen, and her heart had lurched and come back to life. Filled with a sensation unlike anything she'd felt when Todd had kissed her, but something completely new. She'd never felt like this before. She reveled in the kiss, setting aside so much old grief to realize she could feel again.

She pulled back and met his blue eyes. No words passed between them, and yet so much passed between their eyes. Her confusion and amazement, his passion and longing.

"Annie, I don't think we need as much time to get to know each other as I thought."

A smile spread slowly across her face. "Yes, I believe you're right."

"I have such a deep regard for you. It started the first time I saw you."

She well remembered that moment. He'd stepped into the kitchen of the ranch house. She'd looked him in the eyes and couldn't look away. He'd seemed just as enthralled as she was.

That was last autumn.

Moments ticked by as they became lost, each in the other's gaze. She'd forgotten where she was. Who she was. She forgot all her fears because she was much too busy looking at a man who'd awakened a sleeping part of herself.

Now, months later, here they stood. Enthralled by each other.

"Annie, I . . . that is, my *intentions* toward you are completely honorable. I want you to know that. I want us to . . . to continue—"

She kissed him this time just to shut him up.

They were out of sight of the house, but they heard the back door open and close. Cord pulled away, drew her hand back through his elbow, and started walking again.

"Afraid that's one of my brothers?"

"I'd like to have your brothers' permission to court you, Annie."

"They both like you, Cord."

"They do. But the way to earn their blessing is to ask you to marry me."

"I-I . . ."

"Don't say no, please. If you can't say yes right now, then say you'll think about it, that you need more time. But don't say no."

Annie was silent again as they walked on because indeed she'd opened her mouth to decline his offer, at least at this moment in time. But then he'd cut in, pleading with her *not* to refuse him. Still, she could imagine a time in the future when she'd be ready to say yes. She fumbled for the right words.

"I won't say no then, Cord. I won't say I'll think about it either because I'm already quite sure that the time is coming when I will say yes."

He grinned as he turned to face her, his blue eyes shining. "That is very much like saying yes."

Annie went on, "There are lots of things to talk over and

decide before the time comes to marry. Where would we live? Are you prepared to accept Caroline in your life and love her as you would your own child? What about the farm or ranch you want to buy? What about—?"

He pressed two fingers against her lips. "Sure, I'd like to have my own place someday, but for now I'm happy working at the Two Harts as a cowpoke—if that's what you want, Annie. And the farm or ranch I want to buy is something we can plan together. As for Caroline, that little girl is precious and sweet and beautiful, and I'll gladly promise to love her as I would my own child. Do you have any other worries?"

Facing him, she smiled. "Give me time. I'm sure I'll come up with a few more."

He leaned down; she reached up. Their kiss was almost a promise, almost a vow. Annie felt her heart turn to him as old pain became old but sweet memories, those that included her late husband and her life with him.

She found she was able to set the sadness aside. She was ready to step out of a life of routine and work, of teaching and caring for orphans. She'd enjoyed that work, but now she yearned for something different.

THIRTEEN

"You're not going anywhere!" Josh barked.

Yes, just like a cur dog. And Annie apologized to all the dogs she'd just insulted. She'd never laid eyes on a dog as rude as her brother.

"I made my decision, Josh. No one tells me what to do or not do." She mentally scoffed at herself. Someone was sure enough telling her what not to do right now.

"Zane?" Just one single word and Josh sounded like a boy again. A frustrated youngster who needed his big brother's help.

Unfortunately for Annie, Zane was eager to comply. "No. You can't go out into the wilderness with five men."

"I'm not some schoolgirl. I'm a widow who is as tough and knowledgeable in the woods as either of you." That might not be completely true, but she was plenty tough. "You're both busy with work and family. I'm going. Anyway, two of the men are my nephews. That makes it proper." They were more boys than men, though Thayne was real close.

Zane narrowed his eyes. "Those two boys are no better chaperones than your horse."

They were both standing by the table while she was leaning against the sink. She had a juicy roast in the oven, potatoes peeled and nearly cooked. Supper would be ready as soon as everyone gathered.

She glared at her brothers as they faced off, a shootout with words. And she intended to beat them to the draw.

"You've gone for walks with Cord three evenings in a row," Josh chimed in. "You can't ride off with him into the wilderness after that!"

Almost as if he'd heard his name being spoken, Cord stepped into the kitchen. He was wearing his work clothes: blue denim pants and a brown broadcloth shirt, chaps, a battered Stetson, and cowhide gloves. Clutched in his hand was a coiled-up bullwhip.

"Josh, we've finished the branding in the last pasture. Bo asked me to, uh . . ." Cord fell silent, his eyes shifting between Annie, Josh, and Zane. "Something wrong?" He turned back to Annie, his eyes wide. "What's going on here?"

Her arms crossed, Annie went back to glaring at her brothers. "Yes, something is wrong, Cord. My two little brothers are under the mistaken impression that I need their permission to run my own life."

"We told her," Josh said with exaggerated patience, "that it is improper for her to ride off into the woods with five men she's not related to in any way. Including you, who's clearly courting her."

"You're just going to have to wait!" Zane slashed his hand through the air to add weight to his words. "If you give Brody some time, Ellie will be able to go."

"No," Annie said. "She almost went into labor the last time she lifted a heavy pot. She can't go."

Zane tilted his head sideways just a little, conceding the point.

"Tilda won't be suffering from morning sickness much longer," Josh pointed out. "She might not go even when she's feeling better, but I won't feel so bad about leaving her behind."

Again, Annie shook her head. "Tilda's only a couple of months gone on this baby. It can take three months sometimes to get over a fractious belly when you're first expecting. There's no way I can keep those boys and that grouchy professor confined for another month."

"Well, I can't go right now," Zane said. "With the branding done, we'll be moving the cattle to the far pastures. And Michelle's busy finishing up her latest invention, pushing hard to submit her next patent. The earthquake threw her off schedule. I promised I'd help with Leah more. Hopefully, Tilda will be feeling better before Michelle is ready." He looked uncertain, which was odd for him. "Would it be all right to take a baby on the treasure hunt?"

"No!" Annie, Josh, and Cord all shouted at once.

Zane jumped a little. "Then you just have to wait, and so do your companions."

"Um, I have a suggestion," Cord said. He walked over and hung the bullwhip on a wall hook next to the back door, then turned to face everyone.

"You're not a good enough chaperone, Cord." Josh jabbed a finger at him.

Zane crossed his arms to match Annie's posture. "We know you're an honorable man, Cord. But this is bigger than that. It's about how it'd look. People talk; they gossip. Our sister's reputation must be protected. Which means she *can't* go."

"I'm going," Annie countered. "Neither of you can tell me what to do. I'd think you'd have figured that out by now."

Cord removed the Stetson and dropped his gloves onto a kitchen chair. "What if—?"

"Whatever it is, Cord, we're not changing our minds." Josh's face turned an alarming shade of red.

"That's right, we're not," echoed Zane with a jerk of his chin.

"But what if—?"

"Go on now, Cord." Josh nodded toward the back door. "This is a family matter. We appreciate the news about the branding, but—"

"Don't you tell him what to do." Annie dropped her arms and clenched her fists. "You're not in charge of him any more than you are of me."

Josh scratched the back of his neck. "Honestly, Annie, I'm his boss."

"That's true," Cord conceded. "But what if—?"

"In that case, since I'm a one-quarter owner of this ranch, I'm his boss too, and I say he stays right where he is. Cord, say something. You know I've been planning to go after the treasure. You've not objected to it."

"Well, I guess I didn't think about whether it was proper or not for you to go. If we can just—"

Josh swatted Cord's arm. "Are you saying Annie's not proper? Don't you have any respect for my sister?"

Annie turned on Cord. "What? You don't respect me now?"

"All right, you two, get out of the kitchen. I want to talk with Annie *alone*." Cord's face flushed, and his eyes sparked with anger at her two brothers.

Josh flinched. Zane did that little head tilt of his again. Annie really needed to finish preparing the meal, but Cord had a determined look on his face. She waited to hear what he had to say to her as the two brothers shuffled to the door and slipped outside, grumbling the whole way.

With them gone, Annie looked at Cord and crossed her arms again. If Cord thought he could make her to stay behind when her brothers had failed, he had another think coming.

He stepped closer to her. While they hadn't made it to dinner in town just yet, they'd gone out walking every evening since that first time, and they were due for another walk tonight. And tomorrow was Sunday, which left them one more walk before the group rode out on the treasure hunt early Monday morning.

Annie said, "How could my half-wit brothers not realize I was going on the treasure hunt? We've been talking about it all week. It seems Josh thought Brody and Ellie were going, and Zane thought Josh was going. Don't you dare even think about—"

Cord gripped her shoulders, pulled her close, and cut off her rant by kissing her.

It didn't just silence her; it made her questions vanish until she could think of only one thing. How much she'd come to like this man. Much more than like, in fact.

When Cord eased her back, just far enough their eyes could meet, he said quietly, "Marry me, Annie. Then it'll be proper for us to leave together on the dig." He smiled like a clever seven-year-old.

"You want me to marry you so I can go on the treasure

hunt?" Her voice rose with every word. It sounded a little like a train whistle by the time she was finished.

He looked increasingly nervous. "Well, you want to go, don't you? I thought it would be a great excuse to get married."

She didn't believe in violence, which was lucky for Cord. "Get out of this house now. And send Josh and Zane back in here. One of them is going to have to go along with me."

He had the nerve to look like his feelings had been hurt.

"Don't you want to marry me, Annie?"

"It's too soon, Cord. We just started thinking about each other in that way."

"No, we didn't." Cord took her hands in his.

"We didn't?"

He shook his head. "I was in the kitchen, newly arrived from Dorada Rio, and you walked in with Caroline, remember? I couldn't think of a thing to say to you, but I couldn't look away. I was drawn to you so powerfully, I couldn't speak. And you couldn't look away from me."

She felt the burn of tears as she recalled that moment, that very first moment when she'd been struck dumb. "And a week or two later, I came downstairs from helping deliver Michelle's baby and saw you sitting on the floor with Caroline, who fell asleep in your lap. A strong, gentle man who held my precious baby with such care, and you carried her upstairs for me to put her to bed."

Cord smiled. "It's not too soon for us to marry. There's no need to delay starting our future together. I've been wanting to marry you since the first time I laid eyes on you. We've been putting off the inevitable ever since." He kissed her again, longer this time. He must have decided talking wasn't working well.

"All the walking we've done together was just me waiting until it didn't seem like such a headlong rush before I told you I love you. Before I asked you to share your life with me. I love you, Annie. Will you marry me?"

He kissed her again.

This time when he quit, he said, "I'm taking that for a yes." He squeezed her hands tight. "We can get married tomorrow after church. Your whole family will be there. Grandpa can come. Then everything will be perfectly proper for you to lead the group on the treasure hunt."

Annie's brain wasn't working well. In Michelle's experiments with electricity, Annie had heard the term *short-circuit* and its meaning explained. She wondered if that could happen inside a person's brain, too.

Cord leaned down again, his apparent solution to any extended silence.

Moving quickly, she touched his lips with her finger. "Thank you, Cord."

Their gazes met. This time he didn't try to kiss her. With the patience of a saint, he stood there and let her think.

At last, she reached up and kissed him very tenderly, then said, "Yes, Cord. I would be honored to marry you."

Grinning, he slung his arm around her and turned her toward the back door. "Let's call the family in and tell them the good news! Where's Grandpa? Playing with Caroline?"

"I'm right here." Grandpa stepped into the doorway between the kitchen and the main room of the house. "Welcome to the family, Annie." His smile was as wide as the California sky.

Cord laughed. "So you approve of our getting married?"

Grandpa came across the kitchen and pulled Annie into a hug.

Cord saw Caroline come right behind him, and she smiled shyly up at Cord. "Are you going to be my pa? Grandpa shushed me so we could listen to you talk. Ma says that's rude, but Grandpa said this once it was all right."

Grandpa let go of Annie and turned to hug his grandson. Just then the back door opened.

"You talk her into getting hitched?" Josh walked into the kitchen.

Annie's eyes widened as she saw Tilda behind him, eyes brimming with tears, a huge smile on her face. "And the wedding is tomorrow?"

Then came Zane and Michelle, Brody and Ellie, followed by the MacKenzie boys. Goodness, had everyone heard Cord's proposal? Annie considered it a mercy the professor and his assistant weren't coming to supper.

Cord took a firm hold of her hand, lacing their fingers together in a way so warm and affectionate she couldn't wait to say her vows. "Annie has agreed to marry me. I consider myself the luckiest man in the world." Then he looked sideways at her, and his blue eyes flashed with humor. "And it has nothing to do with going together on the treasure hunt. We'd've gotten to this very place soon enough."

She gave a firm nod of her head. "Yes, we would have. We're getting married tomorrow right after church."

Josh said, "I'm going to tell the men to butcher and roast a hog. We'll have a party to beat all." He was gone before Annie could tell him that sounded wonderful.

"You should invite your father and sister out to the ranch

tomorrow, Tilda. We can even let Professor Hardy and Mr. Rombauer come."

Ellie wrapped her arms around Annie's neck and wept. Through the tears she said, "I'm so happy for you."

There was general chaos as everyone hugged the newly engaged couple and congratulated them.

There seemed to be no surprise at all among them. Honestly, Annie herself was a little bit surprised. But no one questioned her decision, which proved she didn't have a ridiculous, addled look on her face.

FOURTEEN

Cord's piano playing at church on Sunday morning had a particularly joyful ring to it. And he couldn't keep the smile off his face.

He glanced out to see his pretty Annie sitting in the front row, Caroline between her and Mrs. Lewis, the parson's wife. Hattie Lewis had helped save Tilda when her brother kidnapped her, a story Cord had heard a few times.

For the closing hymn, he played "A Mighty Fortress Is Our God," and it sounded as though all the voices raised in song might just lift the roof off the small church building. As he played and sang, it felt like a prayer, as if he were beseeching God for His blessing and protection over the marriage he and Annie would embark on later that day. Cord felt the music deeply and put all that feeling into his playing, but today especially, his wedding day, his feelings and the music both soared to new heights.

After the hymn ended, Parson Lewis announced, "For those who'd like to stay, there will be a wedding ceremony immediately following today's service. Our much-loved pianist Cord Westbrook and our beloved Annie Hart Lane are to be married. You're all welcome to join us in celebrating their blessed union."

Cord rose at the same moment Annie did. They met Parson Lewis at the front of the church and faced him together.

"I hope this means you'll be staying with us permanently, Cord," the parson said. "Our services are much enriched by your musical gifts."

Cord looked at Annie, who only smiled in return.

He turned back to the parson. "We don't know what the future holds, Parson Lewis. For now, though, our home is right here in Dorada Rio at the Two Harts Ranch. Our future together is in God's hands."

"Of course. Now, let's have a moment of prayer, shall we?" The parson lifted his left hand high in the air, his right gripping the Word of God.

Cord listened closely to the vows he was taking. He wanted to make his promises solemnly and fully. He stood there holding Annie's hand and didn't hesitate to vow to love, honor, and cherish her for the rest of his life. She promised the same right back with the promise to obey thrown in. Yet she was an agreeable woman, capable and smart, and he wasn't the type to order people around. He suspected they'd deal well with each other.

"I now pronounce you man and wife," Parson Lewis concluded, his smile bright enough to dim the sun. "Cord, you may kiss your bride."

Cord turned to Annie. He probably should have bought her a ring. He wished his ma and his grandparents could have come to the wedding ceremony today. He should have—

Annie kissed the thoughts right out of his head, replacing them with thoughts only of her.

They drew back, then turned to face the sanctuary. Their family. The cowhands, a good chunk of them with their wives and children. The folks they'd befriended as a church family.

The indomitable Mrs. Lewis had moved to the piano and now played a rousing version of "Joy to the World." Though it was considered a Christmas carol, its lyrics were exactly right for the moment.

With a big smile, Cord escorted Annie a few paces down the center aisle to where Caroline stood between Brody and a very pregnant Ellie. They were in the front row, along with Grandpa. Cord shook hands with his grandpa, who offered his congratulations. He'd been understanding about Cord settling in at the Two Harts, but he hadn't exactly approved. But when it came to the marriage, Grandpa had given his hearty approval.

Cord reached out a hand to Caroline. She beamed and rushed forward to grasp his hand. Cord hoisted her up with his left arm, with Annie holding tight on his right. The three of them made their way down the aisle toward the propped-open doors at the back while greeting all those who'd attended the ceremony.

Cord had just joined a big, happy family.

As the afternoon wore on, Annie found herself on the verge of collapse from all the celebrating. Every woman on the ranch, including the bunkhouse cooks, had brought their tables, chairs, and utensils outdoors, arranging everything in preparation for a meal of roasted hog supplied by the Hart family.

Gretel and others had baked bread and potatoes as well

149

as cakes and other desserts to add to the wedding reception. One person had brought a fiddle, another a squeeze-box, and there'd been lots of dancing, laughter, and feasting. Now the music had died down, and the tables and chairs were being carried back inside. With the sun nearly set, a large fire roared at the center of the revelers as the night cooled.

Annie was taken aback every now and then by the realization that she was a married woman again. It made her a little dizzy to think of it, yet it also delighted her.

Cord came up and wrapped an arm around her waist. She couldn't remember the last time she'd seen him. They'd been pulled in different directions by well-wishers and treasure hunters. Mercifully the well-wishers had outnumbered those raring to go trekking into the wilderness.

They'd invited Professor Hardy to the wedding ceremony. He hadn't made it to the church, but he'd shown up for the reception on the ranch. In fact, she couldn't recall his ever attending church in town. But the professor seemed to enjoy the roasted hog, two or three helpings of it. She'd recently spotted him and the loyal Mr. Rombauer riding toward town at a decent pace, almost a canter, and wondered what they were up to.

Leaning close, Cord said, "Caroline fell asleep in my arms during the last dance. I carried her up to bed. Michelle said she'd get Caroline into her nightgown and tuck her in since Leah is already asleep. As for us, Josh said they cleaned their things out of the housekeeper's room, and you and I could stay there for the night, maybe longer. They've been busy building a new guesthouse; he and Tilda may move in there permanently and stay in the ranch house whenever there are guests on the ranch."

Annie's eyes went wide. "I told my brother not to bother making the guesthouse too comfortable, thinking we could have Professor Hardy stay there on occasion. I sure hope it's fit for Josh and Tilda to live in."

"I think the crew building it has been informed it might be for Josh to live in. And you told him that before we had the professor start staying in town instead of here. He's not that great of company, in my opinion."

Annie gave a half smile. "That's a widely held opinion."

"He'll be back here early tomorrow morning to start on what he refuses to call a treasure hunt. It's an 'archeological expedition.'"

Annie groaned. "I'm starting to have my doubts about his coming along with us."

Cord shrugged. "Too late now. He said he'd be here just before first light, ready to head out."

"Too late is right," she agreed around a big yawn.

"Let's go inside, Annie. We're both plain tuckered out, and most everyone has left. The party's winding down." He chuckled. "At last." He leaned down and kissed her.

When he pulled back, she said, "Let's go in, Cord."

Arm in arm, Annie and her new husband started their married life exhausted but full of joy and hope for the future.

In the meantime, they both needed to get some sleep. The *archeological expedition* was to begin first thing in the morning, and it was sure to be a long journey.

FIFTEEN

This time Annie led the group of riders, and instead of bringing up the rear, Cord's horse trotted along at her side. Mr. Rombauer seemed willing and able to watch their flank. And since Annie didn't expect any trouble, she saw no harm in it. Though the man rarely talked, he was strong and a good rider who seemed trail savvy.

They left the ranch by taking the shortcut through Cornerstone rather than following the trail they'd blazed past the green pool and the cave where the MacKenzies' grandpa had met his end.

The professor rode behind Annie and Cord. Thayne and Lock came next, riding side by side unless the trail got too narrow. But it was a decent trail most of the way to Cornerstone, after which they'd start to head into the wilderness.

Annie's feelings for Cord were so different from what she'd had when married to Todd. Everything with Cord was new, exciting, and very sweet. It seemed they could talk forever and never grow tired of it. Along with her, he was now a one-fourth owner of the Two Harts. They hadn't really discussed where they'd end up and if he still wanted to buy a farm of their own. That still needed to be settled, but after their romantic night together, she was well inclined to follow Cord anywhere.

———— ✦ ————

In one long day, they made the trip to the site where they'd found Graham MacKenzie's cabin. There was enough light for the professor to see where they'd dug the last time they were here. The men got busy setting up camp, with the professor mostly sitting and watching while everyone worked around him. Everyone except for Mr. Rombauer, who'd gone off scouting or hunting maybe? No one knew for certain because Rombauer didn't say exactly. He was an overly quiet man.

Annie worked at readying a meal for the group. Everyone was worn out and starving, and they weren't about to wait for Rombauer to wander back to camp before they dug in. For supper they had side pork, eggs, and biscuits, all cooked over an open fire. They drank coffee as they ate, strong and searing hot.

When he'd finished eating, the professor went and took out a notebook and pencil from his saddlebag. He began writing feverishly, muttering about the well and the cabin. Annie thought of Graham MacKenzie and how he'd probably done the same thing many years ago.

The meal was a success, everyone talking about how delicious it'd tasted. Even the professor complimented her on it. Eventually, Mr. Rombauer sauntered back to the campsite, and Annie fixed him up a plate so the man wouldn't go to bed hungry.

Before long, they were all resting under their blankets,

with Annie tucked in warmly beside her newly rounded-up husband.

They were all asleep before full dark.

———— ◇ ————

"I've found something!" Cord heard the scrape of his shovel against iron. They'd risen early for the second day and had been digging carefully for hours, skimming an inch of ground away at a time. This was in obedience to Professor Hardy's overlong, condescending instructions earlier. Hardy watched them all like a hawk as they dug, writing constantly in his little notebook.

The arrogant man did only a little bit of digging himself, mostly to correct the others, showing them how to use the tools and not damage any artifacts they might come across. As they dug deeper, inch by inch, they brought Hardy the odd bits they unearthed. He then recorded the finds with his pencil.

"Looks like it was a chest of some kind," Cord said. "The wood's mostly rotted away, but you can still see by the steel frame of a chest."

Staring at the chest, Lock gasped loudly. "Is it a pirate's chest? There could be gold coins near where you found it?" He was at Cord's side almost instantly.

It was just as well because Cord needed help dragging the rickety thing to the surface. "No, I think it's a chest that once held bottles, foodstuffs maybe. I can't tell what it is, but it ain't for storing gold."

The others had stopped their digging, shifting their attention to Cord and the mysterious chest. He looked from Lock to Annie to Hardy and bit back the urge to roll his eyes. The word *gold* had a powerful effect on people.

Hardy observed intently as Cord, Lock, and Thayne lifted what was left of the fragile chest from the ground. They'd scooped out an area roughly two feet deep and ten feet square around the well. Everyone spread out around the old collapsed well to keep from whacking each other with their shovels.

Apparently, Mr. Rombauer hadn't come along to dig for treasure. Instead, he continued exploring the greater area, vanishing from the dig site for hours on end, then meandering his way back, always at mealtime. Meanwhile, the rest of them had discovered dozens of pieces of steel and now the strange chest. But what Cord really wanted to discover was evidence of a long-lost ship.

"Tell us what you're seeing here so far, Professor?" Annie asked. Her expression told Cord she was genuinely interested in knowing the man's thoughts on the subject.

Hardy stopped scrawling in his notebook and looked up at her. "I'm not sure yet, but the chest may have held bottles of honey." He lifted one of the bottles into the sunlight to illustrate his point, turning it slowly with his other hand.

Cord stepped closer to get a better look at it. "You know, even though the glass is dirty, I can see what you mean, Professor."

Hardy went on to explain that there were a surprising number of things, even three hundred years ago, that could be preserved in bottles.

What was more interesting to Cord was that none of the bottles were broken. They were still intact even after all these years. "If the ship was involved in an earthquake, there would be a lot of shaking. And if the river suddenly dried up, the vessel would tip and probably end up on its side on muddy ground. Much of the cargo and the foodstuffs for the journey would be tossed around. If that's what truly happened, wouldn't these glass bottles have shattered? Why are they not broken?"

Annie took the bottle from Hardy and rubbed the dirt from its neck. "Does that mean you're having second thoughts about the theory of the earthquake being behind the river drying up and stranding the Spanish ship?"

The professor gave them all the first real smile they'd seen from the man, at least that was Cord's guess. Hardy was beaming as he said, "That's what is so very exhilarating about an expedition like this—searching for answers to questions about things and people lost to history. And maybe, if we're fortunate, finding some of those answers. The past is fascinating that way." Then the smile vanished, and he added, "Put the chest over there with the other artifacts. And be *careful* with it. Its remaining wood is fragile. Only the iron straps are holding it together, though not by much."

Cord nodded, then very slowly, with Lock's help, carried the chest the four or five paces to where they'd started the collection of iron pieces they'd dug up that day. There wasn't a speck of gold to be seen anywhere, much to Thayne and Lock's disappointment. Depending on how much was buried at this site, Cord could easily imagine the process of digging taking weeks, months, if not years. He thought even the MacKenzies' interest was starting to wane.

He looked over at the shield, still hanging there about fifty feet away from him. Why had Grandpa MacKenzie hung it in that spot? They'd dug around it some but found nothing. They'd discovered the five graves under the other Spanish shield, so Cord couldn't understand why this shield didn't mark anything important.

He itched to start slinging dirt again from under the shield, this time enlarging the dig, wider and much deeper, but Hardy had insisted they go over everything at the site in a very orderly fashion. Carefully.

———— ✧ ————

"Annie, come with me."

She jerked awake. Lock knelt beside her and Cord, his back to the rest of the camp. She felt Cord stir and knew he was awake, too.

"Shhh." Lock said nothing else, just walked away from the camp and the others who slept on, Thayne among them.

The night was pitch-dark, with clouds blocking the new moon and the stars. The woods surrounded them in all directions.

Cord stood, took her by the hand, and pulled her to her feet. As silently as they could, they followed Lock a good distance from the campsite.

Once they caught up with him, well out of earshot of the camp, he lifted a lantern and lit it. Then he pulled from his pants pocket five gold doubloons. The Spanish coins matched the ones they'd found in Graham MacKenzie's cave.

Annie's eyes grew wide. She tore her gaze from the coins to Lock, then to Cord, but no words were exchanged among them.

An owl hooted overhead. Its rush of wings and the high squeal of dying prey broke the silence.

Finally, into the silence, Lock whispered, "I found these today plus a dozen more in that small iron case I dug up.

I pocketed the coins and gave the case to Professor Hardy. I don't trust him to understand that this gold is rightfully ours. Thayne already knows about my find, and now you do. I don't believe it's stealing if we found them on our land, but . . ."

His voice faded. He didn't have to say more. They were dealing with a moral dilemma here. Annie saw on Lock's face how he was wrangling with doubts mixed with guilt and selfishness. Or maybe it was just his suspicion that he wouldn't be allowed to keep something he clearly thought should be his to do with however he saw fit.

Annie looked at Cord. Once more it all came down to trust. Did they trust the professor to tell him about this find of gold coins? No doubt he'd declare them to be valuable artifacts and wouldn't outright steal the gold. But in the end, he'd want the coins locked away in the museum. He'd tried that very thing with the other valuable coins they'd found. But they'd thwarted him. It had helped that they'd shown him only one gold coin, and with watchful eyes they'd let him study the Spanish coin for as long as he wanted.

Now the situation was a bit murkier. Annie had heard the expression that possession was nine-tenths of the law. Those coins, right there in Lock's hand, were surer of being his to keep.

Cord whispered, "I say we don't discuss this until we get back to the ranch. We'll figure out then what's best to be done, if anything. We can always tell Hardy about the coins at a later time."

Lock's eyes lit up in the night. He nodded vigorously, obviously in full agreement with Cord's wise suggestion.

"Go back to the camp now," said Cord, "and keep that gold well hidden."

Lock slid the coins back into his pocket and headed back.

Annie turned back to Cord, who shrugged and said quietly, "We're in agreement at least, and now he'll do the same with every gold coin he finds."

She wondered what the old Spanish coins' value were in the archeological sense? Were they caught up in hiding an important discovery of the past that might hinder future generations' understanding of history? And what about Professor Hardy and his ambition to become a famous archeologist? She'd noticed that he had entitled his notes *The Hardy Expedition*, and that grated on her something terrible.

Her trust in the learned professor was dwindling.

Annie sighed as she reached for Cord's hand. Unsure whether they'd made the right decision about the gold find, she said, "C'mon, let's go back to camp. I could use more sleep."

Sixteen

"We're going to have to take a break from the digging for a week or so," Professor Hardy announced a week into the treasure hunt.

Cord sat up straight, feeling as if he'd just been poked with something sharp. "Why, Professor? I don't understand. We're finding more artifacts every day, and there's no sign we've found everything." He thought of the shield, hanging there not far away from them. Deep in his gut, Cord knew it had to mean *something*. The place where it hung wasn't by chance.

"For one, I'm running low on paper," Hardy replied. "Secondly, we've collected so many antiquities, it's time we transport them to a place that's safe where they can be properly cared for."

Cord's eyes slid to the sizable stack of *antiquities*, as Hardy called them. While the pieces were interesting to look at, they were a long way from being the treasure Cord had imagined they'd dig up.

Lock piped up, saying, "Well, I'm not ready to quit, not by a long shot. You go on back to town, Professor, and fetch more paper. We'll stay here and keep at it, and we'll be careful with whatever we dig up."

It'd been five days since Lock had shown Cord and Annie the gold coins. After that find, he'd been searching with more enthusiasm than ever. Cord had to wonder if the kid had since dug up more gold and pocketed it. He trusted Lock to be honest about it with him and his brothers and the Hart family, but he didn't intend to share any of this with Professor Hardy.

"No," countered the professor. "I want to get all these artifacts to a secure location."

"If you wanna haul them back to the ranch," Thayne said, "I reckon we could rig up a travois and carry the things that way. The trail here got mighty narrow after Cornerstone." He looked at Annie. "I suppose, once we've hauled everything to Cornerstone, someone could go fetch a wagon and team to get us the rest of the way to the Two Harts. Otherwise going the whole way back with a travois will be mighty slow."

Annie nodded. "I think—"

"I don't intend to take the antiquities to the ranch," Hardy broke in brusquely. "I intend to take them to the university, where they can be analyzed by those who know what's what."

"Wait just a minute," Annie said, directing her ire at the pompous professor.

Lock, who'd been sitting near the campfire in the dying light, looked up at Hardy with clenched teeth. "That's not gonna happen."

"He's right," said Annie. "If we take the artifacts anywhere right now, Professor, we take them to the ranch. Once there, we'll help you with cataloging what we've found, and then we'll decide which pieces you can take on loan to the university and for how long a time."

Cord knew, and Hardy certainly did too, that *on loan* meant paying to borrow the artifacts for a period of time with the MacKenzies still having full ownership of them. It'd been Michelle's idea, concocted after a long talk with Tilda. Because the artifacts had been dug up on Graham Mac-Kenzie's land, by rights they belonged to his heirs. Hardy didn't have the authority to just ride off with their so-called antiquities, not without an arrangement beforehand, one drawn up and agreed to by the MacKenzie family.

Cord also knew that, after a talk with Josh and Ellie, Brody had purchased the land where they'd found the graves and all the armor before they'd headed east last fall. It'd belonged to no one, and being way out in the wilderness, the land had cost only pennies per acre. They'd checked the law in the area, and sure enough there was nothing stopping them from keeping anything found on their property.

The law included a few exceptions, such as if property had been stolen recently and was found stashed on someone's land, like money or gold hidden away that came to be there due to a bank robbery. That money had to be returned to the bank. But artifacts this old were theirs to do with as they pleased.

What it amounted to was that Hardy wouldn't be taking the artifacts anywhere but the ranch.

"The find here goes back to the ranch, Professor Hardy." Annie repeated it with crisp finality.

Hardy glared at her, his hands fisted. "I'd think by now you'd trust me, but clearly when it comes down to it, you don't. This is important. Discovering that the Spanish were in this part of California three centuries ago rewrites history. I need to preserve these artifacts, to record everything, and bring in experts besides myself. You're all still thinking of these pieces as some kind of treasure, but you're wrong. You're small-minded, uneducated, and selfish. These artifacts belong to the world."

Cord surged to his feet, as did the rest of their group. He moved closer to Annie. Mr. Rombauer, who happened to be present at the moment, went over to stand next to the professor. Would the man go on a rampage if Hardy ordered it? Or would he stop Hardy if he started swinging his fists?

Not responding to Hardy's insults, Cord said, "If you feel we must take back what we've found so far, we can do that, but it'll be on our terms, Professor. On loan. Anyway, it might be just as well to stay home for a time." He glanced at Annie, who nodded.

"I've been away from my daughter for too long," she said. "It's time to head home."

The mutinous expression on Lock's face was a clear sign of objection, yet he knew Annie did need to get back to Caroline. She couldn't just abandon her child for weeks at a time.

Thayne didn't speak, but he was watching Hardy with sharp eyes.

Annie went to Hardy and rested her hand on his arm. "I can see these artifacts are important to you, and I—"

Hardy shook her hand away, and Cord got ready to do harm to the man if he so much as touched his wife. Quickly, he stepped between Hardy and Annie. "You wouldn't be studying any of the artifacts we found if it wasn't for the MacKenzies and the help of my family. You need to think about that. You're only along on this little 'archeological expedition' because we invited you. And we did that because we respect your knowledge. There's no call to go and insult our intelligence. Remember, Professor, all these artifacts belong to the MacKenzies. That means they can do whatever they want with them. It's their call."

Annie reached over and patted Hardy's arm again. "We try to keep it in the forefront of our minds that to be greedy over what we've found is equal to 'laying up treasures on earth.' We're people of faith, and we already have riches beyond measure through our faith in an Almighty God. Now, tomorrow we'll load everything up and head back to the ranch. And I'll thank you very much to *never* take that tone with me again."

With that, Annie spun on her heel, walked back to the campfire, and sat. Watching, Cord was reminded how Annie could keep a roomful of children quiet for long hours every day.

The professor had a scowl on his face. It was clear he could hand out a scolding with ease, but he didn't like taking one in return. Without saying more, Hardy moved to the log on the opposite side of the fire from where Annie was. He sank onto it and stared into the glowing embers.

Annie continued, "We've got a long day ahead of us tomorrow—building a travois, packing up, and riding home. Everyone get some rest."

They'd been there digging a full week. Cord had enjoyed the intimacy that had passed between his wife and himself on their wedding night. But nothing of that sort had gone on between him and Annie while they camped with these other folks right at hand. He was ready to go home, too.

He and Annie settled under their blankets side by side.

He watched as the others prepared to bed down. He could tell she was a bit upset, and he was sorry for her tension, sorry she'd had to confront Hardy. But he was proud of how she'd handled herself. He rolled onto his side and wrapped an arm around her waist.

It came to mind to tell her again that he loved her. Normally he wasn't one for such talk, and neither was she. Up to now, they'd had a sensible understanding regarding such matters. Maybe when they got home, though, they'd start to share more with each other.

Seventeen

Cord awoke suddenly, aware of his being bumped or jostled by something. It was pitch-dark, and the world was moving. His head ached, his ears rang. In fact, his whole body hurt.

Then he realized he couldn't move his arms. A few seconds later, his thoughts became muddled, and he felt himself fading away.

The next time he surfaced, he was falling. Had he been hanging before, his head down? Shaking his head to clear it, the pain got bad enough he quit moving altogether.

He hit the ground hard when he fell, and a grunt of pain managed to escape, which made him realize his mouth was covered with something. He couldn't see a thing, as the world around him remained pure black.

He heard another grunt. This one he thought to be female. Annie? Panic filled him as a thud, followed by another broke the silence. A door slammed, and the silence returned.

Utter silence. Utter darkness. He was bound. Tugging on his wrists, he realized then that he was both gagged and blindfolded. He lay on his right side on what felt like dirt.

Another door slammed. Someone groaned beside him.

Forcing his stiff arms to move, he could tell he was bound tightly as he tried to reach for his face. After much effort, he ripped away the blindfold and gag. It was still pitch-black, but he could talk now.

"Annie?"

Another groan. She might be gagged, too.

He reached into his boot and pulled out the knife he kept there. He sliced through the rope binding together his feet. Cutting the ropes around his wrists took some time, but he managed it finally before crawling toward the groaning. He fumbled around until he found the gag and pulled it away, already knowing it wasn't Annie.

"Who is it?"

"It's Thayne, Cord. Thanks . . ." Thayne's words were clipped by his need to cough.

Cord was frantic to find Annie. He was sure she was here somewhere, probably Lock as well. He took a few seconds to set Thayne free, who rolled onto his side and sat up.

After a bit of searching, Cord found Lock and cut him free, but he was out cold. Cord's hand came away wet when he removed Lock's blindfold, blood likely. A head wound. But Lock was breathing steadily, so hopefully he'd regain consciousness soon.

Cord, too, had felt a nasty bump on his head. Thayne probably had one as well. He fought down fury as he crawled around the room, recalling those thuds he'd heard. Where had they come from?

At last he found Annie. Ever so gently he pulled the kerchiefs from her eyes and mouth, then unbound her hands and feet. She shifted after being set loose and moaned quietly.

"Annie, can you hear me? Are you all right?" Cord was

167

fighting to keep his voice steady as he felt tears threaten to spill.

"Cord! What happened?"

He felt around her head and found a wicked bump on the back of her skull in almost the same place as his. Lock's bump was on his forehead, bleeding. Thankfully, Cord felt no sticky, warm liquid on his head, nor on Annie's.

Thayne moved to check on Lock. "Cord, Annie . . . Lock's still breathing."

"Let's pray he wakes up soon," Cord said.

"My head hurts something awful," she said, her voice sounding more like herself with every passing moment.

Cord drew a deep breath and let it out slowly, trying to get his bearings. "I-I think I woke up for a minute when it all was happening. I'm not sure, but it felt like I was draped over a horse. If that's right, they must have moved us some distance away from where we were digging. That no-good Hardy and his man Rombauer attacked us in our beds and then dragged us here . . . wherever that is."

"They're going to steal our treasure," Thayne growled.

Maybe it was the rage or maybe just the noise, but Lock stirred.

"He's waking up," said Cord.

"Did you see where they took us?" Annie asked.

"All I remember is moving with my head hanging down," Cord answered.

"Well, wherever we are, and however we got here, we need to find a way out." Annie started moving forward. "Let's spread out, see if we can figure out what kind of place this is. Maybe it's a cabin with boarded-up windows."

In the darkness, Annie bumped into Cord, and he realized

she was on her hands and knees and had crawled right into him. He felt around until he got ahold of her, then found her mouth and kissed her. "You're the best wife in the world," he said, pulling back a bit.

Annie gave a tiny laugh. "This is a dirt floor, that much is for sure." She pushed away from him. "I've come to a wall and . . . the wall is dirt, too. Are we underground?"

Judging by the sound of it, Annie was feeling her way along the wall. Cord began crawling until he, too, found a wall. He kept moving along it, trying to gauge the total space of their black prison. Then he remembered Lock . . .

"Lock, how are you? Is your head still bleeding? If it is, take off your shirt and press it against the wound."

"I think it's stopped, Cord. Say, are you my uncle Cord now?"

The question put his mind at ease. "I married your aunt Annie, didn't I? Sure, I'm your uncle."

Lock said, "When we get out of here, will you teach me to play the piano someday?"

"Sure I will," he replied, praying they'd all escape from wherever they were so he'd get the chance to teach Lock. "Michelle wants me to give piano lessons to the students. I took piano lessons myself, so I sort of know what to do."

"Thanks, Uncle Cord. I can be your first student."

Cord then came across what felt like stone steps. "I think we're in an old root cellar," he said to the others. He began feeling his way up the steps, eight in all. Reaching the top, he bumped his head against something solid, a roof of some kind. "Is there a cellar under Graham's cabin?"

"I'm not sure," Annie said, "but that Rombauer left the digging and wandered off several times. Maybe all his exploring was to locate a place suitable for a prison. Like a root cellar."

Cord pushed up against what he figured to be the cellar's wooden roof, for it sloped upward. It refused to budge.

"Annie, follow my voice to the steps and climb them to the top. I think I've found the door to the cellar."

A few moments later, Annie reached his side at the top of the steps. "It's narrower here than at the bottom of the steps." She took a shaky breath. "So we were knocked out and thrown into a root cellar."

"Seems that's the crux of it," said Cord. "The door is locked tight, but that won't stop us. We'll find a way out somehow."

Cord's arms came around her. "Let's sit down for a spell. My knees are a bit wobbly. Maybe we should wait till morning. Even a little light through a crack in the door would be a big help. It's hard to figure a way out of a pitch-black space."

Annie rested her head against his chest. "Those low-down coyotes are right now stealing everything we found. But why? They can't hope to get away with it?"

"Unless, like Lock, they dug up a hoard of gold we don't know about. Or it could be those artifacts we found are more valuable than we realize. They might just hightail it back east, sell what they have, and disappear into the crowd in New York City. Or maybe their plan is to board a ship and cross the ocean over to Europe." Cord gave a sigh. "Either way, it's likely we'll never see the two coyotes again."

He felt Annie tense up at the notion.

"What do you suppose artifacts of the conquistadors are worth in Spain . . . including that picture at the ranch of

Cortés himself, which could be the only one of its kind of him as a young man?"

"It makes me right furious even to think of it. All Hardy's scolding about our being careful and digging just right. He only did that so he could be in on the treasure hunt when the whole time his aim was to take for himself what we found."

"*Traitor* is what that man is. Something about him made me question whether he could be trusted, but I ignored it and took the professor at his word."

Cord nodded. "We all thought him to be sincere, what with his talk about California history and his vast knowledge of the past. I guess we put him on a pedestal because he's a professor, well educated, figuring him to be an honest man. In the end, we're lucky those two didn't kill us."

He wondered then just how sturdy the cellar was. Were they stuck down here? Maybe Hardy thought, rather than kill them himself, he'd just lock them all in an old, deserted root cellar far away in the wilderness where no one would find them. What if they weren't able to get out of this hole in the ground. They'd eventually starve or freeze to death, or both. It was only a matter of time.

Annie squeaked, and Cord realized he was crushing her. He relaxed his hold and said, "I say we all rest up until dawn when hopefully we'll have enough light to find a way out of here." He told the same to Thayne and Lock, who voiced their approval.

Of course, they had no idea what time it was. Cord couldn't guess how long he'd been unconscious. For all he knew, it could be high noon right now!

"My head aches like mad," Annie said, "and my knees

want to give out. If we all sleep for an hour or two, we'll have more energy to break out of this awful place."

Slowly, Cord and Annie made their way down the stone steps to the cellar floor to try to get some sleep. He pulled Annie close. Going by their voices, the boys weren't far away from them. Curling up on the dirt floor eased some of the pain.

When Cord woke up later, it was to pitch-dark.

"I'm feeling much better, Josh," Tilda said, resting a hand on her still-flat belly. "I'm worried about Annie . . . well, all of them. I expected the group to be back by now. I think we should ride out to the dig site. I got a bad feeling. Something's not right."

Josh, sitting at the breakfast table beside her, looked up with a sharp snap of his head. "Are you sure? Because nothing's more important than taking care of you and our baby."

With a smile, Tilda leaned over and kissed his cheek. "Thank you, but you're wrong. It's a big wide world out there, and many things are just as important. Maybe not more important to us, but still very important. If I still felt the collywobbles in my belly, I wouldn't suggest going along. I'd say to go without me. But I think a ride in the fresh air would suit me fine. Besides, Caroline misses her ma. I really did think she'd be back by now . . ."

"I know. I'm worried too. We can get to that MacKenzie claim by nightfall if we go now."

Tilda jerked her chin in agreement. "I'll pack some food and water for us. You go tell Zane and saddle the horses."

———— ✧ ————

"If you don't let me out of this bed," Ellie said, "I'm gonna tear this room apart with my bare hands."

Brody frowned. "You sure you're not having labor pains?"

Ellie growled.

Brody came closer, not one speck afraid of her.

She seemed to know it because she calmed down and said, "I'm not having any labor pains. You know I have two months before this baby is born. The pains scared me at first, but then you explained that they're common and now I'm not scared anymore. And I haven't had one for days."

Finally he nodded. "All right. You can get up and return to your normal activities. You can—"

"Ride out to the dig site and see how they're doing. Annie should be back by now. It was a week yesterday. She'd never stay away from Caroline for this long unless something's preventing her. I'm worried, Brody."

"Yeah, I've been expecting them back for two days now. I never thought they'd stay away from the ranch for so long." He gave his head a little tilt and smiled. "I suppose a quiet ride on a gentle horse won't hurt you none. Let's go tell Josh we'll be gone a couple of days."

Ellie threw back the blanket, fully dressed.

He lowered his brows. "You'd already decided to go. You weren't asking for my permission, were you?"

"No, I wasn't. I was inviting you to go with me."

They heard the door to the doctor's office open. Brody groaned, knowing seeing a patient right now was sure to slow them down.

"Brody, can we talk to you?" Josh's voice thundered up

the stairs, but he didn't come up. "Ellie too if she's feeling up to coming down here. We're gonna ride out to see how things are going with the treasure hunt."

Brody headed downstairs. Ellie grabbed her boots and followed him.

They decided to take a wagon to give Ellie a gentler ride. The trail wasn't wide enough all the way to the MacKenzie claim, but they'd unhitch the horses when they had to and ride on horseback the last stretch.

EIGHTEEN

Annie and the others had no food, no water, no light. They had no wood to build a fire with and no matches or any kind of rock to use to strike a spark if they did have wood.

They had explored every corner of the small cellar, probably a dozen feet long from the bottom of the steps and six feet wide. Overhead, the sloped roof was too high to touch, but they had to bend over at the top of the steps or they'd hit their heads.

Overall it was a nasty trap, and Hardy and Rombauer were going to pay dearly for tossing them into it. Not even fleeing to another country would save them. Annie vowed to make sure the two outlaws were brought to justice.

Cord felt his way to the steps and then started climbing. Annie knew this because she was only a few feet behind him, crawling as well.

"Are you boys all right this morning?" she asked.

"My head still hurts bad," Thayne said. "But I'm fully awake now and feel more myself. And I'm not a *boy*."

There was a rustling noise, and Annie had a mental picture of the MacKenzies getting to their feet.

175

"If it helps any, I still think of Zane and Josh as boys. I often yell out the door, 'You boys come on in to eat.'"

Lock spoke, his voice nearer than before. "I've heard you call that out the back door. I figured you were calling to me and Thayne."

Annie smiled into the dark. "Nope. I do think of you as men, honestly. You both do a full day's work when you're out of school. To me, that makes you men."

Cord said, "We've explored this tiny cellar every which way, and I can see no easy way out. But I've got my knife here, so I say we start digging out through a wall."

"I've got a knife, too," Thayne said. "I'll help you."

"I got mine as well," said Lock.

"Me too," Annie chimed in.

"Let's get to it then." Cord had moved to the dirt floor and was feeling his way along one of the walls. "Annie, you go up three steps, Lock up two, Thayne up one, and I'll stay here on the floor. It figures we'll do better when the slope is lower, right? Easier to reach and probably not so hard to dig. We have to dig a tunnel big enough to climb through."

Annie added, "And let's try not to stab each other in the dark!"

— ✧ —

"What are we doing wrong?" Lock sounded demoralized.

"I don't know," Cord said. "It seems like we should've gotten through by now to the surface, but there's not been even a hint of sunlight." He blew out a big breath. "Everyone stop digging."

They'd done a lot of talking while carving away the dirt

with their knives. It helped to keep their spirits up, and it helped so they all knew where each person was standing. So far no one had stabbed their neighbor or sliced off a finger.

"Maybe we should rest for a while," Cord said.

They all sank to the ground, all in agreement with his suggestion.

"You know," said Annie, "we have a root cellar at the ranch; it's out back of the house. Could this one be *under* the house? Because we should have gotten through to the outside by now."

"Could be. The sides do seem to be more stone than dirt." Cord didn't know how best to proceed.

"If we want to eat, we've got to keep digging." Lock was young still and therefore always hungry.

"Let's just rest a minute," Annie said in the sweet voice that was an order.

"If this were my grandparents' root cellar," Cord said, "we wouldn't have had to dig more than a foot up at the highest part of the cellar to reach the outside."

"We've gone at least two feet up," said Thayne. "I shoved my arm in the spot where we dug just to check. And I pushed against the top, and it felt solid. But solid dirt, not rock."

"One thing I know," Annie said firmly. "Josh and Zane will find us. They're probably already looking. If Cord's memory is right, we were slung over the backs of our horses and brought here to be dumped into this cellar. That's going to leave a trail. And I should have been home by now. Ellie will know I would never leave Caroline alone for so long. So they'll come. They'll track us down. They'll read the signs that tell them what happened, and they'll get us out of here. Mark my words."

"Before we starve to death, Annie?"

Cord wanted to swat Lock for saying such a thing, but in the dark he was afraid he might hit the kid on his poor wounded head, so he refrained. "What if this cellar is dug into the side of a hill?" he said, wanting to shift the conversation. "The root cellar at home is on flatland. If this is too, we'd be able to dig up and out fast. But that's not working. Maybe instead we should dig forward, not up. The steps are stone, which means we can move the stones and dig forward. The bottom of the door should become visible before too long."

Annie said, "That might work."

Cord nodded. "You all stay where you are. There's not much space up there, so let me start without all of us together. I'll see if I can pry the top stone step loose."

"Good idea, Cord," Annie said. "What about the door overhead? We pushed on it, but it didn't give at all. But it's wooden. Maybe we can carve straight through it with our knives."

"Another good idea, although I think that wood is made of heavy plank. It's not going to carve easily. Let me try the steps first."

Annie said quietly to the MacKenzies, "Let's pray for Cord to find a way out. I've been praying silently, but maybe we need to lift our voices together."

"I'd like that," Thayne said.

Cord thought just having a plan helped him discover an inner strength. And prayer helped to steady him.

Lock was suspiciously quiet, but Cord decided not to ask why. The kid had an active mind. Maybe he'd come up with a bright idea.

Cord reached the top of the steps. "I've found a seam between two stones. The steps are several stones fitted together, so they should be movable. Keep praying."

Annie had recited Psalm 23 and the Lord's Prayer. She offered prayers for God's help and protection, and for Cord to move the stones away, a very biblical prayer. Cord found strength in it and sensed God's presence there with them in the cool, dark cellar.

He scraped dirt out from between the stones, working where they touched the wall. Finally, one of the stones wiggled, then another.

"Thayne, Lock, come up here. This one's a large stone, but we can move it away if we all pull together. Annie, keep up your praying."

Cord shuffled to one side, making room for Thayne and Lock to squeeze in beside him. They all got a firm grasp on the stone. "Pull it down the steps," Cord said. "I think it'll roll that way."

The three of them pulled. A wave of dizziness made Cord lose his grip. He fell backward and landed with his head on Annie's lap.

"M-my fingers slipped." But it was more than that. They were running out of air in the small cellar.

Cord didn't think resting would do much good, so he climbed back to where the boys were. They'd quit tugging when Cord fell backward, but they still knelt on the steps, holding the stone.

"Let's try again." About the time Cord was ready to quit and see if another of the steps had a smaller stone, it moved. Under great protest, it seemed to him.

Lock grunted from the effort. Thayne heaved until Cord

felt the kid's muscles straining beside him. Cord threw all his weight into moving the stone.

Annie's praying out loud washed over them as they yanked the stone away. It toppled and rolled down one step, then picked up a bit of momentum and went down the rest of the way.

"Are you all right, Annie? We didn't knock you over, did we?"

"I'm fine," she assured him.

"Cord, I see light!" Thayne shouted.

Cord, desperate to see what was outside, leaned away as Thayne began digging frantically with his knife. He couldn't even see whatever hole Thayne had opened in their little prison.

Then Thayne's knife scraped against something. He stopped. "I'm afraid I'll snap the blade. I can see outside, but only a small opening."

"Let me work on it," Lock said, moving toward Thayne.

Cord leaned back against the wall, perched on the lower steps. "I can see now. I've gotten so used to the blackness, I didn't even notice at first." He laughed. He still couldn't see the opening, but it was letting in enough light that his eyes had finally adjusted to it, even if a little.

From behind, he felt Annie rest her hand on his arm. He turned, and she glowed with pleasure at the bit of light and, Cord realized, the fresh air.

His dizziness eased, and he felt stronger. His head was clearer. God had answered their prayers. They'd gotten a hole opened just in time.

They hugged each other.

Beaming, Annie said, "I know we're still in here, still hungry and thirsty, but there's light and fresh air." She inhaled audibly. "It's a feast."

"I'd still like some of Gretel's strudel." Lock was leaning into whatever hole Thayne had opened.

She playfully whacked Lock on the shoulder. "Back up. I want to look outside just for a second. I promise I'll let you back in to work right away."

Cord waited his turn, craning his neck to look out at daylight. It *was* a feast. For the eyes, for the spirit.

Then he pulled away and backed down the steps to sit by Annie as the boys wrangled with whatever stubborn rock they'd run into in front of their little hole.

They should be out of this root-cellar prison in a matter of minutes.

Cord was still thinking that when the sun went down.

Nineteen

"You remember when you said light and fresh air were a feast?" Cord asked Annie. He sounded pretty sour about it. Or maybe he just sounded hungry and thirsty.

She was hungry and thirsty herself. Turned out that light and air weren't nearly enough.

"I remember. I miss that foolish cheerfulness. Why can't we get past that stone?" She'd moved to the back of the cellar in case more stones came tumbling toward her. Probably six whole feet from the base of the steps.

"We've taken out the whole row of steps. Whoever built this cellar here found the one soft patch of dirt on otherwise stony land. The walls are dirt, the roof or door overhead is wood, but everything else looks to be pure stone."

"I've got a chunk chiseled out of that plank." Lock stepped away from his work. After giving up on getting past the stone, they'd begun taking turns carving a hole through the wooden door. "But it's thicker than I thought it'd be." Lock moved to the floor to rest while Thayne rose to work on the stubborn door with his knife.

"I think it's well past bedtime," Cord said. "We best get some sleep now."

Thayne kept at it despite Cord's suggestion. "But if we fall asleep even for a few hours, we'll just be hungrier and thirstier when we wake up."

Lock said, "I suspect being hungry will keep us from sleeping. A growling belly makes it hard to nod off."

"Maybe it's time we come up with a better plan for getting out of here," Annie said.

"I wonder if . . ." Cord began.

The way Cord hesitated made Annie sit up straighter. Her husband had an idea, she could tell. She prayed silently that it would be better than what they'd been doing. It could hardly be any worse. "What is it?" she asked him.

"We've chiseled out a small pile of wood chips from the door. What if we used the chips as kindling, took a couple of loose stones to strike a spark . . . and set the door on fire?"

"Burn the roof over our heads?" Annie didn't see this as a better plan. "Wouldn't the door go crashing down on our heads in flames?"

"And wouldn't we choke to death from the smoke?" said Thayne.

"Cord's idea might just work," Lock said, already moving. "There are a few smaller stones that broke off from the stairs we rolled away, so we could probably make a spark without too much trouble."

Annie eyed the narrow hole where they'd tried to get past the stone steps to the outside world. They weren't able to widen it because of what seemed to be a solid wall of rock. Thayne and Lock had dug like mad in the cellar wall but without success. Annie did her best not to let terror overcome her with the fact they could be stuck down here permanently, buried alive.

"Lock, let's wait to set the fire," Cord said. "With the sun set, we can't see much of anything right now."

"But a fire will give us light."

"True, but I'm worn out, probably due to hunger and from chiseling away on that door. Let's rest for a couple of hours, then work on burning up the door."

Annie realized her hands were trembling. Her throat ached from thirst, and her stomach had gone beyond hunger into a painful throb. She thought of Caroline, who'd already lost one parent. Tears burned her eyes to think she might not see her little girl ever again on this earth. Giving herself a mental shake, she shoved aside all thoughts of a terrible ending and instead focused on how they would use fire to escape the cellar. Lock was right: Cord's idea might work.

Cord curled up beside her on the dirt floor to rest. Lock and Thayne followed suit. Annie could feel herself drifting off to sleep. She drew a deep breath, trying to relax, then closed her eyes and prayed that Josh and Zane were searching for them, once more begging God for His help and protection.

They were all on the verge of collapse; they'd need to get out of this root cellar soon or all would be lost.

Cord shifted so that Annie could lay her aching head against his shoulder. It felt so good to have him there with her. She began to weep silently.

———— ✧ ————

"What happened here?" Ellie said it out loud, but they were all thinking it. Josh had brought them to Graham

MacKenzie's cabin. It was clear that the group had been doing some serious digging at the site, and yet none of them were there. No sign of any artifacts either. Certainly they must have excavated something of value.

"This makes no sense. Lock could hardly be convinced to stop digging when we were here before." Josh dismounted and strode over to the campfire. The ashes were cold.

Brody swung down from his horse to study the turned-up dirt around an old well. A few things were scattered about—the coffeepot and cast-iron skillet—while other things were tidy, like the neatly stacked plates and cups. The blankets were left stretched out, as if the group had left in a hurry. Overall, the camp looked eerily abandoned.

"Cord and Annie would have rolled up their blankets, not left them lying there like that." Ellie's stomach twisted. "Something isn't right. Where is everyone? Why would they leave the site like this?"

Ellie crouched beside a jumbled blanket. "Josh, get over here."

Josh moved fast. Tilda was right behind him. Brody came next.

"I think that's blood." Josh touched the darkened spot on the blanket. Then he reached for a scrap of cloth. It looked like another blanket had been torn into strips. He recognized it. "This is Lock's bedroll." Josh looked at Tilda, then at Ellie. "I'm afraid they're in danger. I'm going to see if I can pick up their trail. We need to track them down, and fast."

"I see only four bedrolls here," Ellie said. "Two are missing."

Brody frowned. "Professor Hardy and Mr. Rombauer." He crouched to get a better look at the ground where Lock had slept. "Whatever happened, they seem to have left to-gether. Going by the hoofprints, their horses headed that way." Josh pointed to a narrow trail and into the depths of the mountainous forest. "Let's ride. We still got a couple hours of daylight."

As they mounted up, Tilda said, "Isn't that a travois trail?" She gestured toward the wider trail they'd ridden in on.

"I didn't even notice it when we came in, but yes. Four horses, each pulling a travois. Traveling toward Corner-stone."

"But two of the horses didn't have riders."

Josh looked at Ellie again. Annie was her big sister. What had they done to her? And to her brand-new husband, Cord, who'd put the light back in her eyes? And the two MacKenzie boys . . . Ellie fought down a scream of terror.

"Not enough blood for murder." Brody sounded sure about that. Still, he had to be plenty worried, wondering what had happened to his brothers. Lock had been bleeding, though not a deadly amount apparently.

Josh rode straight into the rugged wilderness, and the rest of them followed, being careful to give him enough space to search for tracks. Brody brought up the rear.

Winding his way through the forest, Josh made as good a time as was possible. He seemed to follow the group's trail without much trouble. Ellie knew he'd've slowed down if he was unsure. But in a dense woodland like this, with years of fallen leaves and branches, Ellie couldn't see much. She could only trust.

TWENTY

"There's just not enough wood chips to get a decent fire going," Annie said. "They're shredded enough they should catch like kindling, and we've gotten sparks from the stones. I've even torn strips off my riding skirt and gotten that to burn a little, but the wood is damp and won't burn properly."

While Annie worked on getting a fire started, Cord was busy chiseling more chips from the wooden door overhead to add to the fire. She well understood the theory behind creating fire: strike sparks with two rocks, hold something flammable near where you get the sparks to fly, and then stack bits of wood near the easily flammable thing to make the fire grow.

Nevertheless, they were getting nowhere with the fire idea.

Thayne, meanwhile, had dug his way up to his waist and hit rock. Lock had dug on the other side, hoping to make some headway from that angle. Their plan was to dig up a ways, then turn to dig toward the cellar roof. In doing so, they'd find the outside world and freedom.

They were reminded yet again that the cellar was surrounded by stone on all sides, at least that was how it seemed.

How could Rombauer have found such a dependable prison? It had to be luck. They couldn't have scouted out a place before they rode out here. They hadn't even known where exactly they were headed. Well, he'd found this blasted cellar somehow, and now here they were.

The sun was setting again. They'd all taken turns peering through the narrow slit of light, breathing in the clear air while ignoring their dry throats and empty bellies.

Annie couldn't reach her hand through the crack of light outside—it wasn't big enough—but she could see that the light was growing dim.

Please, God, help us.

Her stomach growled, and she pressed a hand against it.

Please, God . . .

She knew a person could live quite a while without food. But a body could only live a few days without water. And they had no idea how long they'd been in the cellar. More than a day for sure.

Please, God, give us inspiration. Give Josh direction. Give me courage.

———— ◇ ————

"Looks as though they rode up this slope, but it's solid rock." Josh swung down off his horse. "Everyone hold back for a bit. I'll do some scouting beyond the rock to see where their horses came out."

"Why would they head this direction?" Ellie asked. "There's nothing up here."

Josh knelt by the last track visible before the trail turned to pure rock. He pivoted on his toes to look at Ellie.

Brody saw the urgency in his expression. No doubt they

were both thinking of Annie. Brody turned toward Ellie, his pregnant wife, as she went to dismount. But she got to the ground faster than he could get there to help her.

Ellie handed him the reins. "I'm going ahead to help Josh."

Brody nodded grimly. They'd been at this for hours. His hope was fading with every passing minute.

Up ahead on the trail, Ellie approached Josh. "I'll walk to the end of this rocky stretch and go left. You go right. Depending on the ground, I should be able to cut your time in half."

Though a tad concerned about his wife's safety, Brody clamped his mouth shut. The truth was, Ellie was doing fine. And she was a better tracker than he was, and they needed every bit of her skill to help save his brothers, Cord, and Annie. He knew being active was good for an expectant mother. Even so, he'd feel much better if she was wrapped in cotton wool and kept to her bed.

Josh straightened and scanned the area around them. "The tracks seem to turn and head straight north, but I haven't been across the rock to see what it's like over there."

"Well, let's go find out," said Ellie.

Brody hung back and helped Tilda down from her horse. He talked quietly to her. Hiding that he was a frantic big brother, worried about his wife and left with no way to help.

Ellie and Josh strode about twenty feet before the solid rock ended.

"No tracks here." Ellie stared at the ground. "And it's loose dirt. All right, you go left. We'll find where they came out." She looked at Josh and nodded.

Moments later, Josh called to the others, "This way! Bring the horses."

Carefully, Brody and Tilda led their horses across the rocky stretch, where, along with the others, they mounted up.

"Follow me," Josh said. "Ellie and I believe we found the trail again."

Pressing forward, they moved on in single file.

Annie woke up with an idea. She lay on her side on the hard dirt floor, Cord's arm around her waist. Was he still sleeping? Hunger and thirst returned to her with a vengeance. Had they slept all night? How many more hours could they go without water? How long had they been locked up in the cellar?

The same questions repeated themselves in her thoughts until she wanted to punch herself in the head.

"Are you awake?" Cord whispered.

"Yes."

"I felt your breathing speed up, your heart start to pound. Are you scared?"

"I'm trying not to be, Cord." She patted the arm he had wrapped around her. "I think we should dig forward and keep at it."

"Forward?" Cord sat up slowly, then helped her to sit. She didn't need the help but thought he liked touching her, holding her. And she liked letting him.

"Yes, let's try digging straight forward a few feet, but widen the area more. If we carve out a big enough hole, one of us can climb in it, turn, and start digging up where there's no stone to block the way."

The boys had stirred by now and were sitting up, rubbing

their eyes. Thayne said, "That's a good idea, Annie. Let's dig forward, make a big hole, then go up from there."

"Worth a try," said Lock as he slowly got to his feet, staggered a little, but then caught himself.

In the faint light, Lock looked gaunt and weak. Annie wanted to hug him and apologize for his suffering and rant about that low-down Professor Hardy. Instead, she got up and grabbed her knife, praying silently for this new plan to work.

The four of them took turns digging forward with the knives. They managed to avoid hitting any stone, enlarging the hollowed-out space inch by inch as time wore on. They were nearing the end of their strength.

Finally, Cord called a halt to the digging. "I think it's big enough—I can get in there now and start digging up." He twisted so that he was facing up, shoved himself into the cavity about to his mid-back, and began hacking away at the dirt.

Lock and Thayne backed away and sank to the floor. Exhausted, Annie leaned against the wall, but her knees buckled before long, and she sat. All she could think to do was to quote Scripture out loud. She thought of a verse from the book of 2 Corinthians she'd memorized not long ago: "'For ye know the grace of our Lord Jesus Christ, that, though he was rich, yet for your sakes he became poor, that ye through his poverty might be rich.'"

Her voice was hoarse, but the words were like water springing forth in a desert, soaking into the dry, cracked ground. Then an old hymn came to mind, and she sang as best she could, "'Come, thou Fount of every blessing . . .'"

A fount, that was water. The image helped to soothe her frightened heart.

"'Tune my heart to sing thy grace . . .'"

They all needed to rely upon God's grace, now more than ever.

"'Streams of mercy, never ceasing . . .'"

Streams of mercy. More water.

Cord's voice joined with hers. He had a beautiful voice, and it gave her the strength she needed to continue singing.

"'Call for songs of loudest praise . . .'"

To praise God in the midst of their being trapped down here, songs of loudest praise. She could do that.

She and Cord kept on singing the hymn while he dug upward.

"'He to rescue me from danger . . .'"

Please, God, rescue us from danger.

The ground began shaking.

"Cord, get out of there! Now!" Annie could see the hole collapsing on him.

Quickly, Cord started backing out of the cavity, but in his hurry, his hands slipped, causing him to stop momentarily. Dirt from above crumbled and broke away, falling and filling in the space around him.

Annie grabbed Cord's feet. "Thayne, Lock, help me!"

The two boys rushed to lend a hand.

But even if they got Cord free, the cellar's structure had weakened and might just cave in on top of them.

They could be buried here once and for all.

TWENTY-ONE

The earth shook. Brody instantly remembered the last quake. It was the first one he'd experienced, and now here came another one already. He wasted no time in swinging down from the saddle, with everyone around him doing the same.

"If the ground collapses, it'll wipe out the tracks." Leading his horse now, Josh hurried forward, his eyes fixed on the trail ahead.

Brody rushed to Ellie's side. "Are you all right? Is this too much for you and the baby?"

Ellie caught his hand and squeezed it tight. "I'm fine. C'mon. Let's follow Josh."

Brody, his jaw tight, nodded. Tilda had gone after her husband. They were deep in a woodland, the ground covered with leaves and fallen branches. It wasn't much of a trail.

Brody had no idea how Josh was able to track anything in the rugged landscape, but he was definitely following something. Grasping Ellie's hand, Brody did his best to keep up with him.

The earth shook harder. Josh staggered but kept pushing forward through the woods. Ellie stopped and braced her legs. Brody imitated her stance. The fierce shaking went on and on, yet no ruptures opened in the ground.

Suddenly Ellie stumbled, but thankfully Brody was right there to catch her. He gently lowered her to the ground and said, "We should wait here till the shaking stops. A fall could hurt both you and the baby."

Nodding, Ellie settled herself on the forest floor amid the scrub brush and decaying leaves. Brody prayed for her and their baby, he prayed for the ones they were tracking, and he prayed for God to give divine wisdom to Josh as he forged onward.

As the shaking carried on, Brody heard a loud *snap* split the air behind them. He spun around to see a huge tree falling straight for them.

———— ✧ ————

Cord broke loose from his dirt prison like a cork popping out of a bottle. He flew backward and landed on his family.

The four of them huddled together on the dirt floor, which was shaking.

"Everyone watch your head," Annie warned.

The immovable cellar door overhead was made of heavy beams, something they'd learned while trying to chisel through it. If one of those beams came crashing down . . .

"Let's quick move to where the roof slopes toward the floor," she added. "If the beams come down, they won't fall with as much force there."

Cord and the boys followed Annie's advice and started for the place in the cellar she'd pointed out. As they did, the ground trembled more violently, sending everyone but Cord backward, then forward like a shot until they reached the end with the low roof.

As for Cord, he'd gone down hard, then quickly got to his feet only to be knocked down again. Glancing up, he saw dirt sifting down from between the beams of the door. He rolled onto his hands and knees and started crawling toward Annie and the boys as fast as he could.

He knew that if the cellar did cave in, it was likely they'd all be crushed to death.

Brody threw himself on Ellie in hopes the falling tree wouldn't kill all three of them. Maybe he'd be struck on the back by the tree, but Ellie and the baby would be all right.

The impact never came. He looked over his shoulder and saw the tree suspended only a few feet overhead, its top snagged by other trees all around it.

"Let's move!" Ellie said. "That tree could still come down on us." She yanked on Brody's arm to get him to move and maybe because he was crushing her.

They tried to crawl forward, but the shaking ground made it hard to do so.

Brody peered ahead and saw that Josh was still upright and leading his horse, amazingly. Tilda had fallen and lay on the ground, her reins still in hand.

Brody didn't see his horse anywhere, nor Ellie's. He wasn't sure if the horses would come back to them, especially in unfamiliar territory, but now wasn't the time to worry about that.

The shaking seemed to double in intensity, forcing Brody

flat on his belly. Ellie sprawled out beside him. He looked overhead and around, afraid of another tree coming down.

Tilda cried out, and he saw her horse dragging her. She'd kept a firm grip on the reins, maybe even gotten her arm tangled in them, and couldn't get herself free.

Josh whipped his head around at Tilda's scream. He ran to her side and dropped to his knees, unwinding the reins from around her wrist while keeping the panicked horse from darting off.

There would be no more attempts at following the trail, not while the ground shook like this. They might lose their only chance to find his brothers, Annie, and Cord . . . if it wasn't already too late.

A heavy timber cracked in half overhead, and Cord dragged all three of his family close to him, covering them with his own body as it dropped.

The beam glanced off his shoulder, and he fell forward. *Please save them, Lord*, he prayed.

Dirt rained down afterward, small stones pelting his head and back. Before he could get up, the weight of one beam, a second, and finally a third came to rest on him, followed by a jumble of stones.

As Cord lay there groaning under all the rubble, barely able to breathe, all he could think was that he'd failed his family.

"Cord, are you alive?" Annie's muffled voice wavered like that of a ghost.

"Brody, did you hear that?" Ellie shouted. "It's Annie! She's close by. We have to get to her. Now!"

He turned to her, a confused look on his face. "What? Did you say you heard Annie?"

"Cord, please, speak to me." It was Annie again. Her voice sounded weak, desperate.

Brody said, "I heard her, too!"

Josh and Tilda approached, each leading a horse.

"Did you hear her, Josh?"

He looked at Brody and shook his head. "No, I hear nothing but the rumble of the earthquake."

"Me too," said Tilda.

"Cord! Wake up!" Annie was terrified. Something terrible must have happened.

"I heard her that time!" said Josh, and Tilda nodded, her eyes wide.

They all rushed toward the sound of Annie's voice and came upon the ruins of an old stone house. On one side was a barn, and between the two buildings a root cellar, collapsing even as Annie yelled.

Ellie ran forward, Brody right on her heels. When they reached the caved-in spot, Brody saw a man's arm half buried in rubble.

"Annie, it's Ellie! We're right here. We'll get you out."

"*Ellie?* Oh, thank the Lord . . ."

Josh turned to his horse and removed a shovel he had tied to the saddle. Then the ground shook again, causing him to stumble and drop the shovel.

"Annie, we see Cord's arm!" Ellie shouted.

"He's on top of me and—" Her words were cut off by coughing.

"No need to talk, Annie. You're probably inhaling grit and dirt. Work on breathing instead." Brody used his doctor's voice. "We see you. Are Thayne and Lock with you?"

"Yes . . . we're all here."

"All right, no more talking now. We'll dig you out. Hang on."

Josh snatched up the shovel and was tossing dirt aside like a madman when a sudden tremor caved in what was left of a sloped wooden roof tucked up beside the stone cabin.

The new cave-in dropped dirt into the cellar, pushing it away from Cord.

"I've got him!" Josh yelled. "Help me pull him out, Brody."

Together, the two men tugged Cord from his grave.

Brody winced at the rough handling of Cord's body, not knowing which bones might be broken or what internal injuries he might have suffered.

As Josh and Brody dragged Cord to the surface, they saw Annie and the MacKenzie boys below, waving up at them. They looked unhurt.

Just minutes later, everyone had been pulled to the surface. They all hugged one another, breaking into sobs and thanking God for His help in rescuing them in time. Cord, Annie, Thayne, and Lock were all very weak, dazed from their hunger and thirst.

Annie threw her arms around Ellie. "You came. Thank God. Thank you all . . ."

Brody had Cord stretched out on his back on the ground. Blood trickled through a coating of dirt on his face. Another trickle came from a cut somewhere toward the top of his head. Brody felt for a pulse, and it was strong. Cord's breathing was steady.

"Ellie, bring water. And grab my bag." Brody looked up, and his eyes landed on his brothers. In a less steady voice, he said, "I'm so glad you're all right." Both boys looked pale and near to collapsing.

At last, the ground quit shaking. Another answer to prayer.

Ellie brought Brody his canteen and medical bag. When she did, she told him all the horses had returned to their owners. Yet another answer to prayer. Ellie smiled. "God is good."

Annie hugged Tilda, then Josh, quietly saying "thank you" over and over again. Then she turned to Cord and dropped to her knees, ready to help however she could.

Brody worked on Cord's injuries as his patient slept. "His heart is steady and strong, but I've found a couple goose eggs on his head. He's taken quite a beating."

"He saved us. You saved us. God saved us." Annie seemed overwhelmed, overjoyed to be out of that dark cellar. She reached for the canteen again. It seemed she couldn't get enough water in her.

Soon each of the escaped prisoners had a canteen in their hands and beef jerky to chew on. They sat Cord up enough to pour a bit of water into his mouth. Everyone breathed a sigh of relief when he swallowed it.

Food and water kept them busy for a time. Ellie got a fire started with Josh's help. The MacKenzie boys pitched in, though they moved slowly. Before long, Brody smelled something cooking while he checked the cut on Cord's head. Annie bathed his face, then pressed a cool cloth to his forehead.

Ellie was the first to ask the question that had been on Brody's mind ever since they'd come upon the abandoned claim.

"What happened out here?"

The boys ran through what they knew. Annie turned around to add her part of the story.

"Hardy and Rombauer must be behind this. What did you find at the dig site?"

"They were gone, along with the horses. We didn't bother to follow them, but we saw tracks leading away from your campsite back toward Cornerstone. So we knew they took you this way."

"What day is it?" Annie asked. "We had no idea how long we'd been unconscious when we woke up in that cellar."

"It's Wednesday. We expected you last Saturday. You'd been gone a week." Ellie began scooping stew onto plates and passing them around.

Brody saw his brothers eyeing the hot food with so much hunger it made his heart ache.

Annie took a plate of food and knelt beside Cord, whose head Brody had bandaged. Between bites she said, "I have to get back right away. Caroline's been without me for too long . . ."

"What about Hardy?" Thayne broke in. "We found a lot of artifacts. It sounds like they were all missing from Grandpa's claim."

Josh sat on a log with his plate of stew. "Well, he's not gonna just ride off with all he stole and not face up to it."

"We'll find him and Rombauer, don't you worry," Brody said.

"Yep, and we'll start by riding into Cornerstone tomorrow since that's the closest town with a telegraph office. We'll send out wires to the surrounding towns with train stations and ask their sheriffs to help find those two outlaws."

Cord stirred at last, his eyes fluttering open. "I-I think there's more treasure there," he said, his voice groggy but understandable. "I don't believe we found everything that site has hidden."

"Maybe Hardy found gold," Lock said.

Cord tried to sit up.

"No, no, lie back down," Brody urged. "You need to rest. You're a battered man."

"I hurt, Brody, but I'm going to be all right."

"You think he found gold, Lock?" Cord asked.

"I never saw it if he did, and you'd better believe I was watching. And with Rombauer being gone as much as he was from the dig site, I can't imagine he found any gold either."

"No doubt he was out searching for a place to lock us away," Cord muttered.

Nodding, Lock said, "He was no help to us, that's for sure. And Hardy didn't do hardly a lick of digging. He was too busy writing about what we found. That makes me think he didn't find gold."

"It's about time we send the law after those coyotes," Cord added. "But I wonder if they didn't run off before we found what was really good."

Brody wondered what Cord considered *really good*.

Lock pulled a small leather pouch out of the waistband of his trousers. "I didn't talk about it after that first time, Annie, but I found twenty more gold doubloons while I was digging."

Brody gasped. "Twenty more?"

"Yep, and it's enough to keep us all comfortable for a long time, maybe the rest of our lives. You said fourteen doubloons would go a long way. That's the number of gold coins Grandpa MacKenzie had on him when they found his body. Well, thirty-four coins oughta help all the more."

Michelle had told them the coins could be worth as much as a thousand dollars apiece.

"Annie insisted we needed to return home," Lock went on. "Hardy may have found something we didn't recognize as valuable. And he knew we weren't going to let him run off with it. Or maybe he did find a stash of gold coins like these ones. Whatever the case, he tried to take away with him what we'd dug up. But we refused, told him it all had to go back to the ranch first to be recorded, and then we'd maybe loan him the artifacts he wanted so he could study them at his university. He seemed to accept that, but obviously he decided to take matters into his own hands."

"Or maybe," Thayne said, "he decided he'd found all he was going to find at that site. We dug up enough to fill six travois, but it had tapered off. It'd gotten to where we weren't finding much around that well anymore."

"I wonder if he might run all the way to Spain," Annie said. "Those artifacts might be extremely valuable to the Spanish people. Remember how he made such a fuss over that badge that might have a picture of Cortés on it?"

They all sat quietly for a bit, wondering what to do next.

Tilda broke the silence. "We're assuming it was Hardy and Rombauer responsible for what happened, but we don't know that for certain."

"Who else could it be?" Annie asked.

Her question brought on another stretch of silence.

Annie finally said, "Send out the wires to try and find them. They almost have to run for the train, don't they? Then I have to go home to Caroline. She already lost her

202

pa. I don't want her scared that something might have happened to her ma."

No one could argue with that.

Then the earth shook again, though not as violently. It was likely an aftershock.

"My last memory was going to bed on Saturday night. We were in the pitch-dark at first, and we had no idea for how long. We were stuck down in that hole for nearly three days." Annie turned to look at the remains of the cellar. "Look at how it was built between two stone buildings. No wonder we couldn't dig our way out."

"The timbers from the cellar door fell on me, and I was hit with falling stones. I'll bet they stacked them there to keep the door secure." Cord ate his stew thoughtfully.

"No food or water the whole time," Annie said. "I was praying with everything I had for God to find us a way out of there, for Him to lead you to us, Josh. And then God sent an earthquake that shook us free."

Cord nodded as he reached up and gingerly touched the bandage on his head. "Let's get some sleep, ride to Cornerstone and send the wires, then head home."

Annie wrapped her arms around him, and they and the others all settled in to rest for a while.

Brody lay there wide awake, his thoughts centered on Hardy and Rombauer. Wherever those two had gone off to, it wasn't going to be far enough. Brody didn't intend to let them go unpunished.

TWENTY-TWO

They rose the next morning with Annie on a mission to get home. Josh wanted to ride ahead fast, straight for Cornerstone, in hopes of catching Hardy and Rombauer, while the rest of them rode to the dig site to pick up their blankets and other supplies and see if they could round up any more horses.

Annie wouldn't hear of it. "No. We need to stay together. I don't like the idea of dividing up into smaller groups. We have to ride past that dig site anyway, and I too want to look around the area, see if they took everything with them. We'll head to Cornerstone from there, then on to the Two Harts."

They all nodded in agreement, deciding it best to stick together. As they set out, riding double, Cord was sitting behind her with his arm around her waist, his other hand gripping the reins.

Annie thought of their life ahead, and something occurred to her. "We've talked only a little about my late husband and how I was widowed."

Cord's arm at her waist tightened slightly. "I'm sorry you had such a terrible thing happen, Annie."

She patted his strong arm. "Have I mentioned that I own a ranch?"

"No. You told me that you and your husband lived on a ranch, but—"

"Well, it's not far from the Two Harts. When our land was stolen and Todd killed, those who did all that also burned down our house. I got the land back, of course. There's a bunkhouse still standing, and Zane and Josh run the place for me. But I haven't been back there since losing Todd."

"Not even once?"

"No, Cord, not once. You said you'd like to be a rancher. Well, how about over there? We call it Lane Valley. The LV brand. But since Todd died, I've abandoned that brand. Now all my cattle are branded with the Two Harts brand. But the ranch is mine . . . I mean *ours*." Annie had to remind herself that she and Cord were married and shared everything now.

"I-I don't know what to say," said Cord.

Annie gave a little shrug. Their horse walked along quietly, the land too uneven to go much faster. There was no trail to be seen. Josh and Tilda rode ahead of them, leading the way.

"There was just no reason to go back there," she added, "but now I have a reason."

Cord nodded. "I'd sure like to see the place. We wouldn't need to live on the ranch if that'd be too upsetting for you."

"How about we ride over there together, and I'll see how it feels? Of course, if we did decide to live on the ranch, we'd have to build ourselves a house. The other one's in ruins, ashes mostly. But staying there in a new house shouldn't bother me overly."

"Let's do that," Cord agreed.

"While I'm being forthright with you about the ranch

property, I should also mention the fact that I sued Horace Benteen, the man who'd ordered my husband's death because he wanted our land. He was a powerful man who didn't think the law applied to him, but he lost the suit and is now in prison, along with his son and his hired men. They're all a bunch of outlaws. Besides having Todd killed, Benteen had intentions to marry Michelle whether she liked it or not. As it turned out, the man was very wealthy. By the time Michelle's lawyer was done with him, I owned his fortune and his ranch, too. And Benteen's got a nice house on the property not far from the Two Harts. We could live there if you prefer."

Cord leaned forward in the saddle enough that she could see his furrowed brow. "Just how rich are you, Annie?"

She gave a little laugh. "I don't give it much thought honestly. Oh, and I'm one-quarter owner of the Two Harts. I haven't paid much mind to my actual financial worth, but I'd say I'm—*we're*—quite rich."

"You know I've got a bit of money myself. I've been scrimping and saving to buy land, and I've never spent it. What would you think of having Grandpa Westbrook, my ma, and my grandparents Rivers come live with us?"

Annie had lived with Mayhew Westbrook off and on for the last year. He loved Caroline. "Can I meet your other grandparents and your ma before I decide?"

Cord smiled. "I reckon you had better. Grandma and Grandpa Rivers are settled on eighty acres just south of Sacramento. I'm not sure if they'd care for the idea of moving."

"Either way, let's not rush into anything."

"That's wise," Cord said as he hugged her around her middle.

Then Josh hollered back, "I found a trail. Let's pick up our pace."

Annie loved her Hart family, and she'd been content living on their ranch. She'd worked hard and made herself useful. But she thought she might finally be ready to go back home.

———— ✧ ————

"Let's pull up here to eat and look around a bit," Josh said. "See if Hardy and that other fella left the bedrolls behind."

Cord said to Annie, "I can't believe how long we were underground." He swung down from the saddle, then reached up to help his wife to the ground. A deep thrill passed through him every time he thought of being married to such a fine woman.

Josh went over and checked the trail that led to Cornerstone. "Looks to me like they took four horses. The four were pulling a travois."

"That had to be slow going," Tilda said.

"We figured we'd need all six horses pulling travois," said Cord, "to get all the artifacts home. With only four horses, those things would've been stacked real high."

A piercing whinny made Cord jump. Then a pair of whinnies not that far off answered back.

"Adding two more horses to this group oughta speed things up." Josh walked toward the whinnies, calling quietly to the horses. "We've got a wagon we left in Cornerstone. Ellie rode on it until the trail became too narrow." Between the earthquake and being abandoned for days, the horses were a bit skittish.

Having two riders per horse had slowed them down some,

and Josh had said the load was too much for the horses to make good time.

An aftershock rocked the ground. They'd been feeling mild quakes all day. That was when Cord's eyes landed on a caved-in stretch of land much like the crack that had swallowed their chuck wagon. And it was right under the hanging shield. Cord's eyes narrowed as he walked toward the rupture in the earth.

"What's this?" He stared down into the crack, which had cleaved the ground twenty or thirty feet deep. "It's a . . . a ship." Tilda stood beside him, looking down, bewildered by what they saw. Josh had gone after the horses, but the others were coming fast toward the rupture.

"Most of the wood has rotted away, but that . . ." Tilda stopped and pointed. "Is that a cannon? And I think I see part of a mast. There are iron beams and other pieces of what used to be a ship. This must be where it went aground after the river dried up in the quake. Over there is a . . ."

Cord looked to where she was pointing. "A skeleton," he finished for her.

Annie came up beside him and peered down into the crack.

It was indeed a skeleton. Stretched out flat on what was once his belly, arms outstretched as if he'd been crawling when death came.

The sight earned a long moment of silence.

At last, Cord said, "'River of death' for a fact."

"We've come across too many dead folks while hunting treasure," Brody said flatly.

"That skeleton is over three hundred years old," Cord reminded him. "Whoever it was, he'd be dead now no matter what."

"Yes, but not dead in the wilderness, far from home. It's a risk explorers take, I suppose, and these men were explorers. Even so, a man oughta die surrounded by his loved ones, not like this."

"Strange, isn't it?" said Cord. "They sailed across the sea all that way, battling storms and whatnot, and then they finally arrive at land only to be dealt a huge earthquake, which ripped open the ground under the river they were on and swallowed up their ship with them in it."

"Those graves we found with the armor," Tilda said, "they had to be tied to this shipwreck. Which means not everyone died here."

"Maybe they were thrown and scattered about when the ground ruptured," Annie suggested. "Or maybe some of them survived, and they put together a scouting party to go hunting for food. Odd they'd wear their armor to do it, though."

"Not if they'd spotted a grizzly bear or two along the riverbank as they sailed," Tilda said. "Before the Lewis and Clark Expedition, no white man had seen a grizzly. One of those bears would have looked monstrous to them."

"Or maybe it's just how conquistadors dressed when out scouting." Cord slowly walked the length of the rupture. "I wonder how many died here. Learning what might've happened is why we tried to do this right. It's why we were being so careful."

Annie crossed her arms, scowling, "And that's why we contacted Hardy. He was supposed to study what we found and learn from it. Write it all up so that others might learn, too. Instead, greed overcame him, and he turned outlaw."

"After what he and Rombauer did, they'll have no part in

this find," Tilda said. She looked up from the ship to Josh. "Do we dare to get another of Michelle's archeologists out here? Is this such a rich find, it'll corrupt the conscience of every man who sees it?"

Josh gave her a wry smile. "It doesn't seem to have driven us toward corruption." His eyes slid over to Lock, who looked ready to jump into the crack and search the shipwreck for lost treasure. Josh laughed and added, "Most of us anyway."

Cord shook his head. "It was right here all the time." He pointed at the shield, hanging between two trees. "That other shield we found marked the graves of those sailors wearing armor. I figured this one had to mark something too, but we couldn't find anything. Until today."

"But we didn't see why he marked this spot with the shield. He had to have seen something, but what?"

They all stared thoughtfully at the shield and with considerable wonder at the ship below.

"When we first got here, we dug around some under where the shield hung," Annie said. "But after we came across the well, we focused all our attention there and started digging. We figured Graham MacKenzie must have discovered what he thought was treasure while looking for water closer to the cabin he built."

Brody nodded approvingly. "I think you'd've all liked Grandpa MacKenzie."

Cord glanced over his shoulder at the remains of the thirty-year-old cabin. It looked as though the woods were getting ready to swallow it up, just like the earth had done with the ship.

But the ship wasn't thirty years old. What had Grandpa

MacKenzie seen here that made him hang the shield in this spot?

"Three hundred years that ship's been buried down there," Tilda said almost reverently. "We've found the true treasure, while Hardy ran off with a few stacks of old iron. For all his education, the man can sure act the fool."

"I saw he'd written 'Hardy Expedition' in his notes," Lock said. "I told him it was the MacKenzie Expedition. That and our insisting the artifacts were ours and had to be taken to the ranch first might've pushed him over into grabbing what we'd dug up and running off with his man Rombauer."

"Whatever pushing he got, it's no excuse to turn violent, to turn thief," Cord said. "They knocked all four of us out, then threw us into that root cellar to die a slow death. No jury in California will stand for men behaving in such a way. They'll both go to prison at the very least."

Annie said, "Those two will be pursued by the law for the rest of their natural lives. If they do make it to Spain, they're going to have to stay there."

"Spain may not be far enough away," said Tilda. "Our country could demand that they be escorted back here, and Spain might well hand them over."

"I see another skeleton." Lock pointed to the edge of the fissure.

"There's an arm and hand sticking out of the dirt." Thayne pointed to one end of the ship while Lock motioned to the other. "And that's . . . that's . . ."

Thayne's tone drew Cord's attention, and he saw the boy's eyes flash.

"That is gold," Thayne finished, but more quietly. "The

man had it clutched in his hand when the ship was swallowed up."

The barely uncovered hand, no doubt part of a body that was still buried, gleamed between the bony fingers with more gold doubloons.

"If I had gold," Lock said, "and the whole world started shaking, I'd think I needed to run or maybe hide . . . and I'd take my gold with me when I did."

Lock turned to Josh. "I'm going down there and get that gold. I know we have to head for home, but not before I grab those doubloons."

Josh met Lock's eyes, and then he looked down at that tragic, lone hand. "I'll get a lasso and lower you down. I'll tie it around your waist. I don't suppose there's anything left of the deck to collapse, but let's be safe just in case."

Lock turned to Thayne. "You don't mind me fetching that gold, do you? I know you saw it first, but . . ."

Thayne gave him a light punch in the arm. "You go. I'll be up here holding the rope. If we have to drop down a second time, it's my turn."

Brody came up to his brothers and put his hands on their shoulders. "Be careful, would you? I'm still not over almost losing you in that old cellar."

Annie clamped her mouth shut as Josh tied a rope around Lock's waist. After all they'd been through, she could vividly imagine Lock landing on the deck of the ship and disappearing forever as it collapsed beneath him. The ship was only identifiable because of the cannon, the iron fittings, and its general shape. He'd be landing on wood that might just disintegrate under his boots.

Her fists clenched as tight as her jaw, she watched Josh, with Brody and Thayne behind him, lower Lock, holding the rope with knuckles white from their tight grip.

It was at least twenty feet, she estimated. The hand Thayne and Lock had spotted was right below Lock. Then, with featherlight care, he stepped onto the ship's deck . . . and one of his feet broke through the rotted wood.

Annie gasped and grabbed ahold of Cord.

"Hang on!" Lock shouted up. But the men were prepared and held the rope taut.

His other foot sank through the rotted deck.

"How could there still be space beneath the deck?" Cord took her hand after prying it loose from his wrist. He stepped quickly behind Thayne to help with the rope.

It wasn't necessary, but she knew Cord wanted to do something. She wanted to grab hold, too.

"I'm bringing you up, Lock, before we lose you," Josh called down.

"No, just a few more inches down, please. I can get those coins."

Annie's heart started racing. She saw Josh exchange a grim expression with Brody. Then Josh slowly lowered Lock closer to the doubloons.

Annie leaned forward to watch her young friend retrieve the gold. He dropped the coins into his pocket, picked up something else she couldn't identify, then shouted, "Pull me up, I—"

The ground shook again, and then Annie was falling forward . . . and down, down into the gaping hole.

A scream ripped from her throat. She landed hard, face-down onto the deck next to where Lock dangled. Their eyes met for an instant before the deck collapsed and she crashed through. It felt like she fell forever, and yet she hit much too soon, flat on her belly. The fall knocked the wind out of her. Debris from overhead fell on her, coating her with dirt and grit.

"Annie!" Cord shouted down.

She'd hit a soft mound of dirt and was all right. As she tried to regain her breath, everyone above was frantic and talking at the same time. She turned her head, fighting to drag in a breath to call up that she was okay, and looked right into the hollow eyes of a skull.

She screamed, shoved herself to her feet, and looked up at Lock, who was dangling there like a giant blond spider.

"S-skull," she stammered. She saw Josh and Tilda, still holding Lock's rope while a second rope descended. Brody was holding it with Thayne's help, with Cord coming to rescue her.

The ground still trembled, and it took her a second to realize it was the earthquake rather than terror shaking her.

"I'm all right." But she wasn't breathing normally even now, and she sucked in a lungful of dust and coughed. "Cord, go back up and lower the rope with a loop for me to slip around my waist. I was spooked when I saw another skull. I'm sorry I fell. I'm sorry I panicked and screamed. But I'm fine."

Not all that fine, yet there was no sense in having Cord fall through the floor after her.

She glanced at the grinning skull. "Just get me out of here!"

Shuddering, she decided she didn't like archaeology much. If skeletons were as big a part of treasure hunting as they appeared to be—first Graham MacKenzie, then those soldiers with the armor, and now this—she was never going to like it.

Cord touched down beside her. She frowned. "I told you to go back."

He removed the rope from his waist and put it around hers. "I'm not leaving you down here."

Another rope dangled beside them. She looked up and saw Lock, standing at the top of the fissure. They'd pulled him back up and lowered the rope again.

"We go up together," Cord said. He pulled the rope around his waist, then glanced up. "Wait! Hold up a minute," he called. He looked at Annie. "Let's quick look around. Right here where we're standing."

"Well, that looks like more armor over there." She pointed to a pile of iron, a helmet, and several shields.

They saw three more skeletons and what looked like iron chests, for supplies probably.

"Maybe those chests are full of gold doubloons," Cord said.

"No, they likely used the chests to hold food or gunpowder."

"I think we should pull at least one of them up."

"What if this ship is more than one story? We could fall through the floor again."

Cord stomped. "This feels like solid earth to me. And the shaking didn't collapse it further." Cord went back to studying that chest.

"What's going on down there?" Josh sounded impatient, his voice tinged with worry.

Annie could hardly blame him for that.

"Is there any more give in this rope?" Cord looked up at Josh. "I see something I want to bring up if we can manage it."

"Are you both all right?" Brody the doctor probably thought this was reckless. And it was. "I think you should get out of there before the whole deck collapses on your heads."

"I can give you about ten more feet, Cord. But I'm with Brody. Grab whatever you see quick and then come up out of there."

"We see four iron chests. If we haul one up and find it contains something valuable, we'll maybe come back down for the other three."

Annie wanted to know what was in them, too.

"Go see if you can lift it, Cord. It might be too heavy for the rope."

But their ropes were made to lasso thousand-pound steers, so they were pretty strong.

Cord went over to the chest and lifted it. "Not too heavy. For sure not loaded with gold."

Annie felt regret and relief at the same time.

He carried it back to her side, then called up at Josh, "Pull Annie up first. You'll all need to be on the rope to lift me up with this chest."

"Looks like a chest a pirate would have on his ship!" Lock shouted down. He sounded thrilled by the find. It seemed the close calls of the past couple of days had done nothing to dim his eagerness for treasure.

"Ready, Annie?" Brody called.

She gave Cord a kiss on the cheek. "Thank you for coming down to save me."

"My pleasure, Mrs. Westbrook."

She looked up at Brody. "I'm ready."

She was pulled up fast since Lock had added his strength to Brody's and Thayne's. Josh and Tilda kept hold of Cord's rope, and she was glad of that in case the ground beneath his feet crumbled.

Once she was on the surface again, she stepped well away from the fissure and grabbed the tail end of Josh's rope along with everyone else, and together they hoisted Cord up.

Lock gasped when Cord set the chest on the ground. "It's hardly rusted at all," he marveled. "The way the chest was buried must have preserved it, maybe because there's so little air or water down there."

There was a hasp that needed to be unhooked, a simple latch that fitted over an iron peg in the chest. It resisted when Cord lifted the latch, but then it moved.

Suddenly, Cord withdrew his hands from the chest. "Nope, this is MacKenzie's Treasure. Brody, Thayne, Lock, you open it."

"It's Westbrook treasure too, Cord. Your family has a claim on half of whatever we find."

"Speaking of finding treasure, we need to get moving so we can get the law after Hardy and Rombauer," Josh said, always the sensible one.

Lock crouched down, Thayne right beside him. Cord scooted out of the way.

Brody said, "Well? Go on and open it already."

Lock and Thayne exchanged looks, and Cord could sense how excited they were. He had to admit, he felt the same way.

With a loud squeal of protesting hinges, they inched the domed lid of the iron chest open.

Everyone leaned forward.

Cord said, "That looks like a journal inside. Just like the one your grandpa sent you."

Lock pulled the journal out of his pants pocket. He kept it tucked in there most of the time. Holding it next to the journal in the chest, he said, "Yep, it's exactly the same."

He looked up at Brody, who gave him an encouraging nod. "See what's in it."

Lock lifted the journal out and very gently opened the leather cover. Across the top of the first page were the words *Anales el Capitan*. He closed it and set it down on an identical book, one of a stack. "This is the captain's log. It's going to tell us everything, isn't it?"

Annie rested a hand on Lock's shoulder. "Yes, it should answer all our questions. And look, the chest is full of journals—or logbooks. They probably contain lots of historical information about Cabrillo's expeditions. These books might even give details that have long since been lost to history, things people would never have learned if we hadn't found this chest today, depending on how long the . . ."

Annie stopped and looked at Tilda. "Is this the captain's chest? He must've been in charge of this one ship, but if Cabrillo led an armada of ships, wouldn't each ship have its own captain? Or could it be that these logbooks were written by Cabrillo himself? He made it out of here, so he wasn't on this ship, right? But maybe he kept his logs on this ship."

"Or maybe the older ones are from him, but whoever captained this ship started his own diary after they became separated." Tilda's dark eyes were wide with fascination. With a bright smile she shook her head. "I don't know, but hopefully by the time I read all the logbooks, I will."

"Hardy was a fool to take a few artifacts and run," said Annie. "He could have been part of a huge discovery. He could've been famous."

Lock gave her a smile over his shoulder. "Instead, we'll be famous." He then frowned. "No gold here, though."

Brody clapped him on the back. "We've got more than enough. And we've got strong backs as well as faith in God, our true provider. We'll be fine even without a treasure trove."

"Before we go," said Cord, "I think we should bring up the other three chests. We need to explore further. I suspect these chests could be the real treasure to be found."

Nodding, Josh said, "Lock, you and Thayne take turns going down there while Brody and I and the others hold the ropes."

The boys were down and up fast, with Lock going twice. They didn't open the remaining chests. Each of the four men tied a chest to his horse's saddle horn.

Josh said, "Let's push hard. Every minute we tarry, Hardy gets farther away. And Annie and Cord need to get back to their daughter."

That got a smile out of Cord. He looked at his wife and thought about how long they'd been underground in that dark cellar, how close they'd come to dying. Once more he silently thanked God for rescuing them.

Minutes later, they were all trotting along when Tilda said, "Josh, stop!" She pointed at the ground, quickly dismounted, and rushed over to the object that had snagged her attention. "Look, it's a dagger," she said and picked it up from among some rocks. She held it up for everyone to see.

Thayne said, "I'll bet that's the dagger that got stolen

from Michelle's lab. Looks as though we can lay that theft at Hardy's feet, too."

"Yep, he didn't turn outlaw just because we pushed back when he tried to take our artifacts," Cord said. "He'd already gone down that path on his own."

"You're dead right," Annie agreed. "I wonder . . . what else has Hardy stolen from us?"

TWENTY-THREE

They rode into the ranch yard at the end of a long day. Annie was barely clinging to her horse. For a time, she'd dozed in the saddle, but she'd hung on and they'd finally arrived home. Ellie and Brody had lagged behind for a while in the wagon but were now catching up fast.

Annie strode straight for the house and Caroline while the men unloaded the chests, carrying them into the laboratory. Caroline was happily playing on the floor as Mayhew looked on fondly, a book open in his lap.

Annie hugged Caroline and held on tightly, until at last the girl wiggled free and went back to her playing. Annie was happy her daughter wasn't upset, but chagrined to realize how well Caroline had gotten along without her ma. Overcome by fatigue, she sank onto a chair near Mayhew and told him all that had happened on their journey.

"There were wagon tracks not far from the place they were camping," Annie added. "They unloaded the travois and filled up the wagon, then hitched their two horses to the wagon and headed out. They left the other horses behind, and we found them."

"Can I see what you found, Annie?" Mayhew asked. He looked as eager as the MacKenzie boys.

Annie brought Caroline and Mayhew—who'd insisted she call him Grandpa as Caroline now did—out to the laboratory to show them what they'd found. Michelle and Zane were already in the laboratory, looking over the items they'd brought back.

Annie said to Mayhew, "Cord told me you have excellent security guards at the bank. He wired them to be on the lookout for Hardy in Sacramento." She turned to Michelle. "And Josh wired Marshal Trey Irving, who helped when we had that trouble with Horace and Jarvis Benteen."

Michelle shuddered visibly and stepped closer to Zane.

"Did you also send a wire to Dorada Rio from Cornerstone?" Zane asked.

"To the train station there," Annie replied, "plus two more down the line. And to Sheriff Stockton. We stopped and talked with the sheriff in Dorada Rio, but just for a few minutes. It was getting late. He said he'd wired you an update."

"That's true," Zane said. "Hardy and Rombauer were spotted loading cargo onto the train two days ago. They'll be past Sacramento by now. But Stockton said he'd pass the word on down the line, hoping they'd catch them before too long."

Annie frowned. "That's mighty bold of Hardy to ride right into our town and board a train. No doubt he was seen and recognized by folks we know. We should find him fast."

Once the group had eaten a hearty supper and drank their fill of water, they all stood outside Michelle's laboratory, trying to figure out what to do next—especially concerning the ship they'd discovered. They decided the right answer

222

was probably to rest up a bit and then ride back there to see what more they could find in the ship and surrounding area.

Annie didn't want to leave Caroline again anytime soon. At the same time, she felt almost desperate to head back to the shipwreck. Yet all she had to do was think of that awful cellar to convince herself to stay home on the ranch with her daughter.

Night was rapidly falling.

Annie wondered if Hardy and Rombauer had plans to ride all the way across the country to the Atlantic Ocean and then board the first ship to Spain. Or maybe they would head to the California coast, San Francisco most likely, a port that wasn't far away by train. Where would they sail to from there, though?

Mayhew held Caroline's hand as he listened to the others share all that they'd gone through in the wilderness. When they got to the part where they escaped from the root cellar, he let go of the little girl and hugged Cord and then Annie. "I'm so glad you got out of there. I'd say God arranged for that earthquake to hit then and there to save you."

Cord clapped his grandpa on the back and gave him a second hug. Though Mayhew had attended church with the family while he was here, Annie knew Cord was worried for the man's soul. Mayhew talking about God sending his grandson a miracle was a sign he was turning to a prayerful and faithful life. She was sure that lifted a burden from Cord's heart.

She decided it was a good thing to have a grandpa around the place.

"What should we do about that shipwreck?" Cord asked.

That was the question they kept going back to. The folks

at the Two Harts Ranch had spent too much time and faced danger too often over MacKenzie's Treasure.

"I'm disgusted with that Professor Hardy," Michelle broke in. "He should've treated what he found out there with more reverence, more respect. For him to steal those artifacts and run off is downright shocking. I'm tempted to send for another archeologist to take Hardy's place, but can we trust anyone else after all that's happened?"

There had been several archeologists interested in assisting them on the treasure hunt, but not one of them was as determined and outspoken as Hardy, not to mention arrogant and stubborn.

Michelle drew a deep breath, then blew it out. "Honestly, I feel like we may have lured Professor Hardy down the path of destruction. We did that by setting before him a temptation he couldn't resist." She looked at Tilda. "Are the things Hardy stole really *that* valuable?"

Tilda gave a little shrug. "I wouldn't have said so, no. The logbooks in that chest, however . . . well, they might truly add to what we know about history and the conquistadors. But it's not like Hardy came upon a stash of gold doubloons—as far as we know anyway. I think he cares more about fame than about amassing a fortune for himself. He wants his name attached to a significant discovery." She paused, shaking her head. "That man has ruined his reputation forever. He's ruined his career, and it seemed as though it was a successful one. Well, it's all over now. Once the law catches up with him and Rombauer, both men are looking at jail time."

The sun disappeared into the horizon as the group filled everyone in and tried to decide when to return to the shipwreck and whether they dared to trust anyone else to help them catalog the discovery. They were still going around in circles when Brody herded Ellie and his brothers off to bed.

Annie was so far beyond exhausted that she wasn't thinking straight. She really needed some sleep.

"While you were away, Annie," Josh said, "we got the guest-house far enough along to be slept in. Tilda and I are staying there. You, Cord, and Caroline can have the housekeeper's rooms." Josh and Tilda headed for a new building Annie hadn't noticed, which was tucked behind the row of cabins.

Cord swept Caroline up into his arms. "Would you like your own bedroom, sweetie?"

Caroline giggled. "Uncle Josh and Auntie Tilda have been letting me sleep in there all week. It's my room now, they said. Except now my ma and pa will be sleeping in the other room."

Pa. The word wasn't lost on Annie or Cord as Caroline threw her arms around his neck. Cord held her tight, his face buried in her dark curls, his eyes closed.

Collecting himself, he looked up at Annie, his eyes shining with love for their little girl. Annie had wondered if she should urge Caroline to start calling Cord "Pa." They didn't talk much about Todd anymore, and she doubted her daughter remembered her father. Sad as that was, Annie didn't want to push her girl to do anything that would hurt her further. Now Caroline had made the decision on her own.

Annie beamed, unable to take her eyes off Cord and Caroline together. He came over and slid his arm across Annie's back, and they went inside, everyone following along.

"Let's go to bed, Ma."

Annie nodded and felt her own throat clog with tears.

On the way in, Cord said, "It seems like every time we

225

think we're finally getting to the end of this treasure hunt, it gets more complicated."

"I suppose finding something unexpected that's been hidden for hundreds of years is always going to be a complicated business."

As they moved to their new rooms, all Annie could think about was letting herself collapse onto her bed, where she'd slumber away the hours till the sun came up again.

TWENTY-FOUR

Annie overslept. Getting buried alive, falling through the rotted deck of an old ship, being nearly dehydrated, then spending hours in the saddle, all in all had left her feeling exhausted.

When she finally awoke and found herself alone in bed, she got to her feet, freshened up and dressed hurriedly, then walked out to a beehive of activity. She headed straight for the coffeepot before engaging with anyone.

She had poured herself a mug of hot coffee and returned the pot to the stove when strong arms wrapped around her waist from behind. Whispering in her ear, Cord said, "Good morning. Do you feel better after getting some rest?"

Annie turned to look into his bright blue eyes and smiled. "I do feel a bit better, thank you kindly. How are you, Cord Westbrook?"

He kissed her on the cheek. "Plan on spending the rest of your life getting to know me, Annie Westbrook."

"I will." It then flickered through her mind that sometimes life could be cut short. Her smile faded.

"What's the matter? You're thinking of Todd, aren't you?"

She saw hurt in his eyes along with his kindness. "I'm going to pray with all my strength that we both live a long life. There are no guarantees, Cord. I'm going to savor every minute of whatever time the Lord gives us."

"Does that include not falling through any more ship decks?"

She chuckled. "I certainly hope so. In fact, if there is another treasure hunt ahead of us, I might just stay home with my little girl. I think my gold fever has been cured for good."

"I can barely translate any of this." Michelle sat at the table with one of the old logbooks open in front of her. "The language isn't exactly Spanish like I know it, and the writing is very hard to make out. But I suppose some of the spellings and expressions have changed from three hundred years ago just as they have with English."

Her brow furrowed as she studied the first page, covered with writing.

"A lot of the words are familiar, but enough are not that it's slow going trying to decipher what's being said. Like figuring out a puzzle."

"Too bad we don't have a professor of archaeology around to help with this," Tilda said sympathetically. "Someone like that would probably recognize most of the unfamiliar terms."

Annie noticed Tilda's father, Carl Cabril, and her sister standing beside Tilda, the two of them whispering to each other. So identical and yet so different from each other. Maddie with her silk gowns and elaborately styled hair, her lace and petticoats and reticule. And Tilda in her red calico dress with white flowers scattered over it, with her hair in a no-nonsense bun.

Maddie looked beautiful, but somehow, Annie, looking

down at her own blue calico dress, liked how Tilda looked more.

"Carl just asked, apparently for the twentieth time, if his son could come to California." Cord had been listening for a while, letting Annie sleep late. "Ben's been writing to Tilda all winter, and she's softened. It sounds like the coyote is coming out here."

"It will be all right," Annie said.

Cord's brows lowered. "What makes you say that?"

Annie remembered then that Cord had spent a good deal of the winter riding the range and staying in the bunkhouse. "When Michelle's family descended on us to see the baby, you met Caleb, right?" He hadn't been in the bunkhouse all that time.

"Yep, he was the leader of the mission group that brought the Stiles sisters here. He married Michelle's little sister, Laura."

"Well, he spent a long time talking through all that had happened to Tilda, and he seems to think things will be better now."

"But Ben was in New York City. How could Caleb talk to him? I guess they could write letters to each other, but—"

"No, he didn't talk to Ben; he talked to *Carl*. He got Carl to realize that Ben had lived his whole life believing he would be kept around only if he did exactly as his father said. Carl and Ben have been writing back and forth, and Ben is beginning to trust his father. Ben's love and respect for him has grown ever since."

Caleb talked with Tilda and helped her write the letters she'd sent, so she could help Ben see what she'd need for Ben to earn her trust. With Tilda's approval, the judge had agreed he could come back. Yet Tilda had been badly frightened by Ben and was slow in trusting him again.

With Caleb's wise counsel, Carl had seen that Ben's misguided quest for his favor was caused by growing up without a father around. Ben and Carl were building a kinder, healthier relationship, and now it sounded like Tilda had agreed to let her brother come back.

"When Ben came out here to get Tilda and she wouldn't go, he grabbed her and ran, thinking it would please his father."

Cord frowned. "That doesn't excuse what he did."

"No, it doesn't," Annie agreed. "Which is why Josh plans to keep a close eye on him. Ben has spent the last year selling all his father's business interests in New York City with the hope he would be allowed to come and join his family. I heard someone say he'll probably settle in San Francisco, invest his father's money, and oversee things from there. So he won't be underfoot all the time."

Cord's eyes met Annie's, and the skepticism he saw there was very clearly shared.

Annie added, "I don't suppose there's much reason he'd pose any further threat to Tilda. Not if the whole idea behind kidnapping her was to take her to her father, and now her father is right here." It was a dubious defense of a scoundrel.

"It's all settled then," Michelle said.

Everyone turned to look at her. Their expressions said that they had no idea what had been settled.

Annie had been late to this discussion, so maybe something had been settled before she got here. Then she noticed the MacKenzie boys' excitement, as well as Josh's skepticism. She began to worry about what might come next.

Cord moved to stand at her side, almost like he needed to support her, which raised her concerns even higher.

"We're all going on one last treasure hunt. The lot of us. And we'll bring Caroline along." The little girl beamed at Annie as if she'd just been granted her fondest wish.

"Tilda's father and sister will go. Mayhew will go, too. We'll gather up everything out there that can be hauled back, documenting it all as perfectly as possible, then take what we found to the museum in Dorada Rio. If any of the professors there want to get involved, they'll have to come to us, do things our way. None of the treasure goes anywhere else, not without our permission and careful supervision."

"The Crocker family pays well," Carl said. "Enough to keep the museum going."

"And everything we find is owned by the MacKenzies and the Westbrooks in equal measure."

"That's probably not necessary," Mayhew said, "but it's something we can settle at a later time."

Annie had noticed that ever since Mayhew had learned that Graham MacKenzie had never repaid his loan before he died, leaving a note saying Mayhew was a partner in his treasure, Mayhew had lost the grudge he'd carried for years. He didn't seem to need the money, and his objection against Graham had been about feeling cheated. Now he'd let that all go.

Annie had misgivings about this massive caravan to collect their treasure. For one thing, she was still recovering from almost being killed. She also wasn't ready to leave Caroline again so soon, nor did she want to put her daughter in any danger by taking her into the wilderness.

But then Annie figured, with a whole crowd going on the

treasure hunt, she and Caroline should be plenty safe. She decided to roll along with whatever Michelle decided, for she was usually right.

"Can we wait a few days before we go?" Annie asked. "I think those of us buried alive need some time to recuperate."

"I'm fine," Lock put in, obviously wanting to saddle up and leave today.

"It's Wednesday," Michelle said. "Let's leave Monday. That'll give us time to go through those chests, too. Carl especially wants a look, and I'd like a little more time for my translating." Michelle arched her brows at Annie. "Since she's not walking yet and can't get into any toddler mischief, I'm taking Leah along, if that makes you feel any better."

Cord's hand closed over hers. Annie realized then that Thayne had come to stand on her other side. He took her hand in his. She looked at him, then Cord. Lock seemed engrossed in the upcoming treasure hunt, yet the three of them knew how close they'd come to dying in that cellar. It was a dangerous business trying to unearth old artifacts in a country prone to earthquakes, especially objects that might be the focus of others' greed.

And they knew Hardy and Rombauer were still at large, though likely miles away by now.

"She's right," Thayne said. "There's safety in a group this big."

Annie squeezed the boy's hand, then let it go. Looking at Cord, she said, "I'll be spending today with Cord and Caroline. We're going back to our rooms for now and maybe take a picnic lunch to eat outside somewhere."

Cord gave a firm jerk of his chin. He released Annie's

hand and plucked Caroline out of the middle of the crowd. "How about we go read a book or play together for a while?"

"I'd like that, Pa." She looked up at Annie. "Do you want to play with us, Ma?"

Such trust. The child never needed to know just how close she'd come to losing her ma and pa. Annie felt tears burn just to think of it. "Yes, Caroline," she answered past the lump in her throat. "I'd love to play with you." Her eyes slid to Cord's grandpa. "Grandpa Westbrook, you can come with us and play with Caroline, too." She'd noticed the sad expression on Mayhew's face when she'd said she was planning a quiet day with Cord and Caroline.

He nodded, saying, "I'll be along after a bit. The three of you should spend a bit of time together first. Maybe we should have the picnic lunch back in your rooms. That would be safest."

Annie went to Mayhew and kissed his wrinkled cheek. "That's a perfect idea to eat inside. Come on in after a while." Then she and Cord and Caroline said goodbye and went to their rooms.

TWENTY-FIVE

They'd come prepared for just about anything, Cord figured as he rode toward the old shipwreck.

They'd left the ranch in the hands of the Two Harts foreman, Shad, and they'd brought along the whole family, including Tilda's family and Cord's Grandpa Westbrook.

They had two wagons, which they'd drive as close to the fissure as possible, and a chuck wagon. Cord had noticed that the trail they'd traveled after leaving Cornerstone was reasonably wide most of the way to the shipwreck site. Neb, the bunkhouse cook, had come along as well. He and another member of the crew would spend time widening the trail to get the chuck wagon close to the site. Until then, Neb would cook the meals, and they'd all ride to the chuck wagon to eat.

With the cowhands along to help and to provide protection, they were a solid brigade.

When they reached the ship, as the sun was setting, everyone moved to the edge of that rupture in the earth to stare down at the awesome sight. Cord reminded them all of Annie falling through the deck and warned them to be vigilant about possible earthquake tremors.

234

It was close enough to bedtime that they decided to wait until sunrise the next morning to begin their search of the shipwreck.

⸻ ✧ ⸻

They'd brought plenty of rope and had a good-sized crew down in the ship before midmorning.

They hauled everything of value to the surface except the skeletons.

Tilda, with help from her pa, Maddie, and Mayhew, busily wrote down every detail of what they found and where they found it, doing their best to keep a thorough record. Ellie, meanwhile, kept watch of the young'uns.

While Cord took his turn helping to investigate and gather up finds, he noticed that Annie had stayed on the surface. Maybe she'd had enough of sunken ships. She spent the time note-taking with Tilda, then chasing after Caroline and Leah because Michelle wanted to be in the thick of things.

By nightfall, Cord figured they'd emptied the ancient ship. They'd gone through what was left of the ship and brought up the kinds of puzzling things that Cord thought an archeologist might find interesting.

Lock held out a small oval object that Cord found familiar.

"That's like that badge Hardy found," Cord said. "He said it was possibly a portrait of a young Cortés and that no such picture of him existed—that he knew of anyway. So if Hardy found it valuable, a piece of history, well, now we have another."

Lock nodded. "And I found another dagger, which looks a lot like the one we have."

Lock studied the knife intensely, and Cord could tell there

was something else on the boy's mind, although he didn't say more.

"There's no sign of a lower level then?" Tilda asked.

Josh, being the nautical one, answered, "Ships change over so many years, of course, but I recognize the general style. It has a very shallow draft."

"Draft?" Annie prompted.

"That means it doesn't need deep water to sail around, which would've made navigating the river easier. I'm almost sure the level Annie fell to is the bottom or the hull. This type of vessel was likely included in the expedition deliberately. They were looking for bays, mapping out water routes into the mainland. They may have sailed up a few rivers, but they didn't find San Francisco Bay. This one ship, though, probably lost its way in the fog that often enshrouds the bay, and they came upon the river by accident. We may find what happened written out in the logbooks, including information about the earthquake and the wreck that stranded them here."

"That information could be in those logs you already took to the ranch," Michelle said. "It's going to take time to translate it all, but I'll get it done. Maybe then we'll have the whole story of this ship."

As the sun dipped down, Neb rolled into the camp with the chuck wagon. He'd carved out a path all the way to the shipwreck site. The two other wagons they'd brought came up behind him, as well as the carriage for Mayhew and Carl. The older men had walked to the site when their carriage couldn't go any farther.

Now they could load all the strange artifacts they'd hoisted to the surface into the wagons and prepare to leave. Cord had thought they might be there for several days, but now it looked as though they'd be able to head for home tomorrow.

Josh, the last one down in the ship still, stood there looking around. The deck had collapsed to some degree, but not entirely. He walked toward one end of the boat until he was no longer visible.

"Josh, come on back where we can see you," Cord called down.

Tilda came up beside Cord, peering down, searching for Josh.

"I'm fine, Cord, but send down a rope. I want to walk to the front of the ship, and a rope might be a good precaution."

They'd begun their search with everyone roped, but as the ship stayed steady, they'd left off the safety measure. The ropes were all coiled neatly right at hand.

Just seconds later, Cord lowered the rope. Josh reemerged from under what was left of the deck and tied himself off. He looked up. Cord realized most of their crew had heard Josh ask for a rope and had come to watch.

"You want anyone else down there?" Cord asked. "I can come."

"Good idea. I see something down here . . . like part of the ship maybe collapsed at some point and was buried. This ship might be bigger than we thought."

Cord tied the rope around his waist, and a couple of cowhands took Josh's rope while two more took Cord's.

Just before going down, Cord noticed Zane was busy unharnessing the wagon horses and getting them picketed out to graze. He turned back to the ship, letting himself be lowered into the fissure. Once on the ship, he walked over to Josh.

"You're right, Josh. Looks like the front of the ship caved in and got buried."

"You can tell by the curve that there should be more of it. I know it's getting late, but we still have the light for a few more minutes. Let's do some digging."

Josh went straight to a wall of dirt that seemed to mark the extent of the ship. As he clawed away at the solidly packed dirt, a chunk of it fell away, and Cord saw . . . something. Possibly more of the same type of thing they'd been finding all day.

"If there was an earthquake big enough to dry up a river, and a crack opened to swallow the entire ship, that's powerful enough to send tons of dirt down on part of it and crush the bow."

"Bow?" Cord said.

"Yes, the front of the ship. There should be a steering wheel, maybe one trimmed in bronze or copper. That would survive, especially as the bow was buried rather than left exposed like the rest of the deck.

"And this could be one of the handles of a steering wheel." Josh quit digging when he saw a skeletal hand.

"We really haven't found too many skeletons," Cord said. "And we know at least some members of the crew survived. The ones we found wearing armor."

"It must've happened fast," said Josh. "The earthquake, the ground cracking and swallowing the ship, the front of it collapsing. This wheel would have been on the main deck, so when the world started shaking and cracking, and an avalanche of earth crushed and buried the front, it pushed the wheel down to this lower level. I'd say this poor sailor died while he was still steering the ship."

Cord sighed. "We're going to have to dig all this out, aren't we? I knew it was all too easy. One day searching, pack everything up, head home."

"It's likely not a large portion of the ship got buried. We may only have a few feet to dig through to find the rest of it."

Cord saw something gleam out of the corner of his eye, lying on the hull nearby. Was it . . . ?

He slowly moved to the spot and crouched down.

Ten gold doubloons.

He scooped them up and turned toward Josh. Based on how the coins were stacked just below the skeletal fingers, the sailor might have had them clutched in his hand the instant he was crushed beneath an avalanche of dirt. Three hundred years ago.

Staring at the gold in Cord's hand, Josh gave a low whistle.

"I'll add these to Lock's collection. Wait . . . what's this?" He held up a thin black coin possibly, so tarnished it was impossible to make out, though Cord thought it might be silver. "I wonder if this is a coin, too. It's about the right size."

Josh moved closer. "And these bits of iron or bronze—I think they're buttons. Very elaborately carved. We may be looking at the captain of the ship. No doubt the ten doubloons were his own. If he died at the beginning of the trouble, and there were other coins, the other sailors might have divided the coins among themselves. Maybe that's why we keep finding a few here and there." Josh gathered up several of what might be buttons.

Cord said, "For now, let's not mention this to anyone. Finding gold like this could get people stirred up."

Josh nodded. "Ten more coins. A strange black circle that might be silver. And the buttons . . ."

"Cord, Josh, are you all right?" Annie called down. She sounded worried.

"We can send down help if you need it," Tilda said. Her voice sounded just as concerned as Annie's.

Cord was quick to call back, "No, we're fine," wanting to put his wife's mind at ease. "We're coming up. We found a bit more down here and may need to dig for a while tomorrow."

TWENTY-SIX

Sure enough, on the second day of digging, they found more to carry away.

Annie wanted to be done with it all. She wondered if, instead of asking anyone to the ranch to study what they'd found, maybe they could do it themselves?

On their way home now, Annie and Cord rode up to Zane, who was leading the way. "Cord and I are thinking of moving back to my land, Zane. If we decide to do that, we're going to need a new house to replace the one that burned."

"We'd be happy to build you a new house, Annie. I'd miss having you and Caroline there. Cord, you've become a dependable cowhand. It won't be long and you'll be one of the best ranchers around."

"I own Horace Benteen's house now, too." Annie wondered if she'd enjoy taking what that polecat of a man used to own or if it would bother her. Right now she thought she'd rather enjoy it.

As they reached a wide stretch in the trail, Josh trotted up and joined their conversation. Ellie was riding in the buggy with Mayhew and Carl. The Hart family dropped back to include her in their talk.

Cord gave Annie an encouraging nod and pulled back so that the Hart family could speak with a bit of privacy. He found himself riding with Tilda, Michelle, and Brody.

"Word is you're thinking of moving off the Two Harts," Brody said.

"We still have some things to decide," Cord replied, "but Annie and I are talking about it. She's mentioned her ranch as well as the Benteen house, which is closer to the Two Harts than her ranch property."

Michelle said, "Only Horace's money and connections kept him and his son from the hangman's noose. I was glad Annie sued Benteen for her husband's death and the damage done to Annie and her home."

"Isn't that unusual? To sue over a death that he'd been convicted of?"

Michelle shrugged one shoulder. "It is, but then most wealthy men aren't murderers, or if they are, they rarely get caught. Benteen got caught. I've never seen the house, but it's said to be beautiful."

Annie must have overhead them because she looked back and said, "I've never seen Benteen's place either. And I haven't been back to our ranch since Todd died. He'd inherited it from his parents. I had no interest in living there with only my daughter when we had family at the Two Harts. And the orphanage gave me satisfying work."

"Annie, we don't have to move if you're happy where you are," Cord said.

Josh added, "You've got a one-quarter stake in the Two Harts, and you'll always have a home there. We've been running your ranch for a while now, and we'd be glad to continue if you want that."

Annie gave Cord a peaceful smile. "I think I'm ready to have my own home again. And, Josh, I hope you understand . . . Cord and I would like to run our own place. I might feel different if we were to move far away, but we'll be close enough to see you often."

Thayne rode up behind them. "I'm going to head to college soon to attend medical school. Looks as though the family is spreading out."

"I guess I'm too young yet to go off on my own," Lock said, sounding a bit disappointed.

They rode along, with Grandpa Westbrook's carriage coming next, Ellie riding beside him. Carl was in the back, along with Maddie, Caroline, and Leah. Next came the chuck wagon and the two wagons carrying their treasure, not counting the coins and buttons in Lock's pockets.

They went home through Dorada Rio, where they were told there'd been no word on any arrest of Hardy and Rombauer. Cord wondered what would become of those two thieves. The truly frustrating part was that justice was out of their hands. The two men had left with a load of cargo and gotten off the train in Sacramento. Then they'd vanished.

If they boarded the train again, no one recognized them. And their cargo, which was substantial and noticed in Dorada Rio, wasn't seen by anyone in Sacramento. If the two men had disguised themselves, and their crates of artifacts stowed along with other parcels, they could easily have gone on with no one the wiser.

Either the two men traveled west to San Francisco and the Pacific Ocean, or they boarded a train heading east all the way to New York and the Atlantic Ocean. The Port of San Francisco, which sent ships all over the world, had been notified. But if Hardy and Rombauer had managed to slip past the lawmen watching for them, they could already be far away at sea by now.

Or they might have stayed right here in California. They could have made plans to stay somewhere in Sacramento, with a place to hide waiting for them. Regardless of the whereabouts of the two thieves, Cord and the others had locked the rest of the artifacts up in the newly secured laboratory. Of course, everything was in a jumble and needed to be sorted, identified if possible, and then sent to the museum for further study.

The museum's name was still being debated. Carl Cabril wanted Captain Cabrillo's Voyage Museum. Tilda thought it should be The MacKenzie Museum. Lock was pushing for The Museum of MacKenzie Treasure, though he admitted a name like that was practically begging for robbers to flock to the place. *Treasure* was the kind of word that could bring out the worst in people.

For all the work ahead and the concern over security, it seemed like the worst was over.

If only Cord could believe it.

He humbled himself before God when he prayed again for their two assailants to be caught and imprisoned. He, Annie, and Caroline could never settle into their new life as long as the dregs of this one hovered around them like a dank fog.

———— ◇ ————

"It's time to move home, Cord." Annie rested her head on his chest as they settled in for the night. "I want to start a new life with you, and I don't think we can do that here at the Two Harts where everyone is so stirred up about thieves and artifacts and future plans for them. Honestly, I'd like to put all of this excitement behind us."

"I'd love to do that, too."

Annie's hopes rose, and along with those hopes, her heart began beating faster. They would start over, a new family, on their very own place, away from the Two Harts. As much as she'd miss the home she'd known for so long, she was ready to make a new home with her husband and Caroline.

"But is it safe?" Cord asked.

Her heart slowed, and her hopes dampened.

"We still don't know the whereabouts of Hardy and Rombauer; we don't know if they escaped somewhere far away or whether they're still in California. There's been no word of their arrest."

Annie considered Cord's words. "We were attacked for those artifacts, and they aren't going to come looking for us if they think they have everything. If we move to the Benteen house, that's not the property I lived on with Todd. Hardy won't know we're there. And we'll have cowhands around us. We'll put together a strong crew there."

Cord patted her hand where she'd laid it over his heart. The touch seemed absent, and she knew he was busy thinking. Cord was dead serious about safety and protecting his family, and their being buried alive recently had only heightened his sense of vigilance.

She continued, "We can ask your grandpa if he'd like to stay with us at the Benteen place and see if your ma would come and visit, maybe bring her parents. If they don't want to move into our house with us, well, we'll figure something out. They could maybe sell their holdings and purchase land nearby, or we could build them something more private on our property."

Cord nodded slowly, not saying anything.

"There's really no reason for anyone to attack us there," Annie added. "If we move, we won't have any artifacts close to hand."

At last, he spoke up. "We're the only witnesses to their assault and their attempt to kill us. That makes us a threat to them. That puts our family in danger."

"Are we witnesses? Truly?" Annie said quietly. "I mean, what did we actually see, Cord, before getting knocked out?" Suddenly she felt less certain about the future.

No matter what they'd witnessed with their own eyes, it seemed their experience in the cellar was a dark tale that connected those two outlaws to their crimes, and it was something Annie and Cord couldn't just shrug off.

Perhaps it was best to put their plans for the future aside. But for how long?

Cord continued patting her hand on his chest. Annie, not ready yet to give up on the idea of setting up a home of their own, tried to control the impulse to pressure him.

Then Cord gave a long sigh and said, "Let's take a ride to the Benteen place. See what we'd need to set up house. If we have to haul wagonloads of supplies to live there, we should probably wait. But if we can pack a few satchels and supplies and ride down there with Grandpa and Caroline, along with a few cowhands for escorts, we'll make the move. Besides, the treasure isn't mine. I've no stake in it except for whatever stake my grandpa has. And I don't see him fighting hard to claim much of it, though he might take one or two gold coins to repay Graham's debt."

Annie's heart sped up again.

"How about we go there after church on Sunday? A few of us will ride to the Benteen place and—"

"It's the Westbrook place now," Annie said, cutting him off. "I don't want to associate Benteen's name with it anymore. It's *our ranch* as of today."

Smiling, Cord said, "The Westbrook Ranch it is then. I'd always planned to be a farmer, but I've found I like working with cattle and horses more. Matter of fact, I have been dreaming of a ranch all winter, ever since I learned to be a cowhand. We could get us some nice Texas longhorns."

"Have I told you that we already have a herd of Herefords on the land?"

"Sure, but Texas longhorns sound good to me."

Annie grinned. "To me too. The ranch is a little east and south of here. We can make it there at a gallop in half an hour." Her smile faded.

Cord pulled her into a hug. "What's wrong?"

"I just remembered the last time I rode into the Two Harts at a gallop. Todd, Caroline, and I were running for our lives. And Todd didn't make it . . ."

"I'm so sorry, Annie. That must've been a very dark day for you."

Resting her cheek on his strong chest helped to ease the painful memory. She realized then that she loved him. She'd known since the day she first saw him that she was drawn to him. She'd come to care for him. But this deep, romantic love was like nothing she'd ever felt before, not even with Todd, whom she'd loved dearly and had considered her best friend.

What swept through her now was the sweetest, warmest thing she'd ever felt. She held on to him, determined that

247

she'd guard him with her very life, as she'd failed to do with Todd. She opened her mouth to tell him that she loved him. What she felt was too big, too generous, and she couldn't keep it inside any longer.

"So we'll ride to the Westbrook Ranch after church, then." Cord's words diverted her for a moment. And then he made her love him even more. "Annie, I promise you, if living in that house makes you the least bit unhappy, we'll build our own. I don't want you to live with something that isn't right for you."

"Thank you, Cord. Going through town is a good idea. If we weren't riding there anyway, there's a shorter route from the Two Harts, but from Dorada Rio we'll ride south and get there fast."

"We'll check around the new place, decide what we need, and see if the house suits us. If it'll work to live there, we'll come back to the Two Harts for a few days to gather our things."

Whatever the history of the house, she'd fill it with love and laughter. God willing, she and Cord would add to their family with more children, conceived in love and raised in faith. And all traces of Benteen's evil menace connected with the place would be forgotten.

Annie pictured herself standing with her handsome husband in their new home and confessing her love to him.

She couldn't wait.

TWENTY-SEVEN

The next couple of days gnawed at Cord. He was ready to see where the future would take them. He was planning to bring Grandpa Westbrook to live with them, and Annie had agreed with her usual kindness. So he'd ride along with them to the new Westbrook Ranch.

Because Josh had good-naturedly fired Cord when he and Annie announced they were moving, he wasn't riding herd anymore. Instead, he spent his time in the laboratory, often with help, sorting through their findings as Michelle continued to fight her way through translating the old Spanish writings, which were on paper so delicate she was afraid to touch it.

Cord found the dagger Hardy had dropped among the rocks along the trail, and he and Lock looked it over. They were frustrated to think of all the artifacts Hardy and Rombauer had gotten away with. Cord hadn't found the badge with Cortés's portrait on it, yet he suspected that Hardy had taken it from the laboratory. What else had been stolen that they didn't yet know about?

While they looked over the dagger, Grandpa came into

the laboratory along with Brody, Thayne, Lock, and finally Ellie, who had a faint smile on her face.

Cord saw the MacKenzie brothers exchange serious looks, and then Lock gave a nod to Brody.

Brody said, "Mayhew, my brothers and I have discussed it." He took the dagger from Cord and offered it to Grandpa. "We want you to have this. We also want you to have half of the artifacts and the gold we found, but this special knife is a token of our gratitude."

"No, thank you, Brody. I'm not taking one bit of this treasure from you and the family."

Cord had wondered, when it came down to it, whether Grandpa would decide to refuse any of the artifacts or the gold.

Brody shook his head firmly. "My grandpa promised you half of whatever he found. Your loan made this discovery possible. We don't intend to break that promise. Thanks to the treasure map he gave me and the one you had, I didn't just find earthly treasure but I found a loving wife as well."

He took Grandpa's blue-veined hand, which trembled a bit these days, and pressed the handle of the dagger into the older man's palm. "We insist you take this. Besides, there's no amount of treasure I can give you compared to what the search for it has given me." Brody paused and smiled. "I'm home again with my brothers. I've married the love of my life, and we've got a child on the way."

Ellie came over to Brody's side and added, "Your money made it possible for Graham MacKenzie to purchase the claim where he found the treasure, and you've given Brody, his brothers, and me riches beyond measure. We want you to have the dagger . . . and more."

Nodding, Grandpa looked down at the knife clasped tightly in his right hand. "This is no regular knife. It's unusually heavy. In fact, of all the things you brought back from the dig site, this knife looks to be the strongest, even more so than the armor. Nothing about it has rotted away. It's pretty much like it was the day those sailors ran aground three hundred years ago."

"Half the gold is yours too, Mayhew," Lock said. "For now, though, at least take that dagger. And, well . . ." Lock hesitated, then reached inside his shirt and pulled out a sheath that held the other dagger.

Cord couldn't hold back a smile. He hadn't known Lock was carrying the dagger around with him the whole time.

Grandpa laughed. "You're carrying a three-hundred-year-old knife. Lock, my boy, you've got more sense than the rest of us. Such sturdy, useful things—if we can still use them, we ought to. But you should wear it so it shows. It's a shame to hide it away like that." Then Grandpa looked at the dagger in his hand again and turned to Cord. "What do you think, Cordell? Should we accept this one little piece of the treasure?"

"If you do, you'll need a sheath so you can wear the knife at your waist properly."

Grandpa gave an inelegant snort. "It would ruin the line of my suit coat." He then extended the dagger to Cord. "But as a western man, a cowboy, you could wear this and make it look right. It'll help you to remember the search for MacKenzie's Treasure. And I'll see it every time I'm with you."

Cord took the knife from his grandpa, then glanced at Lock, who was busily tying his own sheath and dagger around his waist. "Do we dare carry around something this old?" he asked.

Lock finished putting his on and then looked up at Cord, his eyes bright with excitement. "The two of us with these daggers is like a bond between the MacKenzies and the West-brooks, a symbol of the old bond between our grandpas. I like the idea."

Cord smiled. "I like the idea, too."

"I've got a sheath in the ranch house that I think will fit," Ellie said to Cord. "Just be careful with it when you're hugging my sister."

Cord laughed, and the others joined right in, erupting into laughter as well.

TWENTY-EIGHT

"I don't think you should wear that dagger into the church."
Annie seriously doubted it was wise for him to do so. Every
Sunday, her brothers left their rifles in the scabbards on their
saddles and their six-guns in the saddlebags. No one would
think of stealing something from a horse tied up outside of
church.

Then she thought of Hardy dumping them in that underground prison and had to wonder just how low some
people might go.

"You're right," said Cord. "Besides, it might scratch the
piano bench. By the way, I packed sandwiches and a few
other things for lunch."

"I know. I saw you doing it before I could. We should be
at the Westbrook Ranch in time to eat the noon meal there."

"I can't wait to see the place. I'm surprised your family is
all right with us riding off alone."

"I'm a little surprised myself. But there's no way Hardy
could know we own that ranch house."

"Did you talk with Grandpa Westbrook about moving
in with us?"

"I did. He's interested, but he said he'd still be spending part of the year in Sacramento since he's got business interests there that need overseeing."

"I wish he'd retire so he could be with his family all the time."

Cord reached across to hold her hand. "I agree, Annie. I'm hoping once he's moved in, he'll get settled enough that he won't want to leave."

Annie saw Cord adjust his dagger in its sheath.

"That's such an odd-looking knife." She rather wanted to carry it herself. Maybe she could tuck it in her reticule. "Can I see it?"

Cord removed the knife from his waist, sheath and all, and handed it over to her.

Annie held the dagger up, admiring it. It was about ten inches long and fit in her reticule with little room to spare—six inches of blade, five inches of handle. "Why is it black?" she asked.

"Silver tarnishes to black," Cord said. "Remember that one black coin we found? Well, we decided it's a silver coin."

"Is this knife silver, then?"

"It's possible, but silver is a more delicate metal. It wouldn't be a usual choice for a dagger. We think maybe it's plated."

Annie's brow furrowed. "Plated?"

"Yes," said Cord. "The bulk of the knife is steel, but then it was covered with a thin coat of silver. We'll clean it up later and see if the tarnish comes off. Michelle and Tilda have been researching daggers from hundreds of years ago to find out more."

"And on the handle is that strange X again. The Cross of Burgundy. It's barely visible."

Cord nodded. "We saw that same mark on their armor, some of the weapons, the chests, and even in the logbooks. Michelle said it was an important insignia to the sailors at the time."

As town and the church came into sight, Annie hid the dagger in her reticule and noticed Lock doing the same, tucking his inside his shirt.

———— ✧ ————

"Your first trip to the new ranch house should be just the two of you," Grandpa told them.

Cord tended to agree with his grandpa. The idea of an afternoon away with Annie sounded wonderful. And like any overprotective father, he wanted to make sure everything was safe at the house before he took Caroline there. "I'd enjoy the time with Annie. I'll ask her if she doesn't mind leaving Caroline behind for the afternoon."

As he watched Annie and Caroline walking toward him, he said to his grandpa, "The two of us will ride down there and look around, and the next trip can be with you and Caroline along."

Grandpa nodded in agreement at the same time Annie approached with her daughter. "Annie, can Caroline stay with me for the afternoon? That way you and Cord can ride to the new place and enjoy some time alone."

Annie's eyes sparkled. She smiled at Cord, then turned to her daughter. "Do you mind going back home with Grandpa, sweetie?"

"No, Ma. I'll go with Grandpa." She then skipped over and grabbed hold of Grandpa's hand.

After Cord and Annie said their goodbyes, they mounted up and rode off to see their new house. The ride took about half an hour.

"This place isn't far from home at all," Annie said. "I like the idea of living close to family." She turned and smiled at him. "But maybe we've been living a bit too close. I think our being here will be an improvement."

As they rounded a bend in the trail, the Westbrook Ranch spread out before them. Cord gasped.

He was determined not to pressure Annie into living here if it reminded her of the evil man responsible for Todd's death. But it really was a beautiful place.

His grandpa lived in a stately mansion in Sacramento, yet the house here was a Victorian masterpiece: three full stories with a circular tower reaching high above it all. A porch surrounded the front and side of the house, possibly more if he looked behind it. There was another porch on the second floor with glass doors into the house, gabled windows on the roof, along with all kinds of asymmetrical details to make every inch of the house fascinating to look at. There were elaborate wooden flourishes in every peak and around every door and window.

The house was white and looked freshly painted. Had it stayed so pristine despite sitting empty for a few years, or had it been recently painted? Cord couldn't help but wonder what it was going to cost to keep this big fancy mansion in decent shape. No matter, for the house was a real beauty and worth the expense of upkeep. He felt as if he could stare at the house for hours, it was that pretty.

Annie said, "Horace Benteen had all the money in the world to spend on this house. He didn't even live here most of the time. He was in San Francisco, but he liked the idea of being seen as a big rancher, so he poured a lot of cash money into making this ranch a showplace."

Cord heard some powerful emotion when she spoke. He couldn't decide if the sight of the house made Annie anxious, or if she was realizing just now what a beautiful home it was. She said she'd never actually been inside the house.

"Though Benteen owned thousands of acres, he always wanted more. And our ranch bordered his. When we refused to sell him our place, he decided he'd just up and take it."

Annie had tried to explain to him that what the Harts owned had been built with their own hands from the logs and stone that surrounded them. Benteen had hired others to do all his building for him, and doubtless he hadn't lifted a finger to help them, hadn't sweated even one droplet. Of course, no less than highly skilled craftsmen could have erected such a spectacular structure as the stately Victorian house standing tall before their eyes.

"Let's go inside," Cord said. "We might as well see what we're up against."

They rode up to the house, tied their horses to the fanciest hitching post Cord had ever seen, and went up the steps. Annie produced a key.

When she opened the door, Cord suddenly swept her up into his arms and carried her across the threshold. "A husband is supposed to carry his new wife into their first home," he said.

"I don't know about the house," she giggled, "but I do

know about making a home, Cord. I believe we can make a home here."

"I think you're right about that, Annie." He lowered her to her feet and sealed the notion with a kiss.

After a moment or two, they turned from each other and started exploring their new house.

"This place looks like it hasn't been touched in years," she said. "The furniture, the rugs, the light fixtures—everything's coated with a thick layer of dust."

"It's as if they just walked out the front door one day and never bothered to come back," Cord said, pointing at a table with a book open, facedown.

Annie nodded. "That's pretty much what happened. Benteen and his son were arrested and hauled away, and that was the end of it. They never returned here after that day. And after I won the lawsuit against Benteen, Zane sent some cowhands over here to do the chores and care for the livestock. They stay in the bunkhouse at my old ranch. But I'd bet no one's been in here from the moment Benteen and his boy were arrested."

"It feels a little . . . haunted." Though Cord didn't believe in ghosts, he might make an exception this once. "What are we going to do with all this space? Should we close off the top floors, you think?"

Annie eyed the grand staircase in the center of the main room, its wide steps and elegant banister rising in a sweeping curve. The ceiling ran to the second-floor height twenty feet or more over their heads.

"I'm not that interested in using the upper floors. I'm definitely not interested in dusting the whole place."

"If we make up bedrooms here on the main floor, we can

keep all our living down here and leave the top floors be for now. The only way we'd need all that space upstairs is if we had twenty children."

Annie swatted him lightly in the belly with the back of her hand.

"I was just kidding," he laughed.

She turned to him, a grin on her face. "The thing is, Cord . . . we already *have* twenty kids."

His brow furrowed. "The orphans?"

"What if we made this big house the 'Westbrook School for Orphan Girls'? We can bring the girls here, tailor our classes more specifically to their needs, at the same time giving them some much-needed privacy."

"We can hire more teachers," said Cord, "maybe a few of the orphans who have grown up at the Two Harts. Maybe Tilda could come here once a week to teach her history class, and she's been trying to get Maddie to teach more. She might be interested in moving here to teach full time."

"All very good ideas," Annie agreed. "Of course, we'd need to work out all the details, but now I'm excited to have all this space instead of dreading how we'd be rattling around in the house. To start with, we need to look around upstairs and see how many bedrooms we have and what rooms would make good classrooms."

"It's like, without planning to, in his greed and overweening pride, Horace Benteen built a ready-made orphanage in the middle of California's Central Valley. What he built to display how superior he was will now be used to help those less fortunate."

They resumed their inspection of the large house. The dining room included a massive oak table that would seat thirty. The kitchen was huge, like that of a fancy restaurant in San Francisco. Upstairs were eight good-sized bedrooms, big enough for the girls to sleep four to a room with no one feeling at all crowded. The house was perfect.

Annie stood gazing out one of the windows of the turret on the second floor. A girl could dream up here: a fairy-tale princess waiting for her prince to gallop up to the castle to woo her. As she was looking out the window, she noticed two men come out of the barn and walk to a corral of horses, each with the Two Harts brand.

"I recognize those men, Cord. I'd like to catch them and tell them we might be moving into the house. See what they think of having a herd of young girls underfoot."

"I'll run over and have a word with them," Cord said.

Annie stood in her tower and listened to the thundering footsteps on the stairs, followed by the slamming of the back door, which was connected to the kitchen.

Annie noticed the men turn her way and look up at the house. She stepped out onto a balcony and waved to them.

Cord saw her and hollered, "There's a new foal in the barn! Come on down and see it."

She nodded and waved again, then stepped inside and headed for the main staircase.

As she reached the first floor, she heard the unmistakable *click* of a gun being cocked . . . right behind her head. Annie turned slowly around to face Professor Oswald Hardy and Mr. Walter Rombauer.

Twenty-Nine

"Go guard the back door, Rombauer."

Rombauer, his hulking figure moving with surprising grace, went to keep watch at the kitchen window that was beside the door facing the barn.

Eyeing him through an open doorway, Annie's heart sped up when Rombauer pulled out his own gun and pointed it at the ceiling as he waited for Cord to return to the house.

She turned to glare at Hardy. "You sure did a good job acting like a university professor."

"I *am* a professor."

"No, you're a thief and a liar and a would-be murderer. We've got folks searching for you all over California—the ports, the train stations, your university."

"When I stole that dagger, I knew I was changing careers."

Annie remembered then that she'd tucked it in her reticule before church and had never given it back to Cord. "Why the dagger? We had dozens of artifacts to pick from. Then again, you stole them too, didn't you, you thief?"

"Yes, I have in my possession a lot of things, all of which are quite valuable. But the dagger was something I couldn't walk away from. I'll use all those trinkets to gain for myself a comfortable life in Spain, which will include a job in their most prestigious museum. I'll write scholarly books to serve as textbooks all over the world, and I'll become famous as a result." Hardy paused, then added, "But that dagger was what I most wanted. I had it too . . . but then the knife disappeared."

"Disappeared? What do you mean?" Annie wondered what was happening with Cord. She was straining to catch sight of Rombauer at the back door when Hardy drew her attention back to him.

"I brought it along with me to the archeological site. I threw the rest of the armor away, thinking you'd probably guess the theft to be the prank of some mischievous students. The other artifacts we found are fascinating, but that dagger was the most valuable by far. I've seen similar pieces in my life, but they're very rare. And then when we got to Cornerstone and packed everything into crates, I couldn't find it."

"So you lost it. What makes you think we have it?"

A cruel smile twisted Hardy's face. "Because I've been watching the ranch. After we boarded the train in Dorada Rio, we got off in Sacramento and hid the crates, then bought fresh horses and rode back. I searched everywhere, every step of our trip. No knife anywhere. Then we went back and searched the dig site. That's when I saw the ship. Apparently, your family had already stripped the shipwreck of anything of value." He shook his head. "I didn't realize they'd found you and your husband and those fool MacKenzie brothers."

"We were all fools—you're right about that. Not just the MacKenzies, but all of us. Fools for trusting you two."

Hardy snorted. "True enough. Anyway, I recognized what

that dagger was from the first and began plotting how to steal it. Rombauer and I camped out at an overlook near the ranch, waiting for our opportunity. When the earthquake hit, I saw everyone running around in panic and knew that was my chance to go steal it. After I realized we'd lost it, I returned to my lookout post to see if you'd recovered it. I saw your husband carrying the dagger in a sheath—I recognized the distinctive hilt—and looking like a pirate. And I spotted him wearing it to church this morning, so we decided to follow you here. Now, when your husband comes back into the house, I'll get it back and we'll be on our way."

Annie, her heart pounding with fear, wondered if she should hand over her reticule with the dagger now. Would Hardy and Rombauer truly just take it and leave? Or would the two men, who'd been willing to let four people die in an underground cellar, kill them all right that minute without giving it another thought?

"Why?" she asked. "What is it about this dagger? Does it have some historical significance that you didn't tell us about? Why did you throw the armor and other weapons aside and keep only the knife? What makes the dagger so important?"

Hardy's eyes flashed. "The dagger has no more historical significance than any of the other artifacts we found, but what it *does* have is a hollow core in the handle, one that contains diamonds. The end of the hilt twists off if you manipulate it just right. I'd heard rumors that Cortés had a thirst for gold and diamonds especially. He didn't just conquer a land; he stripped it of its wealth. When he sailed back to Spain, he converted the spoils of war into diamonds. And you can be sure that Cabrillo and others shared Cortés's lust for wealth."

"All right," said Annie, having heard enough, "we'll give you the dagger. We'll tell the law to call off the search for you. We'll let you flee to Spain. Cord and I won't even tell my family we were robbed. Just don't hurt us, please. I promise we'll let you ride away with the dagger, but don't hurt me and my family."

He took a moment to ponder what she'd proposed. "We'll need to tie you up in some out-of-the-way room in the house here. We need a decent head start."

It pained Annie something terrible to think of helping the two thieves get away. She knew they couldn't be trusted, but what choice did she have? If she allowed herself to be bound, not much would stop Hardy from killing her if that was his original intention.

She heard Cord's voice as he approached the back of the house. She knew once Cord was inside, within range of their guns, anything could happen. Tragic things.

Rombauer slid back from the door and aimed his gun. Hardy, distracted, watched through the kitchen doorway. It was then that Annie slid her hand into her reticule and pulled out the dagger. She didn't want to kill anyone, hated the very thought, but she'd need to buy herself time to dash out the front door and scream for Cord to stay away.

She gripped the handle of the knife and, using its weighty, ironhard power, slammed her fist right into Hardy's ear. He roared, staggered back, and Annie screamed, "Run, Cord! Hardy and Rombauer are in the house!"

Hardy stumbled, careened into the wall, and went down hard. Scrambling back onto his feet, looking dazed, he turned on her and fired the gun just as Annie threw herself to the floor. The bullet struck the wall beyond her, sending bits of plaster in all directions. She quick jumped up and dove through a doorway and out of sight of Hardy.

She heard Cord shouting and Hardy yelling in rage and pain. Then came more gunfire until Hardy ran out of bullets. Hearing the gun click on an empty chamber, Annie rushed back to the man and brought the iron butt of the knife down hard on the top of his head. The blow sent his gun flying one way and her dagger the opposite direction.

The knife crashed into the wall, and she heard a strange pattering sound but had no time to see what had caused it.

Cord charged in and skidded to a stop in front of Rombauer, who was lying motionless on the floor. He leapt over the man and dashed toward Hardy, who lay on the floor, gasping and grunting. His head was bleeding from an ugly gash from when he'd struck the doorframe.

"Help . . . I need a doctor," Hardy groaned.

Cord turned to Annie as she climbed to her feet. "Are you all right?"

"Y-yes," she managed. "I wasn't hurt."

One of the two cowhands rushed into the house then, and Cord shouted behind him, "We're all right! We're over here."

"Hardy was the only one shooting. He must've shot Rombauer by accident." Annie eyed the dagger lying on the floor. The blade had separated from the haft or endpiece of the hilt, and around it lay what looked like tiny bits of broken glass. Diamonds . . .

"You know, for an educated man, Hardy ain't all that smart."

The cowhand approached and said, "His partner's dead."

Cord nodded. "Figured as much. Tie Hardy there up good and check him for any hidden weapons. Let's throw him over a horse and haul him to the doctor in Dorada Rio."

"Doc MacKenzie at the Two Harts is a better doctor," the hand said.

"A good reason to take him to town." Cord gestured toward Rombauer's body. "We'll need another horse for him. No need to tie him up, though."

Cord went and pulled Annie into his arms and held on tight.

"I need to get to a doctor!" Hardy wailed.

Cord turned with her in his arms toward the injured man on the floor. "You're gonna live, Hardy, but only long enough to face a noose. I don't see why you'd be in any hurry to get to the gallows."

Hardy was sprawled on his back as if he'd given up all hope. Annie thought the man might be crying.

She let go of her husband and walked around Hardy, bent down to scoop up the two parts of the dagger, carefully returned the diamonds to the hollow handle of the knife and replaced the endpiece, then slid it back into the sheath and lastly into her reticule.

With that done, she helped Cord and the cowhand get the two outlaws ready for travel.

THIRTY

Both cowhands brought up the rear as they rode into town.

Soon Hardy was shackled in the jailhouse. The doctor had tended his wounds, given him laudanum for the pain, and left. Tomorrow he'd be facing a murder trial. Because it was Sunday, the trial had been delayed a day. Then Hardy, if found guilty, would be summarily hanged.

And a conviction was likely since Rombauer was stretched out at the undertaker's with a bullet in his chest, and there'd been witnesses nearby who would testify as to the truth of what happened.

Cord and Annie rode for the Two Harts now, both still on edge. Their cowhands rode along behind them. Cord had noticed Annie pick up the two parts of the dagger off the floor, put it back together, and drop it in her reticule. He was glad he hadn't thought to ask for the dagger back. She'd had something to fight Hardy with, and it'd made all the difference.

As they rode into the ranch yard, Cord saw Josh striding out of the barn. He waved the riders over.

"I thought you'd be coming from the south," Josh said. "Did you ride back to town before heading home, because there's a shorter—"

Cord wasn't sure what Josh saw in their expressions, but he stopped talking and went straight to Annie. He plucked her off her horse and hugged her.

Annie, her voice shaking, explained, "Hardy and Rombauer followed us to the Benteen place."

"It's the Westbrook place now," Cord reminded her as he dismounted.

Annie gave him a small smile. "The Westbrook Ranch," she corrected.

The cowhands who'd ridden home with them took the reins of the horses and started for the barn.

"Thanks for helping," Cord told them.

"Mrs. Westbrook did all the hard work." The hand tugged on the brim of his Stetson, and the pair turned toward the barn.

"What happened? Did they hurt you?" Josh grasped her shoulders and held her out to get a better look at her.

Cord heard the door of the ranch house open and noticed most of the family streaming out.

"Hardy's in jail in Dorada Rio. Rombauer is lying at the undertaker's, the result of Hardy firing a stray bullet. We're expected in town tomorrow for Hardy's trial."

Josh gave Cord a narrow-eyed look. "You're leaving out a lot of details."

"I'll tell you everything," Annie said, "but I only want to tell the story once."

The family surrounded them.

"Hardy ambushed Annie," Cord began, running quickly through the details. "He wanted that conquistador dagger, which as it turns out is hollow and full of diamonds."

Annie held out her reticule with the top open. "I've got the dagger here."

Cord continued, "Hardy stole the armor and kept the dagger, and he was hoping to find more just like it. During the struggle with Annie, Hardy shot Rombauer dead, we assume by accident. There's a good chance Hardy will hang tomorrow for his crimes. Miraculously, those two didn't put a single mark on any of us."

He saw his grandpa in the crowd, lines of worry deep in his face. Cord went to him and patted the older man on the shoulder. "I'm okay, Grandpa. Thanks to Annie, I was never in real danger." Cord looked at his precious wife. "Just Annie was."

"Well, I'm glad you're all back home now, and everyone's all right," Grandpa said.

Cord nodded. "Let's all go inside. I could use a hot cup of coffee and something to eat."

———— ✧ ————

"The summer is fading," Annie said. She and Cord were walking arm in arm. Going for walks after they tucked Caroline into bed was their habit now. She cherished these moments alone with him at the end of each day.

"I can see a bit of yellow in the aspen trees," he said. "The whole mountainside will be a blaze of color in a month's time."

Annie loved the way he held her. She loved his voice. She loved his strength and his musical talent. In fact, she loved everything about him.

"I had special plans for today over at the Westbrook

Ranch," Cord said. They shared a smile as they walked on, taking the trail west toward Dorada Rio.

"We never did get to have our picnic lunch, did we?"

Cord shook his head. "Soon," he promised. "You know, I told you I loved you the day I proposed marriage, but what I feel for you is growing into something more beautiful every day. You know how I love music, don't you?"

Annie nodded. "I don't think anyone could play as beautifully as you do without loving it."

Cord leaned down and kissed her tenderly. "You hum in my veins. You're like a chorus of angels. You're the music of my life, Annie. You and I and Caroline together strike a perfect chord of harmony."

A smile spread across her face as he compared her to music. "You could not have found a better way to speak of your love." She stretched up and kissed him as daylight turned to dusk.

The night sounds hushed around them. Crickets chirped. An owl called out. A pair of nightingales sang in the distance. The soft breeze of a California evening brushed past them, and the scent of the pines and the fresh country air were like music to Annie's soul.

"We've spent too much time searching for treasure around this ranch." Annie reached up and brushed the dark hair off his forehead. "I hope we're done with that now. I hope we can settle in to raising cattle."

"In the end, our searching led to gold and diamonds, historical artifacts, and learning some fascinating history. Yet none of that could ever bring us one more bit of happiness than we already have. Holding you in my arms, Annie, I want nothing more—not as long as I have you."

EPILOGUE

Things did eventually settle down. MacKenzie's Treasure was now on display at the museum in Dorada Rio, with various pieces being loaned out here and there.

Michelle had finished translating the logbooks taken from the chests they'd found at the shipwreck, and she'd discovered a wealth of information about the ship and her crew of sailors and explorers. They now had a clearer idea of what had happened to those seamen so long ago.

Tilda's father was busy curating the museum's exhibits. They'd discovered he had a talent for it.

Ben finally showed up and seemed contrite to the point they were beginning to trust him again. While he made his home in San Francisco, he became a frequent visitor to the ranch, occasionally bringing orphans with him to live there and study at the Two Harts School. He also volunteered at the Child of God Mission and donated generously to the cause. Even so, Josh still wouldn't leave Tilda alone with her brother when the man came for a visit.

Ellie's baby, a boy, was born right after Thanksgiving.

They named the child Graham after Brody's treasure-hunting grandfather.

True to his word, Thayne went off to college to study medicine.

Annie, Cord, and Caroline moved to the Westbrook Ranch. Just as they'd hoped, they converted the huge house into an orphanage for girls. All the girls from the Two Harts settled into the upper floors of the house, and Annie and Cord were sent more youngsters needing homes from places like San Francisco and Sacramento.

Cord's mother and Grandma and Grandpa Rivers visited the new ranch and orphanage frequently, but they still made their homes on their own land. Annie hoped that the day would come when they'd decide it was time to cut back on their work and move to live at the Westbrook Ranch permanently.

Grandpa Westbrook had moved his Steinway piano from his mansion in Sacramento to the Westbrook house. Cord taught the piano, both there and at the Two Harts.

By Christmastime, Annie was excited to learn she had another baby on the way, and the whole family gathered for the holiday at the Westbrook Ranch. With the orphan girls living there, it made for quite a crowd in the dining room, yet the table was massive enough for everyone to squeeze in around it. The boys back at the Two Harts were also served a turkey dinner with all the trimmings.

"Let's join hands," Cord said from the head of the table, which nearly overflowed with food.

Ellie sat with her baby in her arms, Brody at her side. Thayne, home from college, sat beside his brother Lock. Caroline sat beside Annie at the foot of the table.

Cord prayed a simple but sincere prayer of thanksgiving. When he said amen, he looked up and smiled down the length of the table, straight into Annie's eyes.

"For all our treasure hunting," he said, "true riches come from God alone. He's given generously to us in the way of family, food, and shelter, but what He's given us most is His love. The glorious gift of His Son, of eternal life. No matter where life takes us, with Him we'll always have riches beyond measure."

Read on
for a sneak peek at

Ambush
of the
Heart

BY MARY CONNEALY

Book 1 of the new series
✦ ROCKY MOUNTAIN MARSHALS ✦

Available in the spring of 2026

July 1872
Near Fort Collins, Colorado

A bullet whizzed past U.S. Marshal Owen Riley, so close he felt the heat of it. Riding beside Delaney Bridger, who he was escorting, along with her brother, to Fort D. A. Russell in Wyoming, Owen threw himself at her to get her off her horse. He held fast to the reins and forced his mustang stallion to lie down on its side.

He saw fellow Marshal Morgan Sawyer hit the ground a second before him. A third Marshal, Tex Mitchel, was already down and crouched low behind his horse, rifle drawn. Tex was bleeding bad. Tex had Delaney's brother, Boone Bridger, down as well.

The Marshals had been paid to escort the Bridgers safely to Wyoming, and fortunately Delaney looked to be all right. She lay beside him, her pistol out, her own horse racing down the hill they'd just crested.

Assessing the situation, Owen saw Boone sprawled on his back, bleeding from a head wound. Clive Duncan, the prisoner they'd been transporting, lay there facedown. He wasn't moving. Duncan was beside Marshal Marley Tweedt, who'd been leading Clive's horse as Clive rode with his hands tied. Just beyond those two was Deputy Marshal Stan Ross, flat on his back, bleeding from a chest wound.

The horses that hadn't been forced down stood as gunfire continued to ring out.

Stan's spooked horse began trotting north in the direction they'd been going. Other horses followed. Only Owen, Morgan, and Tex had managed to hold on to their mounts, using their critters as shields.

They'd all just come out of a draw and were approaching a hill on the trail that led to Cheyenne, riding north out of Denver along the Front Range of the Rockies . . . and they'd rode straight into an ambush.

Five of them shot, four seriously. Marley's leg bled, the wound serious enough that he'd let his horse run away. Marley crawled toward Tex and got his gun out, not paying his leg much mind.

Another glance at Tex told Owen he was in great pain but still in action.

There was a pause in the shooting. Owen had recognized the distinct sound of the Springfield rifle, which carried a load of bullets. One gun.

It wasn't long, though, before more gunfire filled the air. The pause was about the time it would take to reload. But was it just one rifle or the same kind of rifle and multiple gunmen clumped together? Owen had learned not to jump to conclusions. Then he heard something, a grunt maybe, and the gunfire stopped again.

Owen, pinned down near the hilltop, rested his rifle on his horse's back, aiming, readying himself for the next round of bullets.

Yet no one showed himself, no more gunfire followed, and no one came charging over the hill. In the deafening silence, it was as if the whole world had gone still except for the buffeting mountain breeze.

With a glance back at Boone, Owen saw Delaney leaving

the safety of their horse. He grabbed her arm. "Don't you dare go out there."

She turned to him, her eyes furious. "I've got to help Boone!" she cried.

Owen's grip gentled. "He's flat on the ground now where nobody can get another shot at him. But if the gunman who opened fire on us comes over that hill, you need to protect yourself by staying right here behind this horse."

She hesitated, then said, "It'd be foolish, I know that." She swallowed hard and swiped her wrist across her eyes. "I suppose he won't get much worse in a few minutes' time."

"I'm sorry, but it's my job to keep you and Boone safe, and I failed him . . ." It ripped at Owen's heart to see her in tears, knowing her brother was bleeding from a head wound.

But soon she'd calmed down and saw reason. She was a tough western woman. And pretty with her dark hair and those blue eyes. He hated that he'd let her brother down, but he could still protect her at least. Suddenly his hand on her arm felt overly warm. He let go to face the hill again and aim his rifle.

And then she was gone.

"Delaney! No!"

She'd dodged him and was crawling now toward her brother, using her elbows to move forward while staying flat.

Owen added *wily* to his earlier description of her. He didn't go after her but instead focused his attention on the hilltop, ready to shoot at anyone who posed a threat.

After making her way to Boone, she tore a strip off his shirt to bind up his wound. It was an ugly shot to the head, leaving Boone to lay there injured on the hard ground.

He, Morgan, and Tex had partnered up before. Two other

Marshals had ridden with them today, both of whom were lying on the ground like Boone. Stan Ross's eyes were open, staring at heaven because that was where he'd fled. Just a youngster, he hadn't been with the U.S. Marshal Service for a full year yet.

Marley Tweedt, a tough Civil War veteran, was the oldest of them and mean. Alive still but hurt bad. Owen had seen gunshots like this before. Unless Marley got real lucky, it was likely that he'd lose his leg—if the wound didn't fester and kill him first.

Owen felt his temper about to explode, but then his eyes shifted to Delaney once more. The young woman had wrapped a bandage around her brother's head. She looked around desperately, and her gaze locked with Owen's. "He's alive," she called.

Owen had his doubts. Then he did a blamed-fool thing. He left the shelter of his horse and crawled over to Delaney. While he did so, she drew a wickedly sharp knife and slashed at her brother's shirt, cutting another strip of cloth to bind his head and stanch the bleeding.

What Owen saw when he got a better look at Boone gave him hope.

"The wound looks terrible, but it's just a graze," Delaney said as she tied the strip of cloth around the dressing she'd already applied. "He's going to be all right." She said it with such certainty, Owen figured God himself had assured her.

Delaney's pa was newly stationed at Fort Russell. It was said she was a distant cousin to the rugged mountain man Jim Bridger. She sure seemed tough enough to be his relation. Owen suspected she could've survived in the mountains along with the old grizzly hunter. Same went for Boone, and that same toughness might just save the man.

They were on this trail because the train, recently opened from Denver to Cheyenne, wasn't running due to a train wreck that had damaged a stretch of track that included a trestle bridge. No one was making promises about when it would open again. What would've been an easy day's ride on the train had turned into a few hard days' ride on horseback.

Clive Duncan was being escorted to Cheyenne, where he was to hang. He'd broken out of jail a year ago. The Bridgers, Delaney, and Boone had been standing on the train station platform ready to board at the same time as Owen and his group. When they'd found out Owen was changing his plans to ride to Cheyenne, the Bridgers asked if they could come along. They wanted to get to Fort D. A. Russell, where their pa, Colonel Lionel Bridger, was the fort's commander.

"Get back to watching for whoever shot my brother," Delaney instructed, crawling on toward Marley.

Morgan rounded his horse and scrambled on hands and knees back toward the hill, keeping himself low.

Owen, fearing that this time his friend was gonna get himself killed, said, "Morg, no! We fall back. Now. That's an order."

Morgan glanced over his shoulder. The fury in Morg's eyes would have scared a lesser man, but not Owen. Lowering his voice, he added, "We need to find a better spot to make a stand. Sure as shootin' they're after our prisoner."

Morgan gave the crest one more enraged look before turning back. Instead, he moved to the prisoner.

Tex, his blood-soaked arm now with a kerchief wrapped around it, got to work loading Stan's body onto his horse.

They were far enough over the hill that the horses could stand, but no one was going to dare sit up high on their backs, not until they'd put some space between them and whoever was shooting at them.

Mary Connealy writes romantic comedies about cowboys. She's the author of the BROTHERS IN ARMS, BRIDES OF HOPE MOUNTAIN, HIGH SIERRA SWEETHEARTS, KINCAID BRIDES, TROUBLE IN TEXAS, WILD AT HEART, and CIMARRON LEGACY series, as well as several other acclaimed series. Mary has been nominated for a Christy Award, was a finalist for a RITA Award, and is a two-time winner of the Carol Award. She lives in eastern Nebraska with her very own romantic cowboy hero. They have four grown daughters—Joslyn, married to Matt; Wendy; Shelly, married to Aaron; and Katy, married to Max—and seven precious grandchildren. Learn more about Mary and her books at

MaryConnealy.com
facebook.com/maryconnealy
petticoatsandpistols.com

Sign Up for Mary's Newsletter

Keep up to date with Mary's latest news on book releases and events by signing up for her email list at the link below.

MaryConnealy.com

FOLLOW MARY ON SOCIAL MEDIA

Mary Connealy   @MaryConnealy   @MaryConnealy